Also by Shane Kuhn

The Intern's Handbook

HOSTILE TAKEOVER

A JOHN LAGO THRILLER

SHANE KUHN

Simon & Schuster

NEW YORK   LONDON   TORONTO
SYDNEY   NEW DELHI

Simon & Schuster
1230 Avenue of the Americas
New York, NY 10020

First Simon & Schuster hardcover edition July 2015

SIMON & SCHUSTER and colophon are registered trademarks of Simon & Schuster, Inc.

For information about special discounts for bulk purchases, please contact Simon & Schuster Special Sales at 1-866-506-1949 or business@simonandschuster.com.

The Simon & Schuster Speakers Bureau can bring authors to your live event. For more information or to book an event contact the Simon & Schuster Speakers Bureau at 1-866-248-3049 or visit our website at www.simonspeakers.com.

Manufactured in the United States of America

1   3   5   7   9   10   8   6   4   2

Library of Congress Cataloging-in-Publication Data

Kuhn, Shane.
Hostile takeover : a John Lago thriller / Shane Kuhn.—First Simon & Schuster hardcover edition.
pages ; cm
I. Title.
PS3611.U394H67 2015
813'.6—dc23
2014046339

ISBN 978-1-4767-9618-5
ISBN 978-1-4767-9620-8 (ebook)

For Skoogy and Kenners Bear.
When all seems lost, hard work will save you. Never surrender.

Prologue

Federal Bureau of Investigation—National Center for the Analysis of Violent Crime (NCAVC), Quantico, Virginia
Present day

This is the first day of the rest of your life, I think to myself as I squint under the bright fluorescent lights in a windowless interrogation room. In the reflection of the yellowy two-way mirror, I look like a bug in a jar, quietly waiting for a mentally disturbed five-year-old to fill it with water and watch me stiffly gallop to a slow and painful death. But my executioner doesn't come in the form of a bored suburban brat. He comes in the form of Assistant Director Winton Fletcher—a fifty-something FBI poster boy with a scrubbed red face (Ivory soap), machine-precision haircut (Floyd the barber), cheap, ill-fitting suit and prep school knockoff tie (Joseph A. Bank), and high-polish wing tips with skid-proof rubber soles (Florsheim).

"Fletch," as I like to call him, embodies the clean-cut, red-blooded American values invented by square ad execs and political campaign managers of the 1950s. All of it amounts to an intentionally colorless persona designed to put even the hardest criminals at ease and seduce a full confession. If I wasn't an honored guest of Uncle Sam—top hat, tails, orange jumpsuit, maximum-security cuisine, and lethal injection for dessert—I might mistake him for a Lutheran minister or an aluminum siding salesman from Wichita. He saddles up on his high horse across the table from me.

"I'm Assistant Director Fletcher," he says.

"Hi, I'm Dr. Rosenpenis," I reply in homage to *Fletch*, the worst most quotable movie ever made.

He smiles at me, uncertain how to take what I've said, but jaded enough not to give a shit. Someone with his tenure in this place has pretty much seen it all . . . until today. He pulls a crisp new yellow legal pad from his briefcase and begins to awkwardly rummage through it, looking for something else.

"Your pen is in your side suit jacket pocket, Fletch," I offer. "You probably put it there so the guards wouldn't hassle you about bringing a potentially deadly weapon into a room with a homicidal maniac."

He smiles again and pulls out the pen.

"I'm impressed," he says, carefully placing his legal pad on the table next to a thick file folder with my name emblazoned on the tab in institutional block letters: JOHN LAGO.

"You should be," I say menacingly.

He doesn't look at me or react. He's been trained not to react to any negative fluctuations in emotion, only positive. He's been trained to keep all exchanges under complete control. Interrogators can never be looked at as people with personal lives and weaknesses. They are like Fletcher, unassuming and understated in every way, well-spoken robots who do their jobs with immaculate precision. On that note we have at least one thing in common.

Fletcher pulls a clear plastic evidence bag from his briefcase and lays it on the table. Inside is a bloodstained composition book with the following title scrawled in Sharpie on the cover:

The Intern's Handbook.

My original manuscript. First edition. I smile at it like a father would smile at his newborn baby after coming home from a long combat tour. He sees my smile and makes a mental note that I am probably not going to feel any remorse for my sins.

"I'd like to talk about this, John."

"Have you read it, Fletch?"

"Several times."

"And?"

"And what?"

"What did you think?"

"Well, I have a lot of questions about—"

"No, what I meant was, did you like it? Was it a good read? Would it pair well with box wine at your wife's book club?"

He puts on reading glasses, another disarming tactic. Grandpa wants you to sit on his lap, enjoy a butterscotch candy, and shoot the breeze. Here comes the pedantic grin. The feds are also masters of making you feel like you are sick or abnormal. Why do you think they attempt to look so militantly normal? Because to the criminal mind, they strive to be the foil, the mug shot frame that forces you to look at yourself and ask, *What's wrong with this picture?*

"I found it very interesting."

Interesting is another word for *irrelevant* in this context. Probably thinks *Reader's Digest* and *Parade* are cultural oracles. I hate him for evading and I hate myself for caring.

"Like I said, I'd like to talk about it," Fletch reiterates.

"What do you want to know?"

"Is it all true?" he asks.

"Every fucking word."

"You said that you wrote it to help other young people who had been put in the same position as you. Is that the only reason?"

"That was why I *started* writing it. After a few chapters, I realized I needed to write it more for myself than for anyone else."

"You needed to get some things off your chest?"

I exhale a sigh heavily laced with annoyance. It's time to mess with Fletch a bit. He's too into his routine, and I need to jam the signal. I lean in like a film noir confidant, the devil on his shoulder.

"I'm sure you can relate, Fletch. A man in your position. So many secrets. So many things you wish you could undo. For years you've lived in the pressure cooker—but you can't go home and talk to the missus unless you want to put a target on her back. Let's face it, you can't talk to anyone, because what you know is like a plague that needs to be buried or burned with the rest of the bodies. But they don't stay buried, do they, Fletch? Eventually you just . . . unload, like emptying a full magazine into someone's face. It's a bit messy, but undeniably cathartic."

The consummate professional, Fletch leans in as well, playing off my vibe, showing me he's a regular guy. It's like when a pasty executive who's been clipped by life tries to shoulder up at the airport bar to exchange war stories when he's never even been in a fistfight.

"Is that why you wanted to talk to me today, John? You have something you need to unload?"

"In a manner of speaking."

"I'm all ears."

No *shit*, I think, *they'd love those jug handles in my cell block, Opie.*

"May I have a cigarette, Fletch?"

"There's no smoking in here."

"Okay. Maybe I'll go back to my cell." I yawn. "Salisbury steak and potatoes au gratin tonight. After cobbler some of the boys are going to give me a jailhouse tramp stamp."

He lights me one of his own cigarettes. Marlboro Red—the Budweiser of cancer sticks. I draw on it greedily. The nicotine rush dulls the pain in my head but fires up the maddening itch that I cannot scratch under the plaster cast that covers my leg from ankle to arse.

Some of my new cell mates—around eight or ten 'roid-raging lifers who could bench-press two of me—had heard about my former profession and took me for a test-drive my first day inside. I tore most of them shiny new assholes, but they managed to jack up my leg and rearrange my face before the crooked guards stepped in and pretended to give a shit. I try to scratch inside the cast again. No dice. I get all Zen and try to make it go away with my mind but end up looking like I'm having a mild seizure.

"John, do you fully understand your rights and the nature of this interview?" he asks, gently raising a condescending brow.

"No. Where am I again?" I laugh, blowing smoke in his face.

He lights a cigarette of his own to show me he's just doing his job.

"I need to be sure you're of sound mind," he says politely.

I laugh for an awkwardly long time. Just for fun.

"I thought you said you read my book."

"I did."

"Then you just proved that there *is* such a thing as a stupid question."

He ignores me and writes on his pad like an actor on one of those cheesy legal shows.

"When they brought you in, you had been shot and you had a cocktail of narcotics in your blood that would have been lethal to a man twice your size. On your first day with the general population you assaulted numerous prisoners and two guards before they beat you unconscious and shattered your leg. Quite frankly, John, I can't believe you're still breathing, let alone coherent enough to undergo an interview."

"Is that what you call this? An interview?"

"Yes. What do you call it?"

"A bad joke with a jaw-breaking punch line," I say and stub the cigarette out in the palm of my hand.

It's subtle, but I see a slight twitch in his lip, an involuntary reaction. He's beginning to get the picture:

John Lago is in the building.

"That's the kind of thing that might give me the wrong impression about your mental state," he says calmly.

"Why is that?"

"Most people use an ashtray."

"I'm not most people. But you already knew that."

He writes notes, buying a little time to figure out how to regain control of the exchange, but I'm not about to let him start thinking for himself. I'm here for one reason, and it's time to cut to the chase.

"You're not going to find any answers on that legal pad, Fletch. If you're uncomfortable speaking to me, perhaps you should bring in someone with a more expensive tie."

He leans forward on his elbows. Alpha posturing. He's angry. I can see that, at one point in his life, he might have been intimidating. He doesn't realize that he no longer possesses that quality.

"John, there's one very important rule I need you to follow if this is going to work."

"No sex in the champagne room?"

"Don't fuck with me," he says, lightly threatening. "I've seen a lot of guys like you on that side of the table—all with the same attitude, full of themselves. You might think you're special because of who you were *out there*. But in here, you are a man that needs to convince me not to stick a needle in your arm and put you down like the family dog. Am I making myself clear?"

"Let's not fight," I say.

He settles back, proud of his steely delivery and strategic deployment of the F word. Probably a Brando fan. Loves the smell of testosterone in the morning.

"I just want to make sure we understand each other," he says, dialing back the aggression so my anger doesn't make me shut down.

I smile back at him but the light goes down in my eyes and I know that to him I look like a demon in an orange jumpsuit. Intimidation has been my occupation since I hit puberty, and this meat balloon is no different from my other marks. His look of surprise at my sudden change in demeanor is tantamount to a flinch.

"Fletch, if you know anything about me, you know that death is the least of my concerns. Compared to what my enemies are going to do to me, long before I ever make it into a courtroom, your little needle is more like *summer vacation with the family dog.* Forget about what you think will motivate me because I can pretty much guarantee you I'm *nothing* like the others that have sat across this table from you. *And just so we understand each other,* I didn't ask to speak to you because I feel guilty and want to rock floor seats with Jesus at the resurrection. I'm going down—so far I may never hit bottom—and the only thing I care about is making sure I don't go alone."

Now he really is all ears.

"Who do you want to take with you?"

"Alice."

He pauses as a jolt of electricity charges the room.

"You know where she is?"

"I can find her."

"Where?"

Fletch is drooling. Clyde just offered to drop a dime on Bonnie.

"Do you actually think I'm going to bend over for you without asking for a bit of a reach around?"

"We don't negotiate, John."

"Then this conversation is already over."

He is uncomfortable. This is not going as he planned. I get the impression he swaggered around the firing range earlier this week and bragged to the other mustaches about how he was going to school John Lago at his own game. It's laughable. So, I laugh.

"I'll do my best within my authority," he almost whines. "But I'm not making any promises. What do you want in exchange?"

"I want to see her."

"Excuse me?"

"It's pretty simple, Fletch. If I help you bring her in, I want to see her, in the flesh, one last time. Until you can agree to that, we have nothing more to discuss."

"I'll see what I can do."

An hour later I'm back in my six-by-six cell reading the fan mail my fellow cons have written on toilet paper, candy bar wrappers, and anything else that will hold ink and slipped under my door. Of course, every celebrity, even a D-lister like me, has to deal with the entire spectrum of the limelight. Sentiments range from guys telling me they're going to skull fuck me and cut me up into little pieces to guys wanting to pay me to teach *them* how to skull fuck someone and cut them into little pieces. Then, of course, there are the guys who want to be my bitch or my bride and vice versa.

But unlike most minor celebrities, I'm not delusional enough to think I'm a household name and deserve recognition as such. For those of you who don't know me, let me smoke the tires a bit and get you up to speed. I am a killer, professional variety, assassin species. Hey, don't hate the playa. You might have taken this gig too if, like me, you were born with one foot in the grave. But my childhood is a morbidly hilarious story for another day.

Until recently, I was employed by Human Resources, Inc.—a front for one of the most elite contract assassination firms in the world. Our specialty was our cover: the internship. HR, Inc. would place us in companies as interns, the bottom-feeders of the corporate world, and we would use our wallflower anonymity to slither up the corporate ladder like ninja black mambas and smoke heavily guarded, high-value targets—mostly well-heeled Fortune 500 golf zombies who won't be missed at the church picnic.

It was actually a genius concept and the perfect cover for wet work, if you're into that sort of thing. To quote Bob, my former and thoroughly dead boss, "Interns are invisible. You can tell executives your name a hundred times and they will never remember it because they have no respect for someone at the bottom of the barrel, working for free. The irony is that they will heap important duties on you with total abandon. The more of these duties you voluntarily accept, the more you will get, simultaneously acquiring *trust and access*. Ultimately, your target will trust you with his life and that is when you will take it."

Kind of makes you think twice about fucking with the little people, right?

I'm sure you're wondering why the hell someone would choose such a vocation. And if you aren't, then you've got serious problems. But I like to say that this is the kind of work that *chooses you*. Just like with money-grubbing religious cults and the Malaysian sex trade, the trolls of the world are always cruising the gutter for disenfranchised youth, such as yours truly. They know you've got no options. They also know you've got no outside support in the form of parents or even a half-assed state-assigned guardian. When you're on your own as a youngster, you're fresh meat and there's a line of cannibals just waiting to fire up the grill. So, instead of becoming a drug mule or getting sold as a chicken dinner for pedophile conventioneers, I got recruited into the highly unglamorous yet hella lucrative world of contract killing. I have half a brain and I'm fairly athletic, so they applied my talents to the job, scrubbed away any pesky human emotions or empathy that might get in the way, and put a gun in my hand before I had even figured out how to find my dick with it. I was twelve years old when HR, Inc. got its hooks in me and I stayed there for thirteen years.

Three years ago, at the ripe old age of twenty-five, I was about to retire. Bob's philosophy was that anyone accepting an internship past that age would be labeled a slacker by established employees and draw the kind of attention that could jeopardize assignments. Which was fine with me. I was happy to wash my hands of the whole affair, but before I could ride off into the sunset, I had one last job. I should have known not to take it because *one last job* in the movies is always the first step to total annihilation. Always. In the film *Seven*, Morgan Freeman takes *one last case* and ends up in the seventh circle of Hell. Or how about Harrison Ford in *Blade Runner?* Guy comes out of retirement to bag *one last skin job* and finds out *he's a skin job*! Jesus, I should have seen this coming!

Anyway, all I wanted was to move on and try to live something other than a kid-on-a-milk-carton life. I wanted baseball, hot dogs, apple pie, and fucking Chevrolet. God knows I earned it! You know the mortality stats for someone in my line of work? Nearly 100 percent. It doesn't matter how deadly you are because, unless you're the Terminator, eventually one of those bullets coming down like cool November rain is going to find you and paint the world with your insides.

It's only a matter of time.

And I had done my time . . . in spades. I should have bounced when I had the chance. Of course I didn't. Instead of getting my gold retirement watch and landing on my feet with a white picket fence and a satellite dish, I ended up base-jumping from the kettle into the fire. All because of *one last job*. But what's done is done. If you're interested, you can read about the whole hot mess in *The Intern's Handbook*. You won't find it at Barnes & Noble, but I hear the feds have a few copies lying around, and I wouldn't be surprised if you could download it for free on Russian iTunes. I'm told it's an excellent beach/airplane/bathroom/killing-time-after-a-motel-tryst read.

But that was then and this is now. I'm twenty-eight years young and I've ripened like nightshade berries or pungent French cheese. Since having my ass handed to me three years ago, I tried valiantly to leave my foul-mouthed, trigger-happy alter ego behind. Greener pastures were my original destination, but there truly is no rest for the wicked (despite our infectious charms), and I ended up being railroaded into a collision course with, you guessed it, Act Two of my tragic life story. I thought I'd nearly seen it all, but this not only takes the cake, it kidnaps, tortures, and dismembers the pastry chef.

So Kumbaya your asses round the campfire for a little prison bedtime story. If you're already a member of the John Lago fan club, then none of what I'm about to tell you will come as a shock. After *The Intern's Handbook*, you're used to being bound, horse-whipped, and hung from the nearest tree by the prodigious yarns I'm apt to spin. In fact, if this were a movie sequel, it would be *The Godfather, Part II*—better than the original. For all you John Lago virgins, welcome to the party—a raucous affair where they dose your wine cooler with angel dust at the door and you wake up playing a supporting role in a ritual killing somewhere in a swamp outside Tampa.

I guess the best place to begin is with Alice—the beautiful and charming love of my life who deceived me in every conceivable way, beat me senseless, shot me, ripped my heart out and stomped it to bits, and burned everything important to me to the ground. Some of you know about her and can't wait to get your fingers in the dirt, of which there is a veritable truckload. For those who don't, she's just like me—a killer who thought she was heartless but found out the hard way she wasn't when Cupid, that fat, cheeky bastard, shot a 600-grain carbon fiber arrow with a bone-splitting broadhead right through her love muscle, and life as she knew it bled out onto the floor.

When Bukowski said, "If there are junk yards in hell, love is the dog that guards the gates," he wasn't kidding.

1

—

Everyone knows that the best part of any great love story is the beginning. The middle is like driving across the United States—flat, predictable, and offering little more than fast-food culture and rest stop romance. In what other context do men and women live under the same roof and go weeks without sex? The end of a love story is either a catastrophic tragedy or an anticlimactic whimper. And it's the end, so unless it's Jerry Springer–worthy, who even cares? But the bliss of ignorance that comes in the beginning is a drug we all wish we could cook, shoot, and ride till the wheels come off.

When people ask about relationships, they always say, "How did you guys meet?" Not, "OMG, tell me all about your third year!" And when a relationship is in trouble, the desperate couple is always trying to *recapture the magic* of when they first met. The real tragedy is that, without time travel or amnesia, it's impossible to ever get back there. Which is why, to most people, marriage is about as magical as watching David Copperfield make Claudia Schiffer disappear.

The beginning of the love story between Alice and me was a bit more complicated than most. When we first met three years ago, we were mortal enemies, predators lurking in the woodwork of a prestigious Manhattan law firm. I had been sent there as an "intern" to exterminate one of the partners. And Alice, well let's just say she'd been sent there to exterminate me. Hilarity ensued! Despite our impossible circumstances, and the fact that we were interacting with each other using cover identities, we still managed to fall in love in our own twisted way. Predictably, the whole thing ended badly, mainly due to the fact that Alice had been paid to have it end that way. But I was smitten nonetheless, almost literally, and have never been able to shake it.

What's interesting is that our relationship was the perfect metaphor for all relationships. Love is the stepchild of pain and suffering, born of conflict and genetically predisposed to failure. Animals don't love anything but their next meal, and guess what we are and have been for millions of years? Basically, this whole love thing is like a new ingredient added to the primordial soup. So, while we are wining and dining that special someone, buying them flowers and performing feats of strength and wonder in the orgasm circus, we are fighting back our inherently violent opposition to the opposite sex.

A lifetime of living in an emotional black hole, observing people from the outside looking in, made me realize all of this. Knowing I could never have what normal people had allowed me to disconnect from the world and see it through the microscope of reason, unmolested by emotion. But guess what? *Eventually, I wanted what they had.* I wanted it so bad I was like a wolf stalking a blood trail. The way I saw it at the time was that I needed to find love so that I could exist. Relativity is about context. I had no context other than HR, Inc., and that came to an end. Everything else in the normal world seemed like it would drive me to continue killing, but love . . . that was the only thing in life that seemed worth dying for. I felt it with Alice. And I got what I wanted. Ish.

But love is filled with conflict and volatility—especially new love. Of course, when you're dealing with two "normal" people, the result of this conflict and volatility is what you might expect in a burgeoning relationship. You're hot, then cold, fucking, then fighting, making plans, then burning bridges, and so on. Alice and I are about as far from normal as you can get. In fact, she and I are like the two compounds your chemistry teacher told you *never* to mix. We're professional killers! That's taking conflict and volatility to a whole new level. With normal couples, someone might get thrown out of the house after a fight. With us, someone is liable to get thrown out a window.

2

Flashback three years. It was Valentine's Day, for those who enjoy irony with a side of psychosis. I was in Nowhere, New Hampshire, driving through one of the worst blizzards on record, feeling like Dustin Hoffman in *Marathon Man* as my car slid all over the road. I couldn't trust anyone. I knew that death was around every corner, the smiling friend who would invite me in for a hot cup of coffee to get out of the cold. But that was the least of my concerns. Finding Alice was all I cared about. The last time we had laid eyes on each other was in Honduras, through machine-gun sights. She had just finished fucking me over so royally that she made Judas look like Job. In fact, she and my old boss Bob had been in cahoots on the betrayal (long story), so I smoked his traitor ass, and Alice and I lost each other in the chaos that comes with Honduran death squads, a hail of bullets, and high explosives.

After crawling back to the U.S., I spent every waking moment tracking her down. Finally, I got a bead on her in New Hampshire and there I was, a jackass in a snow globe, making my way to Point A. After plowing through half the state, I saw the cabin where she was holed up through the four-inch circle on my windshield that wasn't covered by a sheet of ice. I drove past, hid my car in a grove of trees a mile up the road, and backtracked to the cabin. I approached from the rear, concealing my tracks in the powdery snow with a pine bough. The day was so cold it was like Flannery O'Connor's last breath—raw and as hard as the hammer of divine retribution. I entered through the back door. It was dark inside. I sat in a chair, covered myself with a blanket, and waited like some film noir detective. After an hour or so, I heard tires crunching in the snow out front, followed by the tread of boots coming up the steps. The door opened.

Alice walked in.

Sweet Alice. She looked amazing in her full-length Burberry black leather biker trench coat with a fox fur collar, carrying a bag of groceries. I reveled in her beauty, then greeted her by shooting her in the shoulder with my Walther P22. The groceries went flying and she fell back onto her butt, clutching the wound, a look of shock and confusion on her face. She reached for her gun but saw it was me and reconsidered.

"Hi, honey. I'm home." I laughed.

"John? What the fuck are you doing here?" Alice asked as blood gushed through the fingers wrapped around her shoulder wound.

"Taking care of a loose end," I said.

"Do you think I'd be up here if I was still after you?"

"You're up here because you're working a target. Based on the surroundings, my guess is it's someone in intelligence. CIA. Rogue. About five-foot-ten, a hundred and forty-five pounds. Am I getting warmer?"

"What have you done?"

"I told him to get the fuck out of Dodge before he gets his brains splattered all over Robert Frost country. I told him that his lovely intern is really a cold-blooded killer who is using him to get close to his boss so that she can cut his throat with a tantō knife—yakuza-style, of course."

"Congratulations. Now that you've destroyed my career, please say something hokey about tying up loose ends again and put me out of my misery."

"You're not a loose end. I am."

"Now you're making no sense," she said.

"Maybe this will help."

I set my gun on the floor.

"I love you," I said.

I kicked my gun across the floor, well out of my reach and well within hers.

"All I need to know is if you love me."

I rolled the box with a Harry Winston engagement ring I had given her when I proposed to her months ago across the floor. Ironically, at that time the ring had only been a ploy to emotionally manipulate her in order to gain information about my target. Now it was a symbol of my complete rejection of that part of me, and my complete acceptance of her. Alice just looked at me, waiting for the punch line. Then it was her turn to smile. Even though she had triple-crossed me and left me for dead, there were four carats of flawless clarity in that box that said "I forgive you."

"You're fucking crazy. You know that?"

"Not anymore."

She pulled her own gun and leveled it at me.

"I don't love you," she said defiantly. "And I don't see how you could possibly love me."

"Believe me, if I could walk away from this, or better yet, put a bullet in your head, I would. But I know who I am now. And I know that you're part of that," I said with conviction.

"No, John. I'm not."

"Then pull the trigger," I said, ready for anything. "And I'll have my answer."

"I can't do it," she said quietly.

"Just squeeze."

"I'm not talking about killing you. I'm talking about what happens if I don't kill you. What you want. I can't do it."

She fought the tears that were rolling down her cheeks, mocking her bravado.

"Neither can I," I said. "But I'm willing to die trying. Are you?"

We sat there staring at each other for a long time, both of us wondering what would happen next. Alice answered that question when I saw the muscles in the forearm of her gun hand flex and I heard the faint click of the trigger engaging the hammer.

"I'll take that as a no," I said calmly.

My heart sank and I closed my eyes, waiting for two bullets to double tap into my chest. Then I visualized the coup de grâce, the headshot—a blood, brain, and bone fragment masterpiece adorning the wall behind me—the *Guernica* of my life sliding to the floor in crimson chunks. But nothing came and I opened my eyes, hopeful that Alice was so overwhelmed by her love for me that she couldn't kill me.

Then she pulled the trigger.

3

She fired all ten rounds from her Beretta Px4 SubCompact. They zipped past my head, missing by millimeters, and punched holes in the solid log walls behind me. The sulfur smell of gunpowder hung in the air, burning my nostrils and throat. A flurry of wood splinters blanketed the top of my head like snow. I opened my eyes. Alice was gone. Her gun was on the floor, a cynical wisp of smoke curling out of the barrel. I wasn't exactly sure what to do. I was half-deaf from the gunshots and dumbstruck by the fact that I was still breathing.

The sound of a faucet running jerked me back into lucidity and I followed it into the bathroom. Alice had taken off her top and was examining her shoulder wound in the mirror. A combat grade first aid kit laid open on the counter. She didn't look at me. She just handed me a scalpel, a Magill forceps, and a packet of surgical gloves. I took them and tried unsuccessfully to make eye contact with her.

"What are you waiting for?" she asked, her eyes fixed on the mirror.

I pulled on the surgical gloves.

Alice gripped the bathroom counter and braced herself as I took a good look at the bullet hole I'd put in her shoulder. I didn't feel bad. She deserved a hell of a lot worse. I pulled a syringe from the kit.

"Let me hit you with a local first—"

"No."

"Alice, you—"

"I said no. You going to do this or do I have to do it myself?"

"I'll do it," I said quietly.

She closed her eyes and her light, rhythmic breathing was indicative of a deep, almost sensual meditative state. I gently palpated the powder-burned flesh around the two-inch star-shaped entry wound. She flinched briefly, but then I felt her wounded arm soften, as if she had just mentally separated it from her body. My fingers found the bullet, a hard, jagged lump buried in muscle and soft tissue.

"Got it."

No reply.

I gently inserted my finger into the wound. She didn't move despite what had to be searing pain. I probed deeper, making mental notes on the proximity of larger blood vessels and nerves, clearing a path for scalpel and forceps. Still no reaction. I'd seen breath and focus-induced pain management before but never to this degree. Even if there is no facial affect or muscle tension, there is always increased heart rate and breathing. Not with Alice. By my count her pulse was hovering at around sixty beats or fewer per minute, and her breathing was shallow and relaxed. If warm blood hadn't been dripping down my hand, I would have been convinced that her veins were filled with ice water.

I widened the opening to the wound with my index and middle finger, half hoping I'd get even the slightest wince. Nothing. I put a flashlight in my mouth and looked for the bullet. A slight glint of light told me it was trapped in a web of cauterized flesh that had burned and adhered to it. I slid the scalpel in and gently cut the little blackened tendrils away, freeing the lead mushroom. Then I carefully pulled it out with the forceps, sliding its sharp, superheated edges past the blood vessels I'd noted before. The bullet fell with a wet *clatter* in the bathroom sink. And there was still no movement from her, even when I proceeded to fill and rinse the gaping hole with saline and antibiotic wash and sutured it with more than thirty stitches. It was not until the final piece of gauze was taped over the seeping gash that she opened her eyes.

"How does it feel?" I asked.

She turned and kissed me—not with gratitude, but with the hungry aggression of an animal that has gone for days without food or water. There was surrender in the way she embraced me. Her hold on me was firm, but she wasn't pulling me in. She was hanging on to me, as if she knew that letting go meant falling to her certain death.

I know the feeling, I thought as we fell into bed.

As we methodically consumed one another, I was struck by the newness of it all. I'd been with Alice, but the unfamiliarity of what I was feeling *while occupying familiar territory* inexplicably filled me with mortal terror. And I realized it was vulnerability that ran through both of us like an electric current, powering our desire but threatening to burn us alive.

The point I'm trying to make is that, until that moment, I had never trusted a soul in my life. Instead I manipulated people in order to ensure I had leverage over them. No one has ever had the power to hurt me . . . or love me for that matter. I made sure of that. Mostly because my life depended on it. However, stepping away from the illusion of survival and lying next to a woman who was once my enemy—without a gun under the pillow and with both eyes closed—filled me with a feeling of power that being a predator never gave me. That night, I slept the deep, dreamless sleep of the dead, my resurrection coming in the form of the rising sun and a delicate kiss.

I win, I thought as we made love again. *I saved myself by giving myself up.* Happiness? I felt it. I knew it because I had never felt it before. Not really. Of course I had a hard time trusting it, but when

I looked into Alice's eyes and felt the playful warmth of her smile, I had no choice but to surrender to it. Then her smile faded and her eyes welled with tears.

"What's wrong?" I asked.

"I feel so . . . awful . . . about everything."

"And this is the kind of apology that makes it all irrelevant."

"You're either completely psychotic or you really do love me," she said.

"Probably a little bit of both," I said, pulling her close.

"There's so much I want to tell you," she said. "I want to come clean so we can move on."

"About what?" I asked.

"About what happened. New York, Honduras, me, Bob. You must have *so many* questions. I don't blame you really. I mean, if I were you—"

"Actually, I do have a question, Alice," I said, feigning concern.

"Good. Ask me anything."

"Will you marry me?"

4

"Dearly beloved, we are gathered here today to join . . . I'm sorry, I never got your names."

"That's because we didn't give them to you," I said coldly.

"Come on, padre, let's move it along," Alice said.

"Dearly beloved, we are gathered here today to join this couple in holy matrimony . . ."

Our wedding was a relatively small affair. Like most professional killers, we had no family or friends of any kind, so the guest list was a snap. John. Check. Alice. Check. Nondenominational, guitar-playing ex-convict minister who didn't ask a lot of questions. Check. Smartly dressed hotel staffer poised to toss Juliet rose petals and pop a bottle of 1907 Heidsieck champagne—recovered from the Swedish freighter *Jönköping* after it was sunk by a German U-boat in 1916 (something old)—upon completion of the nuptials. Check. All weddings should be like ours was—the bride and groom, solitary as their cake topper doppelgängers, grinning before Yahweh in bespoke couture.

Even though we spared the guest list, we spared no expense. The ceremony took place in the Ty Warner Penthouse at the Four Seasons in Manhattan. For the price of one night's lodging in that room, you could feed and clothe several villages in Myanmar for a full year. Alice looked stunning in her handmade jet-black wedding gown (something new) that I had a goth seamstress fashion out of exotic military fabrics. It cost me a small fortune (and nearly my pinky finger) but it was worth it. That dress made me want to cut my own heart out and bleed on the sacrificial stone to show my gratitude to the gods. And after all that, I couldn't wait to unceremoniously rip it off her.

I was wearing a tuxedo I stole from a dead MI6 agent (possibly my best-dressed target), and a pair of Vietnam-era jungle combat boots I won in a card game before I killed a roomful of Laotian flesh peddlers with a camp shovel. Alice wasn't into the boots, but I told her letting me wear them was the least she could do after she had tried several times in the last year to put a bullet in my head but only managed to hit my heel. She one-upped me by wearing a pair of Alexander McQueen Titanic Ballerina Pumps she'd had fitted with a razor sharp titanium stiletto heel that could lacerate Kevlar and punch through concrete. They were wickedly beautiful and I couldn't help but wonder how they would look pointing at the ceiling.

"Do you . . . take . . . her to be your lawfully wedded wife—"

"I do," Alice said.

"Seriously?" I said, annoyed. "It's not your turn."

"Why don't we try that again?" the minister said.

"No." Alice glared.

"Don't ruin the moment," I said.

"I don't like the rest of those tired, played-out vows," Alice said.

"To have and to hold, in sickness and in health, till death do us part. Those?" I inquired casually.

"Yep," she snapped, strangling her exquisite saffron crocus bouquet.

"Fine. What do you suggest?"

"There's a very rare bottle of champagne that has waited patiently at the bottom of the ocean off the coast of Finland for nearly one hundred years for us to drink it," she began. "We have actual Kush fresh off the plane from Islamabad, and the Maine lobsters are going to kill each other if we don't kill them first. And let's not forget that I'm so horny I could fuck a mechanical bull. So, with all of these more urgent matters, why do we need to go through with this ritual nonsense?"

"I do," I said.

"We're not there yet," the minister said, annoyed.

"Shhhh," Alice said, pressing her finger to his lips too hard and slightly cutting him with what I could see was a French-manicured nail with a razor-sharp rose-gold edge—adding an instant upgrade to my shoe fantasy. In the interest of expediting the fulfillment of that fantasy, I kissed the bride.

The minister scowled and lit a cigarette while we made out like high school prom dates.

"I now pronounce you man and wife?"

Hands everywhere. Groping. Outside voices.

"Okay. I'm out of here," the minister said. "Congratulations. You two were made for each other."

He took leave of us, along with the hotel staffers, and we took leave of our senses. Just think bacchanal meets Masters and Johnson meets *Penthouse Letters* and you've pretty much got the picture. After several hours of "marital consummation" we put our beautiful wedding clothes back on and had a smoke on the terrace.

"Promise me we'll have sex like that for the rest of our lives, no matter how old, gray, and foul-smelling we are," she said.

"No way," I said. "Maybe if we were chimpanzees . . . on some kind of experimental military drug. Outside of that, I'd be dead in five years if we kept up this pace."

"Maybe that's my fiendish plan. To fuck you to death."

"Okay, I promise."

We both laughed, mainly because the irony of the situation

was as thick as our Sylvia Weinstock wedding cake and twice as sweet. I married the love of my life and former nemesis. We had the most beautiful wedding two totally disconnected psychopaths could possibly have had. We enjoyed unspeakable pleasures. And then it was time for the pièce de résistance, my wedding present to Alice. I opened the doors to the foyer (yes, the suite was that big) and revealed a massive, beautifully wrapped box about the size of a coffin.

"What is it?" she said, licking her lips.

"Open it and find out."

She tore off the wrapping paper and lifted the lid off the box. Her jaw dropped.

"Holy shit, John."

"That's only the beginning."

"Excuse me?" she said, incredulous.

"This is a two-part present."

"What's part two?"

"Are you sure you're ready?" I asked coyly.

"Don't make me shoot you in your other foot."

I looked at my watch.

"Twenty minutes and all will be revealed. Enough time for champagne."

We popped the shipwrecked Heidsieck and toasted. It tasted like unbridled optimism, with a gunpowder nose and a burnt lemon and kerosene finish. After we practically sucked the last drop out of the bottle, we kissed, tasting victory on each other's malevolent lips.

"Ready?" I said.

She nodded, smiling.

I opened her wedding present box and pulled out five shaped charges made to look like little wedding cakes and positioned them in a large circle on the floor.

"John. What are you doing?"

"Sweeping you off your feet."

"Seriously. What are you doing?"

I stopped and grinned.

"This is your present."

I pulled two Israeli Special Forces X95 SMGs with silencers (something borrowed) out of the wedding box, slapped 32-round 9-mm mags into each, and handed one to her.

"It's beautiful, honey, but have you lost your mind?"

"No. You're going to love this. Trust me."

I pulled her close to me and started strapping weaponry to her body with a custom leather holstering harness.

"Okay, now you're making me hot."

"That dress is bulletproof."

"Keep talking . . ."

"My tuxedo is impervious to flamethrowers and chemical weapons."

She jumped up and wrapped her legs around me.

"Save it for later. We need to focus."

"Tease," she said, sliding off.

We busily geared ourselves up.

"How many?" she asked.

"At least a dozen. Maybe more," I said, smiling.

"Who are they?"

"Do you want to ruin the surprise?" I asked.

"No, darling."

"Good. Now, stand next to me here."

I pulled her close to me in the middle of the circle created by the wedding cake–shaped charges.

"You're a sick man, John."

"I know. Isn't it great?"

"Yes."

"Close your eyes."

She did and we kissed. Then she opened them again.

"Can I have a little hint about the target?" she asked, batting her eyelashes.

"The CEO of Human Resources, Incorporated," I answered casually and blew the shaped charges.

The circular piece of floor we had been standing on broke away and we dropped through the ceiling into another palatial suite directly below us. As we smashed into the floor and rolled to cover, bullets were already flying. It turned out I had slightly miscalculated. There weren't a dozen armed men in there. There were two dozen.

Till death do us part.

5

A huge cloud of swirling white plaster dust made it difficult to see and breathe on top of making everyone look completely ridiculous. The Israelis are masters at close-quarters urban warfare, probably the best in the world. Knowing this, I pretty much customized our entire ops weapon package as if we were a couple of Mista'arvim soldiers getting dropped into a Hamas bug nest. Of course, we had the element of surprise with the massive pieces of floor and ceiling smashing down directly into the suite's executive conference room.

Seated at the conference table at the time were several suits from an organized crime syndicate in Eastern Europe. Their heavily armed blockhead security thugs were standing against the walls of the conference room behind them, trying to look all badass with their chinstrap beards and cologne-infused pinstripe suits. At the head of the table, flanked by his own army of murderous goons, was our target, the CEO of HR, Inc. And check this out. The guy's name was Bob! Evidently, he was called off the bench to replace the former Bob after that one's untimely death in Honduras at the hands of yours truly.

The new Bob was nothing like the old one. He was a former military contractor who thought he could pack the same steel as the rest of us. He'd obviously been appointed by whatever mystic cabal, alien brain trust, or Wizard of Oz consortium had been running HR from some ivory tower since its inception. Bob II was a flabby suit.

Which is why it shouldn't surprise you to know what he did when that ceiling crashed down and killed five of the guys sitting a few feet away from him at the conference table. He pissed his pants and crawled under the bed.

Alice tried to go after him, but she got lit up by several shooters and had to find cover. I deployed smoke and flash grenades to throw them off her tail. The bosses who hadn't been crushed to death by falling chunks of concrete floor were choking and disoriented, and I thought I could actually hear some of them crying. Which makes sense, since they were completely abandoned by their tough-fronting velvet rope security apes, who had taken cover all over the suite.

We put a pill in every boss and started looking for a dozen or so of their thugs. The good thing was that they had not only us to worry about, but also each other. There isn't a lot of blood-brother loyalty among clock puncher bodyguards, especially if they're used to getting paid in gristly donkey sausage for doing rusty cleaver jobs in Bulgaria. The bad thing was that this was a recipe for total chaos. Everyone was trampling over one another, trying to find cover. Guess what? There is no cover in a luxury hotel suite! Everything is thin and fragile and expensive. Some realized this and simply made a run for the door. Alice was going to shoot them, but I waved her off. They couldn't ID us and this was probably the only vacation they were going to get before the Boris that was the boss of their Boris boss cut them up for chum.

The brief exodus thinned the herd to eight bearded, Drakkar Noir–pickled human bull's-eyes, and that was more than manageable for the missus and me. The two of us hightailed it to the only *real* cover in the suite—a huge fake Ming vase and a bar cart—both of which had been placed in the room by hotel staff thanks to some very bogus work orders issued by me, and both of which were lined with six inches of titanium and Kevlar composite, impenetrable by anything but a stinger missile. Oh, and they were full of extra mags too, so we basically had some very stylish urban foxholes with sweet ammo stashes.

"Way to plan ahead, love pumpkin," Alice said as she slapped in another mag.

"I think your terms of endearment tank is empty, lamb chop." I grinned.

"This is the best wedding present ever, *sheyne punim*," she said as she drilled a guy who looked exactly like Count Chocula.

"I thought you'd like it, angel puss," I said. "But this is only one of your presents."

"What? John, you shouldn't have!"

"Nothing's too good for my beautiful bride, motherfuckers!" I yelled as I splattered a couple of Borats all over the silk divan.

From that point on it was carny shootin' gallery time. We systematically picked off the remaining thugs, shooting them through walls, decorative partitions, leather club chairs, flat-screen TVs—things that stop bullets in the movies but wouldn't stop a BB gun in real life. Just when we thought it was Miller Time, another problem arose in the form of a .338 Lapua Magnum round that hit the bottle of Grey Goose on top of the bar cart with such force that the vodka inside exploded and incinerated the head of one of our opponents. I quickly found the hole in the window facing Central Park. Sniper. Had to be with Bob II. All the other suits were dead, and there were only two thugs left.

I fired a shot in Bob II's general direction and my position got rattled with a hailstorm of sniper bullets. I did it again so I could judge the angle of trajectory and draw fire on one of the last thugs creeping up on Alice. The thug got his head unzipped by the sniper and I used my green-laser sighting scope to track the powder residue hanging in the air from the kill shot. I followed that until I saw the moonlight delicately reflect off his scope. Son of a bitch was more than a thousand yards away on a rooftop overlooking Central Park.

Then I texted one of my NYPD contacts and gave him the shooter's twenty. City cops *love* bagging a pro, and I handed them a hot snot on a silver platter.

While we tried to lay low, the final thug, of course, had found a way to weasel behind the Sub-Zero refrigerator. Those are heavy, well-made fridges with a ton of metal, so he won the award for smartest meat helmet. We couldn't get a good shot at him and he had Alice pinned down in the twelve inches of space that his bullets and the sniper's bullets couldn't reach. So, I did what any good husband would have done in my position. I shot one of Bob II's toes off. He screamed in agony as the blood poured out of his tasseled loafer. Served him right. Who the hell wears tassels anymore?

"Call him off, Bob Deuce!"

"What?" he yelled. "Who?"

I shot off another toe. He started blubbering.

"The sniper, you asshole!"

"Fuck you!"

Toes 2, 3, and 4. Agony. Large animal wailing.

"Your balls are next!"

"I said fuck you!"

Ball #1. Blasted back to the Flintstone age.

The wet spot on his trousers made for better targeting. At first, he could barely breathe from the pain, and then he started wailing again.

"That's gotta hurt!" I said.

"Just kill him!" Alice said. "I can't take his whining anymore!"

She blasted in his general direction, but the sniper lit her up and hit the end of her gun, destroying the barrel.

"Alice!" I yelled. "You know how much that thing cost?"

"Sorry! Just put that little bitch out of my misery!"

"I'm going to! But first I'm gonna clip his Johnson!"

"No!" Bob II screamed. "I'll call him off."

I heard him fumbling for his phone. Then I heard him whimper something in Russian. I fired a few rounds in his direction to test his truthfulness. He yelped in fear, but no sniper rounds came through.

"Now tell him to shoot that asshole behind the fridge!" Alice yelled.

The asshole behind the fridge took that opportunity to come out, guns blazing. He went straight for Alice, probably thinking a woman was going to be an easier mark. I had a shot but didn't take him out, just so I could see him eat his arrogance. He did when she broke his nose and split his scalp with the heavy vase. When his eyes were drenched in blood, she heart-punched him so hard I heard his sternum snap before he face-planted in the tropical fish tank.

Then we heard Bob II ordering the sniper to reengage.

Since we had abandoned our cover, we were dangerously exposed. When the sniper rounds started whipping through the room, shredding everything, Alice was able to jump back behind her vase, but I was ass in the wind. So I ran into the master, threw the mattress off the bed, and jumped on top of Bob II. Those .338 rounds packed enough powder to go through both of us twice and still plug six inches into the concrete floor. Sniper knew it, and he wasn't about to put a permanent blowhole in his cash cow. Bob II was sucking wind, struggling like mad to get out from under me. Wrangling the fat son of a bitch was like trying to cinch into eight seconds with a pissed-off Brahma. So, I stuck a knife in his subclavian vein and he passed out from shock. I held the blade in place so he wouldn't bleed out. My NYPD contact acknowledged my text but said it would take them at least three minutes to get there because of traffic. That was an eternity we didn't have.

Then my beautiful wife did something brilliant. The windows in the suite had SPD glass—suspended particle devices. These are nano-scale particles suspended in a liquid layer between two panes of glass. When voltage is applied, the particles align and let light pass through. Thus, the glass is nice and clear when it's a cloudy day or if it's night. When the sun is bright, a breaker is tripped and the voltage is removed, causing the particles to move randomly, darken the windows, and block excess UV rays. It's kind of like the bigger, more expensive version of those bowling alley manager glasses that darken in sun and lighten inside. Alice fired a single round into one of the electrical outlets, causing a surge and flipping the breaker for the entire room. Out went the lights and black went the windows.

Then Bob II regained consciousness. Perfect timing.

"What do you want?" he asked weakly.

Blood was starting to pool on the carpet. The sniper was taking blind potshots at us. My plan was going sideways.

"We need to get out of here!" Alice said. "Is he dead?"

"Not yet!"

"What? Why?"

"I need something from him!"

I turned to Bob II.

"You're going to give me your access codes for HR, Bob Deuce, or I'm going to pull out this knife and let you bleed to death."

Everything was exploding all around us. And the sniper had shot out most of the darkened glass, so if he had infrared he'd see movement and that's all those guys need to put a hot tamale right up your ass.

"Go to hell," he said.

"Such bravado. Could it be that it's all done with a fingerprint scan now?"

The look on his face was my answer.

"Adios, asshole," I said and pulled the knife out.

In the distance, we heard gunfire erupt (something blue).

"Sounds like Manhattan's finest!" I said.

I peeked out the edge of the window and saw blue muzzle flashes on our sniper's rooftop. The cops were in a full-on firefight with him. He kept trying to send a few pills our way, but the heat got to be too much for him and he had to concentrate on saving his own nuts. So, when the coast was even slightly clear, we army-crawled out of there and bolted, leaving our weapons and any professional gear behind.

"Well, this dress is definitely ruined," Alice said as we ran down the stairwell and she examined the splattered blood and powder burns on Vera's fine beadwork.

"I think as the new co-CEO of HR, Inc., you can probably afford to get another one."

She slammed me up against the wall and kissed me. I could tell she was deliriously happy.

"Like your wedding present?" I asked proudly.

"Are you kidding me? A hostile takeover is what every girl dreams of on her wedding day."

She kissed me again, so hard it bloodied my lip.

"Can't believe we're going to run HR," she said excitedly.

"Promise me we'll play nice from now on, honey-bunny," I said, wiping the blood off my lips.

"You have my word, schnooky lumps," she said.

"Wow, that's the worst one," I said. "Anyway, let's shake on it," I said and held out Bob II's severed hand.

"Oh, now that's just gross."

6

FBI-NCAVC, Quantico, Virginia
Present day

Fletch is clicking his pen, staring at the notes he just furiously scribbled about my wedding night. He looks like a man attempting to decipher an encrypted message, reading between the lines for threads that might unravel the increasingly complicated cat's cradle of answers to all of his banal questions. The clicking pen is clearly a thinking mechanism for Fletch, a dissonant metronome that focuses his busy hamster-wheel brain. I am acutely aware that he is eager for more information but he is attempting to conceal these motivations with his usual stoic look. He glances at me to see if I am on to him and recoils from my knowing smile, which tells him the answer is a resounding "Yes."

"I've killed no fewer than six people with pens of varying types. They make excellent weapons, Fletch."

He smiles at me to show me he isn't impressed or intimidated . . . and continues to click that fucking pen.

"Nervous habit?" I ask dryly.

He finds that question disagreeable and the smile disappears.

"Does it bother you?" he asks, pausing with his thumb hovering above the pen like a finger teasing a trigger.

"Very much."

He looks down at his notebook and continues clicking, wanting me to know he is unwilling to compromise anything about his process for my sake. It may seem petty, and it is, but it's also a game. Fletch is trying to engage me in this game, hoping I will do something angry and reactive as a result of him ignoring me—attempt to shove the pen into his eye socket perhaps? Instead I return his serve by whistling out loud. And yes, in case you were wondering, I am whistling "Dixie." The only thing he can do to silence me is play his hand and ask the questions he's been trying to suppress.

"John, how did you know they were in that hotel room, Bob's successor and the other men?"

A softball question, motivated by fear or, even worse, a loss of confidence.

"I have my vays," I reply in my best Dr. Strangelove accent.

"Which are?" he asks.

"That hardly seems relevant."

"It's relevant to me. I'm sure that meeting was top secret. Seeing as how you were no longer a part of HR, Inc., I'm wondering how you could have possibly known the exact location and time."

"Or even where to blow a hole in the floor in order to inflict the largest number of casualties," I add helpfully.

"Precisely. So, how did you know?"

"Fletch, I'm not writing a tell-all book here."

"What difference does it make now if you tell me or not, John?"

"It makes a difference because you believe I had help and you want to send out the cavalry to round up the whole James Gang. You got *me*, Fletch. And if you play your cards right, you might get Alice too. Don't be so fucking greedy and let's stay on topic, shall we?"

He is livid—mainly because I just embarrassed him in front of his two-way-mirror drinking buddies. He takes a breath, pointedly rips out the notepad page that might have contained the names of some juicy accessories to murder, and starts a fresh one.

"Fine. If not how, then why?" He touches *The Intern's Handbook* for emphasis. "For someone who seemed quite motivated to exit HR, Inc., you certainly went to a lot of trouble to not only return, but to actually run it."

"Good question, Fletch. You're becoming a regular Charlie Rose."

7

Pretty much everyone at HR, Inc. had a case of the Mondays the first Monday after we had disposed of Bob II and his crew. I think the recruits were simultaneously relieved and terrified to find out that (a) John Lago, author of their banned bible, was now running the show, and (b) he was running it with Alice, his former-arch-nemesis-turned-wife-slash-Chinese-acrobat-Kama-Sutra-sex-panther. Needless to say, we had some serious 'splainin' to do. But after the initial shock, we kept things under control. The nice thing is that no one was demanding to leave HR as a result of the recent *management reshuffle*. Bob II was reviled among the recruits and no tears were shed over his demotion.

"He was a paper-shuffling pantywaist," one of the recruits casually chimed in, "soft church lady hands and a nipple on his bottle of gin. Rest in piss, Number Two."

I instantly liked this guy—first for knowing what the hell he was talking about and second for having the balls to say it. He was a seventeen-year-old black kid with the meanest tattoos I've ever seen and an odd hillbilly way of speaking. He had the squinty, leathery charm of country rearing, but his look was all Bronx torture squad. In his eyes, there was the glint of street wisdom far beyond his years but they were lively and didn't have any of the numbed menace you often see in kids who, like me, were washing blood from their hands before they were old enough to see an R-rated movie.

"What's your name, sunshine?" I asked.

"Sue."

"A boy named Sue," I said, grinning.

"Go ahead, have your fun," he said, grinning right back.

"I take it your parents were Johnny Cash fans," Alice said, audibly rolling her eyes.

"West Virginia cracker variety, if you know the type. Fostered me like the family mutt with a leather strap and table scraps till I was five and then Granny exiled me for running out of cuddle."

"Did you understand a word of what he just said?" Alice asked.

"Did it work?" I asked him.

"What?" he asked.

"The name. Did it work?"

"Here I am, JL. You tell me."

"Contracts?"

"Baker's dozen."

"At seventeen? Bullshit."

"Shortest distance between truth and bullshit is six feet straight down, JL," he said, quoting the handbook.

"A fanboy, John. How charming."

"He knows great writing when he sees it."

"Normally I go for fiction, but the handbook sort of spoke to me."

"Trust me," Alice said, "a lot of it is fiction."

Many of the other recruits murmured their disagreement with her on this particular topic, and I knew immediately I was among friends.

"I think I can speak for most of us here when I say thank you for giving a damn," Sue said.

I could feel Alice bristling, like when ozone lifts your hair off your head just before you get struck by lightning.

"Yeah, well, I can't cut loose of you all. I thought I could but I'm back and this time I brought a secret weapon."

I looked at Alice. All eyes were watching pensively, waiting for her head to explode and fill the room with poisonous snakes. They had no idea how to process her presence, the femme fatale from my masterpiece of murder and intrigue, walking right off the page and into their conference room.

"I know what all of you must be thinking," Alice said warmly. "And you're right. Me being here, in this scenario, is probably the most fucked-up thing you've ever seen. But as you know, John is very persuasive. And if he hadn't had the balls to do what he did, none of us would be standing here right now."

Alice of course had to put an exclamation point on her little speech by firmly grabbing the balls she was referring to—just in case anyone was under the impression I might actually be in charge.

After we gave our pep talk, a lot of the recruits talked to me one-on-one. They *were* actual fans, thanking me up and down for writing the handbook and for coming to their rescue now after the death of the Bobs had left the place in a total shambles. I shared one of the first Bob's hidden bourbon bottles with Sue, and we talked a bit more as the night wore on. Even though we might as well have been from different planets, he was the only recruit in the ranks who reminded me of myself. He had the kind of honesty that only comes from people who've shed a lot of blood walking the razor's edge.

"Never thought you'd be back here, JL."

"Me neither. Old habits."

"Seeing you with her is . . . I don't know, man. Hard to believe."

"Tell me about it."

Sue paused. I could tell he was struggling with something.

"Spit it out before you swallow it, Sue."

He laughed.

"I know I don't know you, JL. I mean . . . I feel like I do, so . . . can we talk man-to-man?"

"Yeah, kid. What's on your mind?"

"Don't get me wrong. I know you're committed to the cause, which is us. You just don't seem like the ambitious type. And Alice, she's got some serious stars in her eyes."

"That's her nature, Sue. But you're wrong about my ambition. I had a few burning bush epiphanies recently that made me believe it's my nature too."

"That bush tell you Alice is someone you can trust?"

"In a way. But it's not really *about* trust, is it?"

"No, sir." He laughed. "I guess we gave that up a long time ago."

"Exactly. I figure I'm with the woman I love, doing what I was born to do and keeping my eyes on you train wrecks. That's enough for me. At least for now."

"Sounds like happiness," Sue said.

"Let's not get carried away."

8

I have to admit it was more than a little weird spending all my time and energy to rebuild a place that I had fantasized about burning to the ground on hundreds of occasions. I had, in fact, planted demolition charges in the subbasement years ago when Bob's goons whacked Eva, the only bona fide girlfriend I'd ever had. I was dead serious about taking that place down like a mothballed Vegas casino. Must have wired it up with over three hundred pounds of C4, enough to blow it up twice.

On Christmas Eve I was all ready to send HR to the moon, but I couldn't do it. It's funny but I was mainly afraid I would kill some poor bastard who was running home after the late shift at some dead-end job so he could play Santa for his kids. Jesus, I'm so Disney sometimes! Anyway, to this day the charges are probably still down there. I took out all the blasting caps and wires, so there's pretty much no way the C4 will pop . . . I don't think.

What was even weirder than me running HR is how much I loved it. I went totally overboard and decided to make whacking someone an artisanal pursuit. Let's face it, there's a right way of doing things and a dumbass way. And it's not really up for debate, because in this business dumbasses always end up dead. So, I focused on putting my money where my mouth is, and instead of just writing some DIY manual, I designed a training regimen that could turn a snot-nosed kid into Billy the Kid in less than twelve weeks. Now I sound like one of those tools on late-night TV. "You too can learn to shoot, stab, strangle, and bludgeon someone to death in twelve short weeks at Human Resources, Inc. And if you act now, you'll get this beautiful Colt Anaconda .44 Magnum with hollow-point rounds absolutely free!"

Seriously, though, I was good at my job. Really good. First thing I did when Alice and I raided the formidable financial treasure chests of HR was build a state-of-the-art training facility in a secluded forest upstate. It was only an hour from Manhattan but provided a profound and much-needed change of pace. I designed the entire facility and most of the training areas inside. It was incredible. There were several interior and exterior *urban combat simulators* inside and on the grounds. The interiors looked like just about any kind of office environment you could think of. Have to kill a guy in an elevator? We had a working elevator shaft and car. From conference rooms to cube farms to executive washrooms and supply closets, there was a simulation zone built to create complete authenticity for every scenario. Oorah.

But then there was my favorite. The *noncombat office skill enhancement zones*. These were rigorous stations designed to teach our recruits—people who might not have finished sixth grade, mind you—how to make copies, file, type, collate, assemble office furniture, operate a watercooler, ship, mass mail, work in multiple computer operating systems, and, of course, make coffee. Again, authenticity was the rule of the day. Interns who show up with zero skills are quickly jettisoned from the workforce in the real world. Our interns had to be excellent at both being an office asset and being a wet-work asset, and our training facility provided them with a serious leg up.

Recruitment was also my area of focus. In addition to finding the brightest and the best—and the most ruthless—in the U.S., our global expansion plans had me hiring in Asia and Europe, two markets with massive upside potential. In Europe, we found recruits from a diverse array of countries, but the young upstarts who impressed me the most were the Norwegians. They were all scary intelligent, perfect physical specimens with the right temperamental mix of methodical rationalism and repressed homicidal rage—both of which they could switch on and off at will. They also spoke many useful European languages and their English carried very little accent. The only problem was that they were too good-looking, but I figured it was worth spending some time to ugly them up in order to take advantage of their considerable talents.

While I was building a pantheon of death and molding impressionable youngsters into killing machines, someone had to maintain client relationships. You can lose relevance in this business overnight, and we continued to send the more experienced recruits out on very selective assignments in order to keep them sharp and maintain our presence. That was Alice's area of expertise. I just didn't have the stomach to deal with clients—power-mongering bloodsuckers who would grind our recruits' bones to make their bread if we were in the beanstalk business. Alice, on the other hand, was acutely aware of the financial merits of befriending power-mongering bloodsuckers and enjoyed wining and dining them until they were pregnant with the HR seed.

Keep in mind that many of them were booze-addled, sun-damaged white men with money to burn and a list of enemies longer than the guest lists for their spoiled daughters' million-dollar weddings. Alice had them eating out of her hand and writing retainer checks of the seven-figure variety in no time. When we were fully operational, we had double the client list and twice the revenue that Bob and Bob II had in their most successful quarters combined. We were, in my white boy hip-hop parlance, *paper'd up.*

9

When it came to the business of running HR, we had a great one-two punch, Alice and me. She was the slick, seductive, consummate schmoozer who could convince the devil to hand over the pennies on a dead man's eyes if she wore the right shoes. Meanwhile, I was running what was basically a chain gang of hardening killers whose ability to execute clean, untraceable hits was as accomplished as their ability to identify over a hundred varieties of coffee based purely on smell. They were also learning to be cool under pressure. I wanted them to be able, like fighter pilots, to laser-focus on the task at hand, even if all hell was breaking loose around them.

But all work and no play makes John a dull (and cranky) boy, so Alice and I made sure we enjoyed the honeymoon phase of our marriage—especially since we never really had time for an actual honeymoon. We bought a killer loft in Chinatown and decorated it like wealthy rock stars from the early 1970s—lots of gold, burled wood, frosted glass, and cocaine. Alice had a fetish for, well, almost all fetishes, so we had a lot of equipment that informed this pastime and transformed our walk-in closet into a dungeon master's armory. I've done a fair bit of shagging in my life, but nothing could have prepared me for cohabitation with a woman who is basically Caligula with a French manicure. I'm amazed I had anything left for work each day, but there was something very empowering about it all. For the most part, we were living like wild animals with no rules and frequent, albeit minor, bloodshed. Someday I may write another handbook for married couples based on this experience, because purely primordial interaction with mercifully little talking is the true meaning of domestic bliss.

"John?" Alice asked me one night after we broke in our vintage Eero Aarnio floating bubble chair.

"Yes, my sweet boudoir contortionist?"

"Are you okay?"

"I will be when I regain feeling in my lower extremities. What's on your mind?"

"I'm . . . this is so hard to say. Not hard, but weird."

"How weird could it be? We're naked in an acrylic bubble chair. We just drank half a bottle of absinthe and we're listening to Jimmy Page play banjo on a super-rare Japanese import eight-track—"

"I don't mean *that kind* of weird. I mean . . . I'll just say it. I'm scared. Okay, happy?"

She punched me in the shoulder. It *really hurt*.

"Not anymore."

She kissed it to make it all better.

"I'm sorry. This is going to sound arrogant and idiotic but I have never really felt this way."

"Scared?"

"Yeah, scared."

"It does sound a bit suspect, but that's neither here nor there. What are you afraid of?"

"This. All of this. Going away. I never cared about a damn thing and now . . ."

"How do you think I feel? Why do you think I would have let you put a bullet in my head? I couldn't bear not having this with you. The idea of that made me want to blow my brains out."

"Stop it. You're gushing." She smiled. "Seriously, though, now that we have this, aren't you terrified of losing it?"

I kissed her, hard and deep. I don't know why, but I was obsessed with communicating with Alice this way. I hated words because they just didn't cut it. There is no way to tell someone that when you're inside them you feel like you've been cut from neck to nuts and hollowed out by the hand of God without it sounding totally mental. It's a feeling, an electric current from the heart to the brain that carries a million words and images like a fast pipe-data stream. And I was trying to zap her senseless with it because I loved her so much it hurt.

"What was that?" she asked, feeling the buzzing on her lips.

"That was my answer."

The next few months were the happiest of my life. Every day I woke up, I faced the day with anticipation instead of dread. Every night I collapsed on my pillow, usually from coital exhaustion, and welcomed sleep with warm resolve instead of paralyzing fear. And even though I knew that having children was both completely insane and out of the question, I could feel that urge, that familial drive to, in a godlike fashion, create two bright, pure eyes to look at us both and remind us of who we really are versus what we'd been made to be. And then one morning, while we drank espresso and cleaned our guns on the terrace, the honeymoon was over.

Just like that.

10

I'm convinced that human beings are just not happy being happy for too long. We thrive on misery and invite it into our miserable lives every chance we get. Of course, the source of the misery is almost always related to something that has nothing to do with love. For most people, money is their Achilles' heel. Either they have too much of it or not enough. For others, it's the ennui that comes with routine. Of course, in the eyes of each person, it's the other person's fault that (a) the sex has dropped off, (b) unrealistic career dreams never came true, (c) the Joneses have a bigger boat, or (d) wifey has been banging the Joneses. And when the blame game begins, you're already past tense. Your relationship is now adversarial and the influence your love had on you just got pissed away.

For Alice and me, I guess I shouldn't be surprised that the source of our marital friction was Human Resources, Inc. After all, if anything could've put a hex on us, it was that place. Hindsight is twenty-twenty, but we probably should have thought carefully about the co-CEO thing. Even though our areas of focus were different, we both had our opinions about the business as a whole and how to build it for the future.

My big issue that Alice gave no credence to was my paranoia that, even though we whacked Bob II, there was still someone out there pulling strings who probably didn't appreciate us taking over HR all that much. Let's face it, Bob wasn't smart or rich enough to keep the business afloat himself. We had a lot of revenue coming in, but HR was always much bigger than your average bootstrap start-up. So, the burning question for me was, *Who was really running HR and when were they going to rain down holy terror on our little lemonade stand?* Alice's counterpoint was that if they were going to do something, they would have done it immediately after our wedding night melee. They didn't, so she figured they were either frightened of us or they had moved on. This was not good enough for me. Each day I was twisting on this issue, waiting for the other wing tip to drop.

Alice had different, equally paranoid concerns, although she would not characterize them as such. Since we took over HR, she had become obsessed with the idea of hunting down and killing an FBI mole Bob was convinced had infiltrated HR on his watch a few years back but who, *she* was convinced, had since returned to the bureau's mother ship. When I met Alice at Bendini, Lambert & Locke, she was *playing* the part of an FBI mole, so the irony of her objective was hilarious to me, but not at all amusing to her. In her opinion, if Bob was suspicious of something like that, it was probably true. I told her that, over the years, I had been privy to dozens of conspiracy theories Bob espoused, and *none* of them ever turned out to be true. But that didn't dissuade her.

To make matters worse, Alice was convinced that ever since she left Honduras, someone had been watching her. She had taken volumes of notes on the subject prior to our meeting in New Hampshire and it all seemed very convincing. Where it went off the rails was when she even questioned the sources I had used to find her in New Hampshire. She asserted that perhaps that information had been conveniently disseminated to me with enough finesse to make me feel like it had not been handed to me on a silver platter? I attempted to explain that I had relied on exactly *zero* outside sources when I tracked her down—because I'm not in the business of telegraphing my moves—but that did nothing to change her mind.

The bottom line is Alice was always right, even when she was wrong.

That morning, a pleasant Sunday on which I had wanted, actually needed, to relax, she casually brought up the topic. Unfortunately, her solution for the so-called problem we had with the FBI was not so casual. Basically, she wanted me to agree that we needed to take steps to whack a mole to eliminate any kind of advantage the FBI might have in potentially launching an offensive that would take us down. I tried to talk her off that particular ledge due to all of the really bad juju that could come about from conspiring to murder a federal agent.

"Even if we kill the mole, whom we're not absolutely certain exists, they can just send another one. It's not going to scare them off. They're the FBI."

"First of all, I'm not trying to scare them off. That's stupid. I'm trying to destroy the one person who might be able to destroy us on a witness stand. Why is that so hard to understand?"

Her hands were on her hips. Not good. I evened my tone.

"It's not hard to understand. As long as there *is* a mole."

"Bob was convinced there was. And it makes perfect sense that they would send one."

"You've really been thinking about this," I said.

She liked my conciliatory tone. The hands abandoned the hips and busied themselves with cleaning up the kitchen, a sign of mental resolution.

"Yeah, and we need to clip that snitch on his or her home turf. Show them who's boss."

My brain had a very difficult time computing that last line.

"Wait, you're not suggesting we go after an agent at the Manhattan field office?"

"Where else?"

"Wow, you're actually serious."

Her hands indignantly shot back to her hips like a gunfighter settling into showdown mode.

"I'm serious about protecting what we have, by any means necessary."

"Then don't try to do an FBI hit. At the FBI."

"John, we risk everything if we don't do something about this. And we have to hit them where it hurts—Mafia-style—so they know not to fuck with us again."

"You may be right, but I need more than Bob's fortune cookie theories that the threat is real."

"I have other intel sources."

I could tell by the look on her face that her desire to be right just trumped her desire to keep that particular bit of information from me.

"From?"

"Reliable sources. Far more reliable than Bob."

"And you expect me to trust that?"

"I expect you to trust me."

There it was. The sanctity of marriage all cozied up with the poison of paranoia. As a husband, you're supposed to have your wife's back, no matter what. That's the unwritten rule. Even if you think she's bat shit crazy, maintaining loyalty is greater than the perils of the sinking ship.

"I do trust you. I just don't agree this is a good use of our time and resources. And if this problem does exist, going after them might make it a lot worse."

"You just don't care. You're a lone wolf. I'm trying to build something here and you're still thinking about number one."

"Alice, of course I care. Don't *you* care about my perspective? You seem so eager to quickly dismiss it."

"Yeah, because you don't think ahead. Your answer to everything is not to act, but to react."

I felt how quickly the conversation was deteriorating, so I tried to adjust to her, to lighten my tone.

"How about we agree to disagree?"

As soon as the words left my mouth, I immediately wished I had them back. Alice was livid.

"Maybe that's why we suckered you so easily in Honduras, John. You think what you want to think and can't see the forest for the trees."

Have you ever heard of something called *imminent impact silence*? That's the eerie moment of silence that occurs just before a bullet tears through your chest or a semi tractor-trailer T-bones you at full speed. Alice's words created one of those silences. For me, the world spun down into slow motion and I was outside of myself, floating above, like the newly dead. I could see myself morph into an instrument of black rage, every muscle in my body contracting like a tightly wound watch spring.

"Truth hurts," she said, smiling maliciously, her voice low and distorted.

"I'm going out for some air," I said.

And it took every fiber in my being to slowly, casually grab my jacket and walk out the door.

11

I vaguely remember walking. The street was a blur of color and noise and swirling plumes of car exhaust. My body was going somewhere, but my mind didn't bother asking where until I realized I was in Brooklyn, standing outside of one of those neighborhood bars with no name, just a crusty old Miller Lite neon sign in the window. At first, I was completely clueless as to why I had walked there. Then it hit me. I mentioned earlier that Bob had my first real girlfriend Eva killed—mainly because he believed love was likely to whip a killer into a soft and submissive domestic pet. Speaking of which, the chicken shit bastard didn't even have the cojones to do it himself. He just gave the order and did his best to make it look like she'd been raped and strangled by a bunch of junkies desperate for money. I never bought it. The whole thing stunk like Bob to high heaven.

Eventually I tracked down the Neanderthals who *actually* did the deed. They were a low-rent set down in Bensonhurst. Mostly janitorial and dirty laundry types for the mob. Think lower than prison snitches and you're about halfway to the bottom where these guys feed. I didn't do anything about it at the time, because I was afraid of the repercussions from Bob. But I never forgot about them and there I was, standing outside the bar I knew they frequented and used for "business." It all made sense. I was going to channel all of the rage

I was feeling for Alice and Eva into those unsuspecting goombahs. Kind of like going to get your aggression out on the heavy bag at the gym but with a heavy bag that has a mustache full of soup and a diamond horseshoe pinky ring.

As soon as I walked in, I was a wolf entering the den of a competing pack. All the pockmarked nut crushers in the place practically snarled at me. I strolled up to the bar and took a seat on an open stool.

"Piña colada, please."

The bartender glared at me, then looked at the patrons out of the corner of his eye. Then his right hand disappeared under the bar.

"Get the fuck out of here, fairy. We don't sell umbrella drinks."

"You Terry?" I asked casually.

"Who the fuck wants to know?"

"I was banging your ma last night. She told me you never call anymore."

He took a Ted Williams cut at me with the baseball bat he'd been gripping under the bar since I sat down. I stopped the bat barrel with one hand and knocked him out cold with the other. And it was on. Weapons were flashing. Guys stepped to me quickly, even the fat ones, and tried to get a piece. You should've seen the looks on their faces when I kicked them so hard to the deck they were pissing blood and crawling for streetlights. Some of them pulled knives and guns and I quickly disarmed them before breaking their jaws or limbs and chucking their weapons through the bar windows, showering the sidewalk with glass.

When the cops finally came, the looks on *their* faces were even more hilarious. I could see by their reactions that this was one of their payoff spots—probably worth a few grand a month to give the guys in this bar a pass. So, they showed up more to protect their investment than to enforce the law. I disarmed them both and hand-cuffed them to the bar rail with their pants down. Then I doused them with Bacardi 151 and told them to shut it or we'd have us a proper pig roast.

When everyone had either run or passed out, I sat myself down back at the bar—just in time for the bartender to wake up and stagger to his feet, totally disoriented. Terry. I knew he had killed Eva and I could imagine his sweaty fat face hovering over her when he did it.

"How 'bout that colada now, Jimmy Buffett," I joked.

"What the fuck do you want?"

I showed him a picture of Eva that I carried in my wallet. She took it in a photo booth when she was drunk and gave it to me as a joke. He tried to pretend he didn't recognize her but he wasn't very convincing.

"No one will ever know what really happened to her. But they're going to know what happened to you, Terry."

He reached for his gun and I let him wrap his fingers around it under the bar counter. I wanted him to feel the false sense of power one gets from gripping what I'm guessing was a .357 with the serial number filed off—straight from the police impound, courtesy of his copper friends. I heard the hammer cock and the cylinder rotate. I allowed him to get the gun up from behind the counter and I even let him point it at me. But like most nonprofessionals, he hesitated for a half second. And I took that opportunity to pull my S.T. Dupont Elysée fountain pen—a platinum and black mother-of-pearl work of art that was partial payment for a job I did when I was nineteen in Paris—and (reluctantly) slipped it into the end of his barrel.

Then I ducked behind the bar and he pulled the trigger. When the hammer came down, the revolver exploded in his face and the fountain pen buried itself in the back wall. *C'est dommage*. I looked up and saw him standing there, surprised because he no longer had a jaw, a tongue, or any teeth. The lower half of his face was a ragged suckhole.

"Say hello to Bob for me."

His surprise turned to the expressionless wax visage of the newly dead and he fell facedown into the ice trough. His life drained into the sweating cubes in fertile red blooms as he melted like Dorothy's Wicked Witch. I heard the sound of police sirens and I ran. I kept running flat out until I was back home. I sat on the stoop because I was beginning to black out from lack of oxygen. My head was exploding and my shoes were full of blood. When I got back to the apartment, Alice was gone. She had left a note next to a bottle of bourbon: *I'm looking for you. Stay put and have a drink.*

I cleaned my feet and poured myself a fist of whiskey. I didn't try to call her or text her. I wasn't sure I was ready to look her in the eye without losing my mind for good. What she'd said still rang in my head like a gong.

Sucker.

I tried to shake it but I knew I never would. When you've lived as long as I have on pure survival instinct, your brain instantly catalogs all things that it sees as a potential threat. Even though it was said in anger and meant to cut me to the quick—an argument technique used by pretty much every couple on the planet—I couldn't help but focus on the arrogance in her voice. There was a kind of satisfaction to it, as if deep within Alice some part of her was ultimately proud of her "work" with Bob, the work that had been designed to eviscerate me.

Distrust almost always begins with a question. In my case, I was asking myself, *Is Alice using me to get what she wants? Is this just part of another con? Will she dispose of me when she feels my usefulness has run its course?* I tried to talk myself down in the hours that I waited for her to come home, but the persistence of those questions was more powerful than my lame attempt at self-reassuring answers.

When she walked in, she looked exhausted and strung out. I

12

After that night, things were different. It was subtle, but different nonetheless. We had lost some of the playfulness we had before, and I noticed Alice being careful about keeping her emotions in check with me. When I brought it up, she passed it off as growing pains. She said couples need time to get to know each other and learn the most positive way to interact. All of it sounded reasonable, but a little on the self-help book side of the aisle. I think we were both thinking the same thing but were afraid to say it. Had we jumped into this thing prematurely? We could have just worked together and waited to get married. After all, we never really dated like normal people, and neither of us had any experience to apply to the situation. So, we started treating our love like a complicated explosive device that could go off at any moment.

On a more positive note, our work relationship improved exponentially. Alice was a lot more open to my views on how to run the company and less apt to attempt to steamroll me into submission. And we promised each other that, once we really got HR up and running, we would address Alice's FBI mole issue and my HR puppet master issue — giving each the same amount of consideration. But we both agreed that the first thing we needed to do was ramp up our efforts to bring in much bigger clients, and replenish the coffers we'd raided to build the new training facility.

braced myself for an altercation, but instead she held me, wrapped herself around me, and pulled me in tight.

"I'm so sorry, John," she said.

She kissed me and tears were running down her cheeks.

"I love you. Do you forgive me?"

I was overwhelmed and couldn't speak, so I nodded, pulled her close to me, and carried her into our bedroom. We lay on the bed for hours, just holding each other. We were both terrified at what had happened and we were clinging on for dear life.

For better or for worse . . .

As soon as we put some lines in the water, we hooked a massive fish. An anonymous entity approached us with a five-million-dollar retainer as a calling card. When Alice and I saw who the target was, we could barely contain our excitement. I've said many times in the past that our targets have more than earned their status as such, but this guy was going to turn revenge into a dish best served hot with several courses and a sublime Bordeaux.

Admit it. We all secretly hate tech billionaires. Sure, they slaved over a hot workstation for a few nights and lost a wink or two while they punched in code and drank eighty-four-ounce gas station jugs of The Dew. But it's not like they built the rail-road, invented iEverything, or Kentucky Fried three generations of chickens. That's tycoon-style. Say what you want about people like Gates, Jobs, Ford, Sanders, and Mellon, but they're in a class all their own, standing on a foundation of brick, mortar, blood, sweat, and tears. Starting Facebook is more like winning the trailer trash lotto. You might have more money than God, but no one's going to name a library after you or display your bronze bust in the town hall. Tech billionaires are the bourgeoisie of today, spending sucker money on all manner of fine clownery, having their self-aggrandizing autobiographies ghostwritten for them in their late twenties, and pouring more money into tech garbage to digitally enslave the masses.

Alice and I landed the mother of all nerd moguls. As you know, there are some very popular online dating sites and apps out there. Even though they are infested with robot pimps catfishing with tranny lures, these sites are wildly successful. And our target was the CEO of arguably the biggest and most successful online meat market in the U.S.—and other countries where marriage doesn't mean a father gives away his teenage daughter to a man his own age in exchange for a couple of goats and some shiny stuff.

Dr. Love, as the press referred to him, was the first to introduce the *100 percent match and marriage guarantee*. The deal was that if you didn't meet the love of your life, get married, and stay married for at least five years, he would not only refund your money, but he would also write you a personal check for $10,000. And his record was perfect. In fact, it was so eerily flawless that it gave birth to a litter of conspiracy theories ranging in theme from alien intelligence to pharmaceutical mind control.

When Alice and I read Dr. Love's dossier, light dawned on Marblehead. It was actually quite sinister, even to a couple of professional cynics like us. The guy used to be a high-level geek in the NSA domestic surveillance program. He had been in charge of writing programs that would analyze observed behaviors in people and identify trends that would serve as predictor models for their future actions. Basically, because of Dr. Love, the NSA knows us better than we know ourselves and can predict within a high range of statistical probability what we will do tomorrow, next month, or even a year from now. Everything was going swimmingly in their Orwellian dystopia until Love resigned and basically replicated his own tech to build an electronic dating empire. Think about it. If the machine knows a person inside and out—from purchasing behavior that identifies wants and needs, to medical history that defines body type and psychological profile—pairing that person with someone compatible is a piece of wedding cake.

And it's got nothing to do with *love*, brothers and sisters. It's all about the partnership paradigm. Most people marry to build a fortress that keeps loneliness out and enables them to stockpile social obligations within. It's all part of the program they've been following since childhood and usually has nothing to do with their true desires. What person, in his or her heart of hearts, wants to have a big family? Try pumping out five kids and you'll see firsthand what it's like to experience a complete loss of self. But people inherit those absurd check boxes from someone else who they probably knew would withhold real love if they didn't check each one dutifully—like a parent.

Of course, strict adherence to *the program* creates a (false) sense of security that people will fight to protect with much greater zeal than they ever would the preservation of love. What's the number-one reason people divorce? Money. If Fred Flintstone stopped bringing home the brontosaurus bacon, Wilma would have started banging Mr. Slate. The point is, Dr. Love had the partnership aspect of relationships dialed in. If someone worships money and possessions, fortune cookie says they will end up with the same species and both will protect the arrangement they have with their glorified roommate at all costs—at least for a time north of five years. Like I said, sinister.

The anonymous client who greenlit Dr. Love tried to appear mysterious, but it's easy to smell the ham on the hand of the seasoned bureaucrat, and dollars to doughnuts said it was the NSA itself that wanted him sucking dirt. They've had their share of raging tabloid embarrassments and it was a good guess that they probably didn't want anyone to know about the technology they were using to turn the U.S. into the USSR, so a quiet snuff job was the order of the day to keep the tower ivory.

Dr. Love's well-documented reclusive, bordering on hermitical, lifestyle was a good indicator they had already tried to take him out—most likely on a number of occasions—and failed. He was rarely seen in public, and when he was, the grainy photos taken yielded such generic images that if you didn't know who you were looking at, you could easily believe they were all of different people. He lived like Pablo Escobar, very difficult to pin down and almost completely inaccessible without breaching many layers of security. An execution scenario at the office was doable, but definitely the path of most resistance. And our deep-pocketed client was paying us handsomely for our ability to be highly discreet, so we wanted to impress them with our finesse and sophistication in order to keep the wheels greased on Uncle Sam's gravy train.

After spinning our own wheels trying to find an opening, an opportunity finally presented itself on a silver platter—Dr. Love's annual sales and marketing meeting in Las Vegas. A corporate meeting! At a massive Social Networking Con no less! We couldn't believe our luck. He would be out of his office cocoon and vulnerable to any number of potential attacks. This was going to be fun. Unfortunately, getting into the event as interns or employees was a long shot due to the fact that Dr. Love had a relatively small and loyal workforce—roughly four hundred people who had been there from the start-up days—and someone with his stratospheric level of paranoia would sniff out an unfamiliar face in a heartbeat.

As we worked every possible access scenario, we kept hitting the walls we knew Dr. Love would have in place if he was a spook worth his salt. I was about to commence a time-honored ritual of beating my head against the wall, when Alice, in her sweet attempt to calm my nerves with warm affection and a cold drink, was inspired with a brilliant idea.

"We're a match made in heaven," she said, smiling and casually lighting a cigarette.

"That's a little corny, but I couldn't agree more, darling," I said, taking a drag.

"No, dummy, we can get into the Dr. Love Con if we're one of his Match Made in Heaven couples."

"Like those slack-jawed breeders he had on *Oprah*?"

"Exactly. Every year, he invites ten guinea pig couples to the meeting who have passed the five-year mark and that he feels are great success stories. Then he parades them around like 4-H livestock, wines and dines them, and brings them up onstage for his keynote address. We'd be joined at the hip with Dr. Love!"

"Just when I didn't think it was possible for me to love you any more, Alice, you drop this mad genius trip on me."

"I know, right?"

So, we worked with Sue and set the wheel of cheese in motion. Getting into the group of couples was the easy part. Regional sales reps submit candidates, so we hired some heavy hitters to "convince" the New York rep to submit us for the Northeast region and keep his mouth shut about it or his wife would find what was left of him and his mistress in her yoga bag.

The hard part was building our execution scenario. First, we needed a great hitter profile so the NSA would never be suspected of pushing his button. Second, we needed to find a way to whack him that was elegantly subtle. A bloodbath would have been counterproductive, as it would have opened up an investigational can of worms with the FBI and the press. Imagine the shit storm you'd create if you pulled a drive-by on Mark Zuckerberg—the media would follow that blood trail like a pack of rabid dogs until eventually they had your sorry ass up a tree.

To find the right execution scenario we turned the tables on Dr. Love and put *him* under the microscope. He didn't have a lot of enemies from his NSA days because he was a think tank jockey and anyone who had been wronged by him would have had no idea who he was. And in any event, we wanted to avoid a connection to the NSA in the interest of shielding our client. So we dug into his life as the matchmaker CEO and opened the door to a veritable clown car of potential enemies. The best of these was a former Mossad agent whose wife had had a brief affair with Dr. Love. The affair resulted in divorce and the wife was never seen again. The Mossad agent was at large, but it was suspected he made it back to Israel and was under protection there.

We liked this scenario for a couple of reasons. First, Mossad agents know how to kill efficiently and discreetly and disappear as soon as the job is done. Second, this would bring the affair to light and the press would have a field day with adultery being the reason for Dr. Love's death. Kind of like Dr. Oz choking to death on a Ding Dong. Finally, the Dr. Love Con was happening during the week of the Mossad agent's wedding anniversary date, so motive was locked and loaded. The narrative would be your garden-variety hypocrite, fall from grace tragedy, and the resounding chorus would be "He got what was coming to him." We put Sue on to work out the logistics.

13
―――――

When Alice and I arrived in Vegas for the event, we were treated like royalty. They put us up in a suite at one of the nicer hotels and packed our days with appearances and activities. The perks were nice, but spending time with the other couples was worse than torture. They were a gaggle of milquetoast suburban zombies who finished each other's sentences and turned karaoke night into a PDA blitzkrieg. Who tongue kisses in the middle of an "Islands in the Stream" duet? Alice and I seriously considered doing the world a favor and killing all of them as a bonus. When one of the wives asked Alice if she was a stay-at-home mom, I thought my wife was going to shank the cow-eyed dullard right then and there. It became clear fairly early on that Dr. Love's system probably weeded out more intelligent people who had pesky mental complications, like an above-average IQ, that might get in the way of myopic devotion. Love is indeed blind when you're dealing with someone who gets all hot and bothered about the early-bird special at HomeTown Buffet.

Dr. Love fancied himself a progressive business guru, so he subjected his employees and us to several farcical team-building and training activities designed to show us all how to maximize our potential—upside-down painting (from point of view to point of you!), trust-fall workshop (there's no "me" in team!), ropes course (fear is a four-letter word!), and the list goes on. The trust-fall workshop was probably the most fun because Alice deliberately dropped me just to horrify the other couples.

The ropes course provided our first potential opportunity to smoke Dr. Love. Predictably, he favored the extreme version, and he liked to do it at night to really get people pissing in their Dockers. A fall from the highest platform was a good fifty feet, but that alone wasn't enough to ensure a kill. We needed a little insurance.

Mossad is big on wire garrotes, so our plan was to rig a wide loop of the safety wiring they used on the course at neck height above the platform. It would be impossible to see in the dark, and since we would be up there with him, Alice was going to distract him while I attached the end of the loop to his harness rope. A last-minute change in the beginning of the course would cause him to immediately lose his balance, and the fall would trigger the wire loop, causing it to rapidly cinch and relieve Dr. Love of his head. A dangling piece of anchoring hardware would be enough for the Vegas PD to call it an accidental death, but the wire guillotine would leave the Mossad bread crumb trail for the feds.

Everything was going according to plan until Dr. Love decided that doing a zip line from the roof of our hotel to another was more extreme, and we had to send Sue back to the drawing board. The good doctor appeared to be fond of Alice (shocker), so we toyed with the idea of having her lure him into a tryst in which foreplay would involve putting a .22 slug in his head—also a Mossad favorite due to its quiet, close-range killing ability. But Sue discovered that the guy had metal detectors fitted around his hotel suite doors and windows, and any visitors—like the escorts that were ordered to his room each night—were required to completely disrobe before entering. Since Alice was not fond of the idea of keistering a vial of neurotoxin—another Mossad party favor—we scrapped that plan as well.

Time was running out and with it our options. So I dipped into that treasure trove of resources known as the movies, and wouldn't you know it, one of my all-time favorites provided inspiration for our kill scenario—*The Godfather*. Specifically, the scene where they tape a gun for Michael Corleone to the back of a toilet in a Brooklyn restaurant so he can come out blasting after excusing himself to take a piss. If we hid a gun somewhere in the staging prior to Dr. Love's highly anticipated keynote address, we could retrieve it and pop him during one of the evening's many absurdly theatrical moments. Sue found out that there would be a lot of pyrotechnics (rekindle the fires of romance!), strobe lights, and loud music, so we could theoretically take him out and vanish undetected before they served the champagne toast.

Getting the gun into the staging area, however, turned out to be a bigger problem than we anticipated. The stage was already assembled and heavily guarded. Anyone bringing anything in or out was subject to search and metal detectors. So, we had to get creative. Back to the movies—*In the Line of Fire*. John Malkovich is the clever assassin who builds a composite gun in order to smuggle it into a fund-raiser and kill the president. Since then, composite has come a long way and there are some firearms almost completely fabricated from exotic carbon fiber recipes. But whether it was made of plastic or butter, it would still look like a gun, so we needed to smuggle it in piecemeal. It just so happened the cheap-ass award trophies Dr. Love was going to give each couple were big acrylic hearts shaped like wings mounted on wood stands. Sue was able to find a way to hide the gun parts in our trophy, but we still had no solution for bullets, something we would not be able to smuggle into the room in a rabbit's foot key chain.

Sue paid a visit to one of our exotic gunsmiths in Reno, and he suggested we take an old-school cap-and-ball approach. The gun chamber could be fitted with a plastic casing full of powder and a powder cap that uses chemical release, versus a hammer strike, to ignite the powder. All we needed was a projectile, and my lovely wife was going to supply that in the form of a four-carat diamond on a ring that closely resembled her engagement ring. A diamond would ensure that all the king's horses and all the king's men couldn't put Dr. Love's egg head back together again, and thematically, it was a home run.

The night of the keynote address, everything was in place. Sue was able to get our trophy in with the others due to the original trophy maker's sudden illness, and Alice was sporting her deadly bling. As you can imagine, the entire affair was a cacophonous cheese fest, replete with saccharine testimonials and a full-frontal media blitz. Dr. Love was a hybrid of Tony Robbins and Jerry Springer, moving around the stage like a self-help carnival barker.

Then the warm cold duck was passed to everyone in plastic flutes and Dr. Love brought all of us Match Made in Heaven couples to the stage. The video wall behind us was aflutter with animated winged hearts circling like a crimson cloud of monarchs on a summer day. We were all handed our trophies by a band of bikini-clad ladies in impossibly high heels, and Dr. Love took center stage. While he blathered through his address, misquoting Shakespeare and comparing Cupid to Jesus, Alice and I very carefully removed the gun parts from their angelic housing and she blindly assembled it in the pockets of her black ostrich feather Dries Van Noten skirt.

As we waited for the big finale that Sue had said would incorporate all the pyro and noisy distraction we would need to do the deed, something unexpected happened. Dr. Love made a special speech about Alice and me.

"All of these couples are matches made in heaven," he started. "But I want to call attention to one couple in particular that made an impression on me this week. Doug and Karen Goldstein, can you please join me for a moment."

We were Doug and Karen Goldstein, named after the foster parents who once locked me in a woodshed for two days with a bag of dog food and a bucket of dirty water.

We stepped forward and stood proudly next to Dr. Love. He smiled warmly, shaking my hand and kissing Alice on the cheek for an uncomfortable amount of time.

"Doug and Karen showed me this week that sometimes compatibility can be fueled more by conflict than harmony."

He had no idea.

"It speaks to a more animal part of our makeup that wants the heat of passion, but doesn't require the comfort of being too like-minded."

The other couples' faces turned slightly sour and they stopped petting and kissing each other like deranged kittens.

"Because I've been inspired by Doug and Karen, I'm going to incorporate an element of friction into our system. And you know what happens when you have friction?"

He stared down the crowd, challenging them to answer.

"Anyone?"

Silence.

"Fire. Just like if you rub two sticks together, if you rub two people together, sparks will fly!"

Cheers from the audience. Then the lights went down and the pyro started exploding all around us, accompanied by Katy Perry's seminal pop hit "Firework" playing at max decibels. In the heat of the moment, Dr. Love leaned over and whispered in Alice's ear.

"Dump that stiff and let's go fuck like jackrabbits on my private jet."

Alice took that opportunity to lead Dr. Love by his throbbing gristle into a dark portion of the stage and put her own diamond of wisdom through his leering eyeball. Viva Las Vegas!

14

After the Dr. Love extravaganza, we decided to spend some of our hard-earned dollars and jetted off to the Amalfi Coast for a belated honeymoon. As we lay basking in the Mediterranean sun, we were feeling optimistic. Alice was looking at her iPad and quickly sat up in her chaise.

"John, we just received payment for Dr. Love," she said with an ear-to-ear grin.

"I don't think I've ever seen you smile that wide, not even when I asked you to marry me . . . twice."

"Guess how much Mr. Anonymous Moneybags just forked over for the job."

"I thought he kittied up five mil?"

"We got a bonus for creativity," she said excitedly.

"I hate guessing. Just tell me."

"No way. This is too good."

"Fine. I'll just throw out a ridiculous number. Eight mil."

"Try seventeen."

I sat up quickly in my chaise and knocked over my glass of Barolo.

"You're shitting me," I said.

"I shit you not, John Lago."

"That is some serious cheese, me lady."

"Cheese? That's a motherfucking dairy farm."

"I think a celebration is in order," I said and flagged down the cabana boy for a magnum of champagne.

When it arrived, we were making out so hard we practically fell out of our chairs. The waiter filled our glasses and we raised them, looking at each other behind the cascade of crisp dry bubbles.

"Not bad for a day's work," I said.

"I think we deserve a raise," Alice said.

We drank and kissed and drank some more and kissed some more and ended up back at our villa. We drank and made love until the magnum was gone and smoked cigarettes naked under the moonlight.

"We're going to be all right," I said.

She rolled onto me, her tan, sun-drenched skin hot against mine.

"John, we're going to be more than all right. We're going to be rich and fabulous. We already are, come to think of it."

"No, I mean us. We had a bit of a rough patch there."

"Ancient history, darling."

She kissed me again and gave me a drag of her cigarette.

"I love you, you twisted son of a bitch." She sighed.

"I love you, you sick freak," I whispered.

Our last days in Italy were so good I really didn't want to go back. I suggested to Alice that we just keep the money, set the recruits free, and live happily ever after. But, like Sue said, Alice had stars in her eyes, and I saw them come out that week. Our new client already had more jobs lined up for us and others were lining up as well. Like I've always said, word travels fast in our very small world, and when everyone knows you're the best, they won't settle for anyone else. Fine with me. What the hell else was I going to do? I didn't care about money the way Alice did, but I cared about her and wanted to be with her. Basically, I would have followed her into hell in those days and that's exactly what I did.

15

When we got back to Manhattan, we had to hit the ground running. Sue briefed us on the assignments he'd been supervising and they all required our attention. Alice and I were completely backed up with requests from existing clients, a long list of potential new clients, and our new anonymous moneybags client. Retainer money was flowing in mogul style, and Alice was chomping at the bit to expand. With the stringent training regimen I had established, I was reluctant to do this too quickly. Back in the day, I had seen Bob pack the place with a bunch of snot-nosed rookies when the workload got heavy and half of them got popped. I wasn't about to revert to his old churn-and-burn model on my watch.

Alice agreed in principle, but making big green was clearly one of her lifelong dreams and she wasn't going to let anyone or anything derail that. I started to feel the distance I felt from her before the Dr. Love gig. The hardest thing to take was her tendency to circle the wagons around what she wanted and defend it like a junkyard dog with a bone. That kind of behavior was common among other HR recruits. Being desperately poor for most of one's life tends to make one want to gather up as many shekels as possible before the fat lady sings and eats your bony ass for lunch. It was just human nature but it sucked coming from Alice because

I wanted her to be different, despite the crushing influence of the past.

And it put me in a weird position. John Lago as the voice of reason? Please. Of course, when it rains it pours, and while I was trying to find my footing in the mud, my lovely wife decided to hit me up with my favorite pain-in-the-ass topic: her FBI mole hunt. Evidently, she had been making inquiries and trying to gather intel on the subject in the background since we'd had an argument about it. And by in the background, I mean behind my back. She had even gone so far as to ask our powerful new anonymous moneybags client from the Dr. Love gig for assistance, a move that I felt was extremely risky.

"What's the big deal?" she asked, knowing full well what the big deal was.

"They're probably NSA. They play golf with the FBI!"

"Don't be ridiculous. Those guys despise each other."

"Maybe, but you know how small that world is. If you're right and there is a mole, the more outsiders know about it, the more likely it is that the mole will go underground or the feds will decide to make a move."

"So *we* make a move," she said, full of bravado.

"How? We don't even have a target."

"Maybe we do," she said, smiling.

The smile at that moment was the one she used when she wasn't sure if something was going to make me happy or enraged.

"Meaning what?" I said, knowing the answer.

"Meaning we have a name."

"What?"

"You heard me."

"Just like that?"

"Just like that."

"Who is it?"

"Client is going to send an encrypted dossier. Right from the FBI personnel files."

"Great," I said, trying unsuccessfully to hide my ire.

"Honey, don't be mad," she said.

"I'm not. I'm glad it worked out."

"But I should have talked to you about it first," she placated.

"This is a partnership, right?" I asked.

"Come on, John. It's a great partnership."

"Then let's do what partners do and work together. I don't want to be someone you feel like you have to tiptoe around."

"I was just afraid you would say no."

"Because I would have. For good reason."

"Baby, look at me," she cooed.

I looked in her eyes. They were so bright and intelligent, she was like a snake charmer, wrapping me around her little finger.

"Trust me, okay? I know what I'm doing."

I did trust her and she did know what she was doing. But it wasn't her judgment I had an issue with. It was her gunslinger attitude. When I met Alice, I had been working within a system, an organization with a set of rules. HR, Inc. was by no means perfect, but there were checks and balances in place. We were employees, and with that comes a hierarchy and politics. Alice had always been freelance. Yes, she worked with Bob and probably had been trained by him to some extent, but she had never been part of our recruit ranks. She was used to making her own rules in the field and felt weighed down when she had to consult or collaborate with anyone. Even though she was my wife and loved me, when it came to the business I got grouped in with all the others who didn't just sign up to the Alice way.

At that point, I had to make a choice. I could either continue to butt heads with her, exerting my own will and opinions to serve my ego, or I could just acquiesce and choose my battles sparingly. I couldn't help but laugh about it over a couple of beers with Sue.

"JL, that's pretty much how all relationships work. 'I Got the Pussy I Make the Rules' didn't end up on a T-shirt for nothing."

We laughed but it didn't last. Sue got us a couple of whiskeys to try to smooth out the permanent crease on my brow.

"Need you to have my back, Sue."

"You know I do, JL."

"I love Alice but she can go off half-cocked and we can't afford any spilt milk right now."

"I hear you. Not into this FBI thing either. Waste of time. Like you say, whack a mole and up comes another."

"Logistics. If she's going to force me into this circus, I want to be the ringmaster."

"I been thinking on it since you all brought it up," Sue said. "Got some ideas. None of them good."

"Lay 'em on me."

Sue had already drawn up a plan that was so out-there crazy, I could hardly believe it made any sense to me. But if you really think about it, how many ways are there to break down the door of one of the biggest FBI field offices in the country and smoke one of its agents? Even coming up with one was a miracle. As we saw it, there was just no way to do it the usual way, with subtlety and finesse. We needed shock and awe. So, we spent the next thirty-six hours working round the clock to fill out the details in the framework of Sue's preposterous plan. It was either going to work or be the most epic fail in the history of HR.

When it was fully cooked, we pitched it to Alice. I half expected her to laugh in our faces, but she was actually impressed by the plan and fired up to execute it right away. On that note, we were in total agreement. The longer we waited, the more likely our target might be moved or reassigned. Plus, we needed to sit on that like we needed a hole in the head. The mole was standing in the way of Alice and me being happy, and I couldn't wait to put a serious hurt on that punk.

"John, thank you," Alice said that night in bed.

"For what?"

"For being on my team with this FBI thing. I know pretty much everyone at HR thinks it's a terrible idea, including Sue."

"They don't run the company. I don't care what they think."

"I appreciate you saying that, but I know you do."

She kissed me and I felt a little like an irresponsible father who just reluctantly bought his daughter a Porsche 911 for her sweet sixteen. "Thank you for having my back," she said.

"Of course. Thank you for having mine," I said, hinting at our agreement.

"As soon as this is off our plate, we're going to just focus on the future and get filthy rich," she said, totally missing my hint or just avoiding it all together.

"Alice . . ."

"Yes, my love?"

I wanted to remind her that I wasn't just helping her out and having her back, although that was part of it. I wanted to ask her if she had thought about the issue I wanted to chase down, the issue of the puppet master running HR, the issue that really did represent a threat to everything we had built. But I didn't. In retrospect, I realize that I had assimilated into Alice's world, not vice versa. I did what she wanted me to do in order to avoid unpleasantness between us. She didn't do what I wanted because I never cried bloody murder like she did if I didn't get my way. It was like brainwashing. Whether she knew it or not, she had changed me into something I didn't want to be, *someone* I didn't want to be. And I resented her for it. When she kissed me that night, the sweetness was gone. I smelled the garlic and wine on her breath and found it revolting instead of slightly endearing.

I felt distance from her, mainly distance I myself was creating. Of all the times she had hurt me in the past, none of them felt as sinister as the slow transformation she had created in me, a transformation I hadn't even noticed happening. I told myself I would confront the issue with her after the FBI gig. If she refused to change, I was going to walk. I had no desire to leave her or HR, but I had been to hell to find myself and I wasn't about to go back.

16

After a couple weeks of preparation, we were ready to rock. We chose a Friday night before a three-day government holiday weekend to take advantage of all the goldbrickers who would slip out early or be absent altogether because they were "working at home." It was also the night of a major sporting event and guy's guys can't resist the siren call of wings and beer. Last but not least, our op window was during a two-hour period wherein there would be a shift change at the FBI field office—from full-day crew to skeleton crew—followed closely thereafter by a shift change at the closest NYPD precinct.

The intel on the mole offered by our anonymous client had been solid and verifiable and had enabled Sue to pinpoint her—yes, I said *her*—location in the building. All we had to do was flawlessly execute the umpteen steps involved in our wildly complicated and dangerous plan and we'd be home free.

The first part of the op was the most dangerous, but also the most fun. Decent entry points in a highly secure building are, by design, few and far between, but there is always a weak link in the chain and, as with most facilities, in this case it was the roof. It's very difficult to secure a roof in a city like New York, mainly due to the dense bird population. There are hundreds of bird species in Manhattan, from pigeons to peregrine falcons, and they own the rooftops. Any kind of electronic security system would be compromised hourly in New York, so, unless you're dealing with a bank, you don't see them that often.

We were dealing with the FBI, so Sue had done due diligence and located some physical entry systems and video surveillance units, but nothing we couldn't handle. But getting *in* to the building was not the problem. The problem was getting *on* to the roof. You're not going to just scale the side of an all-glass building with suction cups, and speed roping down from a chopper would surely raise some eyebrows.

Oddly, it was within our discussion about New York birds and security systems that we came up with the solution: wingsuits. The lunatics from the Red Bull Air Force fly those things at two hundred miles an hour about ten feet from the face of a rock wall. It's amazing tech. Closest you'll ever get to being a bird without sprouting wings of your own.

For our purposes, we needed wingsuits that were heavily modified for lift versus speed. We were on the roof of a building five blocks away that was probably two hundred feet higher than the FBI building, with a clear shot to the FBI roof. Our goal was to glide on the updrafts and float down to the FBI rooftop like hawks vectoring in for a kill. Easier said than done. The buildings in Manhattan create an environment similar to canyons with closely spaced rock formations. Wind patterns are unpredictable *at best*, especially due to the fluctuations in heat and air pressure created by traffic, solar reflection, eight million human beings living, breathing, and fucking, you get the idea.

As we stood on the precipice of the building, we went through the checklist. Sue was monitoring everything from an empty apartment in the building across the street. He was going to be our eyes and ears during the op, and he was our ride home when the deed was done.

"Sue, you set?"

"Yeah, chilling in the rear with the gear," he answered quietly over our closed-channel radio systems.

"Don't sound so glum," Alice said. "What we're doing is definitely the short straw."

"She says as she gets ready to fly over Manhattan in the baddest-ass op ever invented," he answered back.

"We have you to thank for that, Sue," I said. "How's the wind pattern?"

"Still swirling like a mother. Twenty knots up, down, all the way around, JL."

"Clock is ticking," Alice said. "Let's go."

"Hold on," I said. "We'll get a window. One freak downdraft and you'll be the secret sauce in that falafel cart on the corner."

"Okay, Dad," she said, smiling.

"Looks like we'll have a pressure shift in about thirty seconds. Cool wind just came off the river and when it hits your position you'll have a nice fifteen-knot headwind for about three minutes."

"Wow, feels like Christmas," I said.

I kissed Alice.

"Don't kiss me like that, John. We're going to be fine."

"I didn't. I just—"

"We were born to do this."

"Yeah," I said. "Lucky us."

"Now!" Sue barked in our earpieces.

We jumped. The headwind lifted us up another fifty feet or so, immediately putting us in danger of overshooting the building.

"Bring it down a bit," Sue said, "or you're going to end up in Queens."

We had to point down into a descent position, putting us in danger of ramming headfirst into the building's thick plate glass doing ninety.

"Now you're coming in too hot!" Sue yelled.

"Jesus, get it straight!" Alice yelled back.

"Switch to canopy!"

"Too visible," Alice retorted.

"If you don't, you're gonna hit the side of the building and bounce."

"Let's try the pilot chutes first," I said.

We pulled our small pilot chutes, which slowed us down and got us back into trajectory.

"Good," Sue said. "Bogey, two o'clock."

A police helicopter was in the distance, closing on our position.

"I see it," I said.

"He's going to see our chutes, John," Alice said.

"I know. Almost there," I said.

"He's coming right at you," Sue said.

"Sue, get on the police radio and call in a ten eighty-eight with an Amber Alert in Battery Park."

"Copy."

The chopper was getting closer, its searchlight barely missing us. We heard Sue call in the bogus high-speed chase/child abduction.

"We're dead," Alice said.

"Chill. It's going to work," I said.

Chopper was less than half a mile away when he turned sharp south toward Battery Park.

"Pretty slick, John," Alice said.

"I try," I said.

"Eighty feet and closing," Sue called out. "Deploy canopies."

We could see the FBI roof in front of us. We pulled our full-size chutes and slowed our descent. For a second, it felt like we would have a soft landing, but then a sudden downdraft folded our chutes and we hit hard, rolling across the roof and noisily smacking into some air ducts. We quickly detached our suits and stuffed them behind the ducting.

"You think they heard that?" Alice whispered.

"No alarms coming from inside," Sue said.

We took a minute to collect ourselves and gear up. The mole was on the seventh floor. Once we breached the rooftop access door, we had twenty floors to descend to get to her. We figured we had about ninety seconds to get there before we'd be trapped in the stairwell, which is tactically about one notch above standing in front of a firing squad. I looked at Alice and I could feel the static electricity coming off her tight nylon-and-Kevlar catsuit.

"That's a good look for you," I whispered.

She kissed me and put my hand on her ass.

"Just remember," she whispered back. "If you don't make it out of here alive, you'll never see this ass again."

"That's the best pep talk I've ever had," I said.

Then I blew the hinges on the rooftop access door and we sprinted into the stairwell.

17

We moved quickly down the steps, ready for anything they threw at us. After the first fifteen seconds, we didn't hear anything out of the ordinary outside the stairwell. We also didn't hear any internal building alarms, which they would have definitely deployed to evacuate employees. Alice and I looked at each other, both of us thinking the same thing. It was just too quiet, the kind of quiet that brings about paranoia because you know goddamned well it isn't going to last. The farther down we went into the shaft, the more we could feel the air being sucked away into the vacuum of whatever was about to blow up in our faces. We stopped for a second to listen. And, of course, as soon as we noted the lack of response, that's when it came.

Agents began rapid-firing up the stairwell. Slugs were bouncing all over, lighting us up like a pinball machine. We were two fish, shit out of luck in a barrel. Alice and I started popping smoke grenades like mad and hurling them down at the agents. We heard coughing, cursing, bodies falling. Then we followed that up with high-velocity .40 S&W rounds from our SIG MPX submachine guns. Our random fire patterning, coupled with the smoke grenades, created a lot more confusion and panic than we'd even hoped for. The agents tried to return fire, but our relentless volley sent them scrambling for the exits. This gave us a window to sprint—albeit in total blindness—the final fifteen floors to our target location.

Then we heard Sherman's March coming down the stairs behind us. Bad. Very bad. You never want your opponent above you. They have every advantage and you have dick. It sounded like at least a dozen or so stomping down. We stopped dead, threw our gas masks on, and chucked some CR gas canisters up at them. CR is nonlethal ordnance, but it's still pretty nasty. It causes intense skin irritation, temporary blindness, uncontrollable coughing, gasping for breath, and panic.

We heard the canisters pop and the stairwell immediately filled with thick yellow smoke. The agents started coughing and choking and blind-firing down the stairwell. We hit the deck as a bullet maelstrom pockmarked the walls around us. I got nicked on the side of the neck—nothing serious but an annoying amount of blood. Alice slapped some QuickClot Combat Gauze on the wound, instantly stopping the bleeding, and we kept moving. With the agents yelling and puking and trying to get out of the stairwell, it made it possible for Alice and me to head down our last three flights of stairs unmolested. We slapped in fresh mags and stopped by the door to our target's floor.

"Ready?"

"Let's get some," she said quietly.

We busted through the stairwell door and sprinted across the office, spraying bullets and pinning agents down in their cubicles before they could even draw their weapons. We were still on schedule, despite the war in the stairwell. In fact, we were about three minutes ahead of schedule, which gave us a little more room for error in accomplishing our objective. As we searched for the target, we addressed all aggression with assault rotation—backs to each other, checking six, nine, three, midnight. Nobody but us got off a clean shot.

First-line responders tried to take out our flanks, but their beer bellies and bad reflexes were no match for our speed. We pinned them all down in time to pop another couple of CR cans. That made them come to Jesus. They were coughing and gagging so violently they didn't dare try to challenge our hellish cover fire. For a brief moment, I drank in the scene—clouds of burning paper swirling in the yellow smoke. FBI agents on all fours pissing in their pants. I'm sorry, but it was a thing of beauty.

Then we made it to our target's glass-walled office. Alice got eyes on her shoes sticking out from under her desk. Her door was locked and the lights were out. *Amateur hour*, I thought. It was almost killing my buzz that it was going to be so stupid easy to whack her after all that foreplay.

"May I?" Alice asked, chomping at the bit.

"By all means," I said and laid down more cover fire for her.

Alice advanced to the target's office, blasting through the glass doors. One of the bullets hit the target's shoe, and it flipped out from under the desk. That's when I saw that the shoes had been placed there as bait. The office itself had no windows and only one way in and out. It was a trap. Just before Alice was about to go through the door, I saw agents come out from two cubicles like hunters in a duck blind. They had been waiting for us.

"Get down!" I yelled.

Alice turned and saw the agents and hit the deck just as they opened fire. I returned fire, but they blasted my position until all I could do was crawl, desperately searching for any kind of cover. I found some cubicles and got under one of the desks. I looked for Alice but didn't see her. Then I saw her hand shoot out. An M68 fragmentation grenade was in it.

"Okay, that sucks," I whispered to myself and tucked into a fetal position with my hands over my ears.

Seconds later, I heard the agents yelling warnings to each other, but then the grenade exploded, rocking the place like an earthquake, and I didn't hear them again. The smoke was so thick it was impossible to see two feet in front of me. I felt my way to a door and ducked inside. The power went out in the building momentarily and the emergency lights came on in what I realized was a women's bathroom.

"Don't move, asshole."

A woman's voice, behind me. I heard the sound of a safety being disengaged on a Beretta 92. I turned slowly. She was standing in the shadows near the stalls but stepped out into the light. At first, she looked like she was going to shoot me, but then her face changed to the shock of recognition.

"John?"

Jesus, what are the odds? I thought, and she stepped closer so I could see her face. She looked like she expected me to recognize her, but I didn't. At least not at first. Then it dawned on me.

"Juno?" I whispered, my blood running cold.

She looked somewhat familiar, but barely. When I knew Juno before, she was nineteen. She worked at HR and Bob put me in charge of babysitting her on a job. When we got to the job, Bob told me to whack her. At the time, I thought it was because she was inept and becoming a liability. So, I showed her some mercy and put her on a slow boat to China. Literally. Our target was a shipping exec slash human trafficker whose office was in a commercial port. She got into a shipping container and I never saw her again until that moment at the FBI field office. The reason I hadn't recognized her in the dossier was because many of the important features I remembered about her—hair color and length, eye color, weight—had changed dramatically. Her overall style now was "Bureau Bland." Then it dawned on me.

Juno was the mole.

That's why Bob had wanted her dead in the first place. And I saved her ass, just so I'd have to come back someday and shoot it off. I guess it's true that no good deed goes unpunished.

"Don't you remember me, John?"

"Yeah, I'm just surprised to see you."

"Me too. What are you doing here?"

"Selling magazine subscriptions."

More gunfire outside.

We ducked at the sound of machine-gun fire, which was followed by another explosion.

"We need to get out of here," I said to her.

"Come with me," she said.

"Where? If they see me out there, I'm a dead man."

"I can show you how to get out."

She grabbed my arm.

"Why the hell would you do that?"

"Returning the favor." She smiled.

I should have put a bullet in her head right then and there, but the idea of saving someone just to kill them years later was ludicrous. Alice would never know I let her live because Alice was either dead or hightailing it to our exit strategy. Juno led the way out the bath-room door. The building power had been cut and the faint yellow glow of emergency lighting created a bizarre theater of chaos all around us. The cozy corporate FBI field office had become a black-ened, burning war zone. Juno pulled me behind a wall. She pointed to the far end of the office.

"The elevators are straight that way. If you can get into the shaft, there's a parking garage at the bottom."

"Thanks for the tip," Alice said behind me.

And then she shot Juno in the head.

18

I turned and Alice was standing beside me, smoke pouring out of the barrel of her SIG MPX. She didn't look at me, only at Juno. She put a few more rounds into Juno for good measure.

"Check that one off my bucket list," she said. "Let's go."

We ran to the elevator shafts.

A dozen or so G-men in full strike gear were doing formation sweeps of the hallways. We stayed out of sight until they passed. *Ding*. The elevator door slid open like a gleaming android mouth. The elevator car wasn't there, just a dark hole waiting to swallow mankind and take it to the basement for mandatory euthanasia. We slipped past the clueless storm troopers and into the elevator shaft. The doors closed behind us, making it as dark as a tomb. We put on our night vision goggles. One of the elevator cars was four floors up and moving down toward us. Just after it passed, we jumped on top of it. We rode it down for two floors, but then it stopped suddenly when it lost power.

"Fuck," Alice hissed.

"They shut down the elevators, which means they won't come looking in here anytime soon," I whispered.

"That's great, but we're still five floors up," she said.

It was a solid seventy feet to the bottom of the elevator shaft. The vertical lift cable for the opposite car, caked with decades of grease, was in sight and gave me an idea.

"The lift cable," I said. "We can jump over and slide down."

"There has to be a better way," she said and radioed Sue.

"Sue," Alice said. "We need you to look at the elevator shaft schematics and get us out of here."

Static on the radio.

"Great," she said.

"The concrete walls in here are too thick," I said.

She pulled out her phone. She was about to call Sue when she stopped short and stared at the bright screen.

"What is it? No bars?" I asked.

"No. I just received a message from our client."

"What's it say? We're fired?"

She was silent, still staring at the screen, her eyes dancing back and forth as she read something.

"Alice, what's wrong? What does the message say?"

She turned to me, a grave look on her face.

"'Kill John,'" she whispered.

I waited for her wry smile to appear, or any kind of sign that said she was joking.

"Let me—"

I reached for the phone, but she put her gun in my face instead.

"Alice, honey, what the hell are you doing?"

"You set me up, John. Our client tried to warn me about you."

Her eyes were welling with tears of rage and sadness. I felt like the floor was giving way below me.

"No. Alice, what—?"

"You knew the target. I heard you talking before I shot her."

"I can explain that."

"Shut up!"

Then the tears were streaming down her face.

"You were working with her before. When Bob was alive."

"That's ridiculous! Who is saying that?"

"Didn't you help her leave the country when Bob wanted you to kill her?"

"I felt sorry for her. How could you possibly know that?"

"Bob knew you let her go. The only reason he didn't kill you for it was because he was short-staffed at the time."

"I let her go because she was pathetic and I thought Bob was having me waste her because of that . . . or to test me. So, I did the only good thing I've ever done in my life and I let her go. Tell me, what would you have done, Alice? Would you have chopped her to pieces with a rusty meat cleaver? Are you that cold-blooded?"

Alice had stopped listening. Her animal brain was demanding a quick, instinct-driven decision. I was quickly becoming just another option to be weighed and potentially discarded for a better one.

"Maybe your silence is my answer."

Then I could feel tears of my own. Our eyes met, and that's when I could see she had turned the corner. I was on trial and the situation warranted speedy sentencing.

"No wonder you were resisting me when I wanted to take her out."

She was in a full rage, feeling vindicated for what must have been many hidden suspicions, ready to throw everything away to feed her belief that none of what we had could have been possible or real. I tried to remove my own anger and disbelief from the moment and attempted to deal with her in a more passive and empathetic way. I was nowhere near ready to throw any bit of our relationship away.

"Alice, please. I love you. I'm here with you. Why would I ever—"

"Good-bye, John."

And just liked that she pulled the trigger. Being completely bewildered, my reflexes were not as sharp, but I managed to slap her gun out of my face and she fired a round into my shoulder. I kicked her legs out and we fell to the roof of the elevator shaft. She lost her gun in the fall, so she was punching, kicking, and gouging at me with everything she had. My arm was bleeding and weak and I tried to hold her off, but her anger had reached a fever pitch and she kicked me in the chest with both legs. I slid across the roof of the elevator car, my hands grabbing for anything to keep me from falling to my death. I looped my good arm around one of the electrical cables, and it caught me briefly, but my momentum partially jerked it out of its coupling. Sparks cascaded into the shaft as I pitched over the side.

Alice gathered herself and found me hanging on the side of the elevator car by the arcing, fire-spitting electrical cable.

"Marrying you was easily the stupidest fucking thing I've ever done," she said coldly.

My hands were slipping and I barely had a grip on the cable as I tried to shake the cobwebs out of my head.

"So I guess you could call this a divorce," she said quietly.

"Thank you," I said.

"For what?"

"For making it easy to stop loving you."

I jerked the cable out of the motor and fell into the darkness. Above me, an explosion of sparks ignited the grease on the lift cable and flames spread up and down it like a giant fuse. The fire was a deep orange with white tips that birthed long demonic snakes of black smoke, transforming the elevator shaft into a brightly lit tunnel to hell.

As I waited for impact, memories of my wedding night with Alice flooded my mind and I was thinking, *If this is my life passing before my eyes, then God is an even bigger asshole than I thought.* Turns out I was the asshole because God or Buddha or Steve Jobs actually had my back in that elevator shaft in a big way. I figured I was just going to plummet to the bottom and bounce. The feds would scrape me up with an overpriced defense contractor spatula and bag me like roadkill. But wouldn't you know it? Lucky for me, there was another elevator car two floors below that broke my fall. Don't get me wrong, that was a solid twenty-footer and I didn't know the elevator car was there, so I hit full force on my back and the impact turned my heart off like a switch. It's called commotio cordis and it's a V-fib cardiac arrest caused by a violent blow to the heart.

I immediately stopped breathing and everything went black. As I was lying there on top of the elevator car, twitching the death tango, I suddenly had the sensation that I was on fire. In fact, my body felt so hot I thought I might explode. I figured I was one more lipstick-smeared butt in the devil's ashtray, but it turned out the live electrical wire I jerked out of the other elevator car that was spitting and twisting like a snake followed me down the shaft and whipped against the car where I was laid out. *BOOM!* The live wire juiced the car and defibrillated me right back to the land of the living before it landed on the bottom of the shaft and shorted itself out in a pool of petroleum muck. Roll away the stone, motherfuckers. Thanks to Jesus and a few thousand volts, I was back from the dead.

19

When I came to, I didn't know who or where I was. Then the fog lifted and I looked up the shaft. There was no sign of Alice, which was good, because I was really banged up and couldn't have held off a sneeze. At a geriatric pace I managed to climb down the service ladder rungs all the way to the basement and bust out through the motor pool garage. I took a manatee-gray FBI Crown Vic from the motor pool that smelled like a decade of chili dogs and beer farts and drove myself to my underworld chop shop hospital. After a ghoulish doc with a Boris Karloff accent and the bedside manner of a lobotomy patient patched me up, I went to the bathroom to take a leak and looked in the mirror. There was a gash below my eye that looked exactly like a bloody teardrop. It reminded me of the Bible verse, *And if your eye causes you to stumble, pluck it out.*

Truer words. Never spoken. I stumbled, I even fell, but I caught myself before I drowned in the fantasy that was Alice. The burn I had in my chest for her was gone. She had beaten it out of me. And what's worse is the whole thing was so spectacularly surreal. The last person I expected to see in that field office was *Juno*, let alone as the mole we'd come to exterminate. I would chalk it up to horrific luck, but the games we play are not often games of chance. I learned a long time ago that coincidences are the things you start believing in right before it just so happens a bullet is crossing paths with your head.

Speaking of which, it occurred to me that Alice popped Juno pretty hastily, even under those circumstances. One would think that if Alice finally bagged the super spook who, in her estimation, had been threatening our entire operation, she would demand a few questions be answered before pulling the trigger and spraying the answers all over the Mr. Coffee machine. That was the first thing that stopped making sense when I finally had a chance to get my head together.

The other thing that rang about as true as a cowbell was the whole setup accusation. Riddle me this, Batman, if I was trying to set Alice up, why the hell would I go to all that trouble? I was the one who didn't want to do the FBI hit in the first place. I risked my neck as much as she did, maybe more. And she was the one with the direct line to the mystery client, the soon-to-be-dead client who told her to kill me.

The more I thought about all of it, the more the whole thing stunk to high heaven, and either Alice's nose was too far up her own ass to smell it . . . *or she set me up*. The latter actually made a lot more sense, so I choked down my emotions and forced myself to play devil's advocate. First, the FBI mole hunt would have been a perfect way to take me out without any danger of tipping me or the rest of the recruits off—kind of like when a family hunting dog is taken out for a hunt and conveniently never comes home. Second, like I said, *she* was the one in contact with our mystery client, who might very well be anything but a mystery to Alice. It *was* rather convenient that the invisible man just happened to be able to give us some helpful tips on the identity of a target we'd been trying to pin down for months and then turn the tables on me when I was most vulnerable and not on candid camera. Finally, the hardest thing for me to admit was that Alice was capable of being so bloodthirsty to own HR that she simply chose her ambitions over me. I wouldn't have believed it myself at the time, but I sure as hell did after the FBI gig.

Jesus, I was such an idiot.

Alice told me back in New Hampshire that she wouldn't be able to give me what I was asking for, and she was telling the truth. I just wasn't willing to listen. So, in the wake of her betrayal, I didn't waste time crying in my beer, thinking that she may have just been using me all that time to get what she wanted. That was very likely true but it was a moot issue at that point anyway. I made better use of my time drinking firewater and thinking about how pulling the trigger was as easy for Alice as telling me she loved me and wearing my ring. But she was going to find out she wasn't the only one for whom taking a life was as routine as taking a breath.

20

FBI-NCAVC, Quantico, Virginia
Present day

Fletch is smiling. It's one of those fatherly smiles that a dad wears for his son when the kid strikes out and blows the Little League game.

"What?" I ask.

"I didn't say anything," he says.

"I'm talking about the smirk on your face."

He tries to give me the *I don't know what you're talking about* look.

"Really? You want to play me like this?"

"I don't understand—"

"Fuck it. I'm going back to my cell. Guard!"

"Hold on, John. Let's talk about this."

"Yes, let's. I want to know why you had that look on your face or I'm out of here."

I slam the table with the palm of my hand. Fletch jumps and his hand moves to where I presume his gun is holstered. He stands and backs away from me. A little well-placed anger can be very effective. In this case, it creates a question in Fletch's mind about my level of volatility. His simplistic view of "guys sitting in the chair across from him" causes him to underestimate to what degree everything I do is calculated. Despite all of my strengths, to him I have a weak mind with a loose screw. To him, I am like a wolf that could turn on someone at any moment, as evidenced by his flight reaction.

"Are we going to have a problem, John?"

"Share and share alike, Fletch. Or did you drop out of kindergarten?"

Fletch pulls his chair back to sit down and slides it a little farther away from me. I resist the urge to jump at him just to make him flinch.

"I was smiling because I was a little surprised at your incomplete assessment of Alice's betrayal."

I'm a little surprised by his eagerness to offer information. It's contrary to his normal approach, but he can't help himself because he *needs* to save face with me in front of his colleagues.

"Do tell."

"Didn't it seem odd to you that Alice would choose this method of taking out the mole?"

"Are you admitting that Juno was a mole?"

His excitement fades a little knowing he has already said more than he should.

"Let's say, for the sake of argument, that she was."

"For the sake of argument."

"Attacking her in the FBI field office would only bring down more bureau pressure on Alice. You don't really believe that Alice thought we would be intimidated by her brazen act, do you?"

"Just spit it out, Fletch, before you pop."

"Alice had a reason for killing you, John."

"Is there an echo in here?"

"It wasn't just because she wanted to take over and you had served your purpose. Your purpose was to take the blame with the bureau. That way, Alice gets rid of the mole *and* pressure from us. If you're dead, we have no one to hunt down."

"She was there too."

"Wearing a gas mask most of the time, deftly avoiding cameras. And even if we could identify her, she's not in our system. As far as we would be concerned, she would have been your Patty Hearst, along for the ride."

I return Fletch's fatherly smile.

"Not bad, Assistant Director Fletcher. Not bad at all."

I allow him to bask in his proud glow, glancing up at the two-way mirror from time to time.

"I'm thinking Alice's head would make a nice addition to your trophy room, Fletch. What do you think?"

"Like I said, John, I'm working on it."

He starts a new page in his nearly full notepad.

"What happened after you made it out of the field office?"

21

After I got cleaned up, I assessed the damage, and things were actually a lot worse than I thought. My phone had been deactivated and I couldn't access my bank accounts. That night, I went to our apartment and the locks had already been changed. I knew Alice wouldn't be sleeping there, so I climbed in through the fire escape. Most of her clothes were gone. She had packed in a hurry, taking only what was near and dear, and left the apartment probably for the last time. Something caught my eye, glittering in the trash can. It was her engagement ring. I started to pick it up, but then left it in there. I would never go back. I *could* never go back. She'd tossed us out just like the ring, and in that moment I hated her for it, almost as much as I hated myself.

Then I went to HR. Same situation. My security code didn't work. I had installed webcams in the office when we renovated and I could still access those. I watched the place for a couple of hours and saw Alice fortify it with a small army of mercenary types to cover her ass. Made perfect sense. People like Alice and I may kill people, but every hour of every day someone is looking to kill *us*, someone professional. We live it and breathe it. She knew if she got rid of her husband, the only person who truly had her back, she would have to beef up her security big-time to keep the vermin out, especially since the FBI would be putting a truckload of money on the street to turn every player with a record into a snitch. Eventually she remembered to cut off my external password access to the system, and my camera feed, along with everything else, went dead.

I called the banks with my accounts to assess the situation. Alice had emptied all of my accounts, even the ones I had no idea she knew about. She hadn't wasted any time scrubbing me from the face of the earth. I wanted so badly to give her a twelve-gauge shotgun divorce, but that was pretty much impossible. I had no money and no immediate access to weapons. I didn't even have any clean clothes. Also, I was pretty sure that after she shot me and saw me plummet down a flaming elevator shaft, Alice was under the impression I was dead, and I intended to keep it that way for the time being. The smart thing to do was to disappear for a while and find a hole to crawl in so I could lick my wounds and regroup. But before I blew town, I needed to pay someone a visit.

Like a good recruit, Sue always entered his apartment through the basement service entrance and took the stairs. I was waiting for him when he walked in the front door. I injected Ketamine into his jugular vein and dropped him before he had a chance to put his keys down. When he woke up he was zip-tied and bound tightly with heavy gauge plastic, lying in his bathtub, which I had filled with highly flammable ethanol gel. I couldn't take any chances with his loyalties, which at that point were almost impossible to predict. Showing disloyalty to Alice or me could easily result in death, so I needed to leverage him to get some answers. In spite of all that, he was really glad to see me.

"JL, you're alive!"

"Keep it down. You'll wake the neighbors."

"Listen, man," he half whispered, assessing his situation, "I'm really glad to see you and all, but why do you want to kill me?"

"I don't want to kill you, Sue. I need information."

"All you had to do was buy me a beer."

"We're way past that, kid. I need to know one hundred percent that you aren't bullshitting me. There's too much at stake."

"What's that smell?"

"Butane gel. There's enough in the tub to incinerate the whole building."

"JL, they got kids living here."

"I know. Three of them next door. I needed that component in case you decided you didn't care enough about yourself not to burn alive."

"That's one hell of a bullshit detector you got going, JL."

"Never failed me."

"And it won't now, man. I have no reason to lie to you. What the hell you want to know?"

"Does Alice think I'm dead?"

"Yeah. After I got her out of the FBI office, she told me the feds shot you and you fell down the elevator shaft. Nothing she could do about it. Lying bitch."

I laughed.

"What's so funny?"

"Business as usual," I said.

"What really happened, JL?"

"It's a long story and I'm short on time. Do the other recruits know about my untimely demise?"

"Don't think so. She'll probably tell them tomorrow."

I lit a match and held it over him.

"Yo, what the fuck?"

"Did you have anything to do with it?"

"With what?"

I got closer with the match.

"Like I said, with what?" he said defiantly.

He didn't have it in him to assign his loyalty to someone like Alice. I may have had a blind spot with her but not with anyone else. He blew out the match, and I couldn't help but laugh.

"Got any weed?" I asked.

"Vape's in the medicine cabinet."

I took a hit and gave him one.

"Permission to speak freely, JL."

"Granted."

"I'm glad you finally cut loose of that psycho. I'd call her the C word, but that ain't Christian. So, I'll just be a gentleman and say she's a rotten, soulless whore with a mean streak a mile long. No offense."

"None taken," I said, laughing through another hit.

"And if she fucked you over, I got beef with her too and I'll help you make things right, believe that."

"I believe it, Sue. Gotta go."

"You going to cut me out of this?"

I pulled a stiletto and popped the blade. I pointed it at his eye.

"You didn't see me," I said gravely. "As far as you know, I'm dead. I'll be watching you and Alice. So, if she suddenly thinks I'm alive, I'll know it's you and I'll come back here and hang you upside down over low burning coals, Apache-style, so your eyeballs boil and your face melts off while your brain poaches in your skull. Feel me?"

"I feel you."

"Good."

"Where the hell you going, man? Let me up out of here and let's both go waste her and be done with it. I'm not playing."

"Open up."

I held out the knife and he clamped it between his teeth.

"You're a good kid, Sue. Keep your head down and your mouth shut and you'll be all right."

22

On the way out of Sue's place, I took his Beretta and a couple of hundreds he had in his pocket. I was twisting in the wind, so I needed to get my hands on money, weapons, and any other contraband that would help me vanish undetected as quickly as possible and sustain me until I could regroup. I kept stashes all over the city, most of them well stocked with all manner of assassin sundries. A hitter never knows when the real shit is going to come down and being prepared is the best way to keep from getting buried in it. That's one of the few useful things Bob taught me, and it saved my ass on more than one occasion.

While I played scavenger hunt in all the boroughs, I thought about a job that could have been my last if I hadn't had stashes. Ironically, the assignment had been to smoke a big-time drug dealer. No, he didn't have gold fronts, two chainz, and a six-four. In fact, he wasn't a *he* at all, you sexist bastard. *She* turned out to be one of my most interesting and memorable marks. You may have heard me speak of duality before? Well, Kiana Nguyen, a half-black, half-Vietnamese Wall Street gunslinger with baroque music tattoos and an entourage of MMA fighters, was the double-edged sword of duality, with each blade razor sharp. By day, she was a partner in a wildly successful boutique hedge fund. And by night she was one of the heaviest hitters in the East Coast heroin trade, known on the street as Kali, after the Hindu goddess of destruction.

Her hedge fund did legit business but, unbeknownst to her partners, she was using it as a Laundromat for her drug cash. Evidently, her partners in the brokerage found out about her skag lord alter ego and paid HR to put a pin in her before she got busted and the feds seized everyone's lobster pants and cigarette boats. Of course, they wanted us to do it when the coffers were swimming with drug money they could easily absorb as a Christmas bonus. I swear Wall Street has more scumbags in suits per capita than a Mafia wedding.

I started my internship at what I'll call Goldman & Smack on a Monday, and by Friday I had managed to weasel my way into the bull pen within spitting distance of my target's posh corner office. On the surface, she seemed like a mild-mannered numbers nerd with no interest in the poncey clothes and male fetishes—golf, sports cars, Kobe steaks, barely legal hookers—that the rest of her office worshipped with mouth-foaming cult zeal. She was routinely ostracized by the rest of the suits and held a solid lead as the butt of most watercooler jokes. But after hours, when all the other douche tools were off at ball games and booze cruises, she was still at the office, doing business and just about every drug she could get her hands on. Anything she could snort, shoot, pop, or gulp was fair game, and she would consume copious amounts all night while she ran her empire. I thought I liked drugs. Compared to this maniac in horn-rimmed glasses and orange juice–can curls, I was like a middle school kid trying a sip of his dad's beer for the first time.

Like most rich drug dealers, she had a lot of heavies to watch her back. As I mentioned, she had a taste for pinheaded MMA brawlers and seemed to collect them like scarves or snow globes. These guys sat in the bull pen with everyone else, wore suits and ties, hacked away at computers, and talked on the phones all day. But, like my internship, it was all a cover. They didn't know a short sale from Shinola, but they were convincing enough to the untrained observer. I, on the other hand, could have picked them all out of a lineup. Suit jacket sleeves and pant legs just a little too tight. Tattoos peeking out of collars and watchbands. A slight bulge on the back of the hips and the ankles from concealed weapons. All the other brokers peeled their jackets the minute they sat at their desks. These guys kept them on all day, even in July when the AC wasn't keeping up. Their hands were also a dead giveaway—scarred, knobby, meat hooks from punching, stabbing, and shooting their way through life, with dry dead skin from all the times they'd had to scrub off the blood.

Trying to figure out when and how I would hit her really depended on the meat hook boys. A night job would have been the most convenient, but that was when she and her crew were thick as thieves. The day presented a trickier option because of the volume of guys in the bull pen, the noise, and the overall chaos potential. On the one hand, if I could use the crowded room to my advantage, her bodyguards would have to fight through bodies, most of them aggressively overweight, to get to me. Bob used to call it a smash and grab, when you hit someone in broad daylight with a lot of people around and use the resulting mayhem to your advantage to slip out unnoticed. But Bob was an idiot and with all the terrorist response teams within three minutes' striking distance of any Manhattan landmark, I wasn't all that comfortable playing OK Corral at a busy Wall Street office in broad daylight.

Finally, as it often does, opportunity presented itself but at the worst possible time. I had been sent on a run to pick up dry cleaning, cigarettes, tampons, Viagra, cinnamon dolce lattes, and a lot more items the suits thought it was funny to make the intern go buy, when I passed a small sushi restaurant at around lunchtime. I stopped short when I saw a Yorkie in a monogrammed Burberry sweater tied up outside. That yapping rat went everywhere with Kiana. It was like her baby, which meant that day, lunch was going to be on me. I let the mutt go to town on all the crap in my errand bags and strolled inside—where I quickly noticed my target and her pilot fish whooping it up behind the rice paper screen of one of the large private dining rooms.

They were sitting ducks and the closest thing I had to a weapon on me was a can of Aqua Net I had picked up for one of the traders' three-hundred-pound mother-in-law. I thought about radioing Bob, but he would have kicked my ass for half stepping on the job with no piece, and he couldn't have gotten anything to me in time anyway. I had to think quickly or blow a golden opportunity before they asked for the check. Then I remembered I had a stash box a few blocks away. I wasn't sure what was in there, but it had to be better than the dick I was currently holding in my hand.

I sprinted to the stash, which was in a YMCA locker, and saw what I had to work with: an ARES FMG submachine gun and two mags, a bottle of ether, a .38, and what looked to be close to $10,000 in cash. I took everything but the cash and sprinted back to the sushi restaurant. I slid quietly into a table in the back, with an open view of Kiana's private dining room, and made preparations while I drank a large Asahi. So dry. So crisp. So refreshing. Asahi!

The FMG is a total James Bond weapon. It's basically an Uzi that folds up into what looks like a very small briefcase or a très chic woman's handbag. I thought about just spraying them with bullets, but the FMG, although cool, basically pukes copious amounts of slugs, which come out of its extremely short barrel spinning end over end. So, if you're not point-blank, there isn't a lot of accuracy. And once you start shooting, you're not going to kill them all at once so they're going to start shooting back. I didn't really want to be in a firefight with a bunch of pros when my own firepower was suspect at best. And I didn't want it to drag out long enough for the cops to show up. I'd brought in a flask of ether as my element of surprise. In addition to being a strong anesthetic—way more effective than chloroform—it's about ten times more flammable than gasoline.

I poured the ether into my empty Asahi bottle and stuffed a cloth napkin in the top. Then I lit the napkin with the table candle and chucked the boys a serious curveball through the rice paper. The flaming bottle ripped through the rice paper screen like a comet, smashed into the jaw of one of the thugs, and exploded like Nagasaki. Next thing you knew, the whole private room was engulfed in flames and black smoke. The wretched smell was like sucking on the exhaust of a Tokyo taxicab. Predictably, the meat hook boys opened fire, but they were shooting at my table, where I had tied down the FMB and jammed the trigger in firing position. While it laid down cover, I picked them all off one by one with the reliable .38.

When the smoke cleared, though, I couldn't see Kiana. The floor around me was covered in beer and broken glass and had basically become an ice rink full of razor blades. Then I noticed the sushi chef was just standing there staring at me. I was about to ask him for some hamachi to go when I saw his hand jerk, followed by a metallic flash of light. The son of a bitch chucked one of his sushi knives at me! Goddamned thing stuck in my thumb and made me drop my gun. The second knife was headed for my eyeball but I stopped it with the palm of my hand. You can't imagine the pain of an eleven-inch sushi knife sinking point-first in your palm and piercing bone. I screamed like a little girl. This made the chef laugh his ass off. In the interest of wiping the smile off his face, I whipped the knife back at him and it plunged into his thigh. He crumpled to the floor and passed out from the pain.

It was about this time when Kiana swung down from the ceiling and kicked me so hard in the head that I smashed into the hostess stand and blacked out for a few seconds. When I came to, I saw a blurry image of her jumping down from the sprinkler pipe she had been hanging on. Then I saw the blurry image start beating the shit out of me with a flurry of punches, kicks, and elbows thrown in the Vietnamese Vovinam fighting style. This is known as a "hard and soft" system, so her strikes were like iron, but each time I tried to hit her, she either deftly avoided me or expertly absorbed my energy.

After sweeping my legs and sending me headlong into a hot sake machine, she pulled the sushi knife from the chef's leg and turned to me. I knew this was my last chance to make a move, so I didn't hesitate. Before she had a chance to advance with the knife, I ran at her full speed, like a free safety going in for a bell-ringing head tackle. She tried in vain to get out of the way, but I gave her a forearm shiver to the side of the jaw (NFL fighting–style) with all my weight behind it. The hit lifted her off the ground and knocked her back about five feet into the sushi bar—hard wood and three-inch-thick glass. It exploded when she collided with it. I knew she broke her neck because she fell to the floor twitching and gasping in the beer puddle like a fish on a boat deck.

None of it was pretty or even all that professional. Bob was really pissed because I had not implemented the execution scenario we had discussed—Cuban necktie to indicate South American competitors—and the police and FBI spent a few weeks making the case a priority. Eventually they ran out of coffee and doughnuts and filed it as a cold case, but I always remembered that you never know when an opportunity will arise and you always have to be ready to take full advantage. Which is why one of the best rules in the handbook is Rule #7: Get your shit together.

23

That old stash box that helped me pull off the sushi hit was my final stop on my way out of town. The $10,000 was still in there, along with some spare ammo, and a bag of narcotics I lifted from Kali's Theory suit jacket. I'd also snagged a driver's license from the slimmest of the MMA thugs. Whenever possible, Bob always had us take IDs because we could wipe the magnetic data strip and use them for our own purposes. In this case it was a godsend because I needed to get on a plane and the dead thug bore a close enough resemblance to make that happen. Good thing I had followed Rule #7 fairly well because, all told, I pulled around $300,000 and change from my stashes. It wasn't going to keep me off the feds' radar screen forever, but I was happy to have anything buy me some time.

I chartered a flight out of Newark to San Diego and drove into Mexico the next morning. Trying to go anywhere else would have required a passport and customs and I couldn't risk having my face show up on a Homeland Security screen. You can drive right into Mexico without showing any kind of ID, which was perfect for me, but I knew by doing it I was going to have to jump through serious hoops to get back to the U.S. The good thing was my money would be long there and I needed a few days in the sun to clear my head.

I holed up in a small beach town called Puerto Peñasco and slept for nearly two straight days in a tiny apartment near the ocean. The sea breeze was like an opiate, making my limbs so heavy I could barely move. When I was finally able to get up and move around, I saw that the bullet wound in my shoulder had become infected, probably from me lying on it for so long, sweating in the dirty bedding. I tried cleaning it with drugstore antiseptics, but it didn't help and I ended up with a high fever. I stumbled to a local doctor and bought some expensive gringo antibiotics along with new dressings. I also paid him to send his nurse to my apartment a couple of times a day to clean and redress my nearly gangrenous wound, feed me, and keep me hydrated.

I spent the next thirty-six hours in a horrible fever dream that quickly turned to a nightmare. I was visited by nearly all of the people I killed over the years, ghoulishly taunting me every time I would fall asleep. It wasn't some obscure dream either. I could see them in the room with me, clear as day, making themselves right at home. At first they would look normal, then they would turn or the light would hit them just right and I would see the horrible damage I had inflicted upon them—exit wounds, acid burns, deep lacerations . . . I'm surprised the nurse kept coming back because half the time I was screaming when she got there and she had to knock me out with Valium.

The worst part was when I would see Alice. I would wake up and she'd be next to my bed, dabbing my forehead with a wet cloth or giving me a sip of water. When she was done comforting me, she would sink her teeth into my neck and tear out my throat. I would usually wake up vomiting in a bucket on the side of my bed and cry myself back to sleep.

When the fever broke, it was a Sunday morning and I could hear church bells. I forced myself to get out of bed, pulled on whatever clothes I could easily grab, and walked outside. The beach wasn't far and I had this idea that it was like the Sea of Galilee that was going to wash away my sin and sickness. When I got there, trash and diapers were strewn up and down the sand and sewage and an oil slick floated on top of the water. I brushed used needles aside and sat in the filthy sand, watching the glittering wave tips much farther out at sea. A little girl walked up to me and tried to sell me Chiclets and screamed when she saw my face.

I went back home and looked at myself in the mirror. I looked like a corpse. I had lost at least twenty pounds and my body fat had been nearly zero to start with. My cheeks were sunken and I had dark circles under both bloodshot eyes. I felt so weak, I could barely stand. I force-fed myself some of the food the nurse had left in the refrigerator and opened a bottle of mezcal I had bought when I first arrived. Bad idea. I had barely eaten anything for days, and after a few glasses, I felt like a hole was being burned in my stomach. I lay down on the sofa and fell asleep watching Mexican soap operas.

I woke up to the sound of glass breaking. I stood up too quickly and nearly passed out, steadying myself on the coffee table. Two dark figures darted through the back of the house and ran to my bedroom.

I yelled something unintelligible and headed for the bedroom, but a fist flew out of the darkness and tagged me on the jaw. I went sprawling across the Saltillo tiles, unable to break my fall. The guy came at me again, this time with a gun, and I pretended to be half-conscious. When he got close, I throat punched him with every ounce of strength I had left and he fell back, clutching his shattered windpipe and turning blue. The gun he was holding fell out of his hand and skidded under the couch. I went to grab it when I heard his partner yell from inside my room.

"Luis!"

Before I could grab the gun, Luis's compadre emerged from the bedroom holding the backpack that contained all my money. He looked like a Mexican version of Mel Gibson from the *Lethal Weapon* days—bugged-out eyeballs, Brillo mullet, and acid-washed jeans. I dove at him, and he kicked me with the pointed toe of a cowboy boot right in the stomach. When I doubled over, he kicked me in the head and I fell to the floor, drifting in and out of consciousness. I waited for him to finish me off, but he just spat on the ground next to my head and walked out the door with my $300,000.

24

When I woke up and remembered how FUBAR I was, I decided I was done. The gods were hitting me over the head with the message that this was the dead end of the road, and I didn't disagree. Without money, there was no way for me to survive. I was too weak to try to pull a job, and after the fever nightmare, I didn't really want to. I also realized that what happened with Alice was weighing on me much more than I thought. As much as I tried to tell myself I really didn't love her anymore, without her in my life, my future looked pretty bleak. I tried to imagine myself at forty, like Jean Reno in *Léon: The Professional*, drinking milk and sleeping in a chair with a gun in my hand, and I knew I would rather die than fulfill that prophecy.

So, my plan was to drink as much mescal as possible and chase it with a bullet from the dead bandito's gun. My last hit. *At least it will be an easy gig,* I thought as I went to work on the bottle. By sundown, I was stumbling around like a Bowery bum, singing and punching holes in the walls. I reached under the couch and grabbed the gun.

"*Dios mío,*" I shouted at the *cucarachas,* scattering them.

It was a gold-plated .45 with a platinum Virgin Mary inlaid in the grip, a filigree of roses on the barrel, and the words *Flores para los muertos* inscribed on the top of the slide. *Perfecto,* I thought. *Looks like Jesus loves Luis but everyone else thinks he's an asshole.*

I gathered up my bottle and my shiny new gun, and walked along the beach until the lights of the town were in the distance behind me. I sat down among the rotting piles of litter and drank the rest of the rotgut mescal, swallowed the worm, and watched the moonlight filter through the clouds and dance across the water. I was about to give myself last rites when I heard loud voices and the sound of a car coming up the beach. A pickup loaded with a bunch of young people partying in the truck bed tore past me.

At the wheel was Mexican Mel Gibson.

I thanked the Blessed Virgin for my fortune and shot out his front right tire. The pickup swerved violently, pitching most of the revelers and booze bottles into the sand, and skidded to an abrupt halt. While the women cursed and gathered themselves, the men drew their weapons and searched the darkness for something to kill. They never saw me coming. The Virgin Mary and I dropped their sorry drunk asses in fewer than thirty seconds and I put a bullet through the mouth of Mexican Mel Gibson just as he opened it to curse my name. The women scattered and I got my money out of the truck.

As I walked away, I looked at the litter of bodies. They were all a bunch of kids, late teens, early twenties at most. All of them carried the ridiculous gold-plated hardware indicative of cartel boys. Looking at them, I thought about Sue and the other young HR recruits. Was I just going to abandon them all and leave them at the mercy of Alice? Hell no. I'd worked my ass off to try to save theirs, and throwing myself away with the used condoms and Doritos bags on a filthy Mexican beach felt like a betrayal of epic proportions. Not to mention the fact that it meant I was going to throw in the towel to Alice without a fight. She had proved she had it in her to run those recruits into the ground if her hair-trigger temper got the best of her, and I couldn't allow that to happen.

I walked into town and made a collect call to a fixer I had on the West Coast, an Irish gunrunner who I had used in the past to acquire military hardware. Guy could get you an M1 Abrams Tank within twelve hours if you had the cash. I told him I'd gone dark in Mexico but needed gainful employment to stay sharp and prep for a big job in a few weeks. I asked if he knew anyone looking for a decent triggerman. He mentioned a farm boy named Griner in Sonora, but was reluctant to hook me up with him because the guy was some kind of hardcase son of a bitch. I told him I could handle it. The Irishman took down my address and told me I'd be contacted within a few days.

Next morning I woke up to a black cloth hood being shoved on my head by two of many gloved hands that quickly bound me with zip ties and duct tape and stuffed me into what smelled and felt like the hungry maw of a black, nondescript panel van. The familiar prick of a needle sang me to sleep while visions of Alice being riddled with bullets danced in my head.

25

Gran Desierto de Altar, Sonoran Desert
Six weeks later

S uck dirt, Nancy."
Griner strode around me, his huge, mud-encrusted boots
stomping heavily on the grass, crushing the helpless blades to
green pulp. I pumped out twenty one-handed push-ups while
he jabbed his rock-hard finger into any part of my body that was
exhibiting incorrect form. When I was done, I leapt to my feet
and he was already walking away from me. For six long weeks I
had been the reluctant pupil of a black-eyed Arkansas hillbilly
who wore overalls and no shirt and looked like the love child of
Charles Manson and Aileen Wuornos. The day I arrived via the
black bag express at his sweltering wasteland of a training ground
in the middle of the most godforsaken desert in the world, he took
one look at me and told me he wouldn't send me to kill a rat in
his mama's shitter.

I agreed to train with him because I had no place else to go and
figured I could use a brushup. I had also had the distinct feeling that
if I refused, he would have buried me up to my neck in a fire ant
hill. Being a professional for so many years, I thought I was hard. I
thought I was at the top of my game. *I was wrong.* As an HR intern,

I'd been beaten, shot, stabbed, burned, electrocuted, and nearly drowned, but all of these things combined paled in comparison to Griner's training. In six weeks, he peeled away the layers of weakness until there was nothing left but bone and sinew. He built me from the ground up with a relentless onslaught, the likes of which I am guaranteed never to face in the field. In this respect, it is the finest training I could have ever received. If my hatred for him hadn't been so venomous, and my desperation to get out of there and get on with Alice so urgent, I would have thanked him from the bottom of my black heart. But he had taken most of what was left of my money for his "services" and still hadn't sent me out on a job. So much time had passed I was beginning to worry that when I got back to New York, Alice might already be dead by someone else's hand, along with Sue and all of the recruits.

The other problem I was beginning to see was that Griner figured because he trained me, he owned me, and I owed him a debt. And being in his pocket was about the last place on earth I wanted to be. So, as I went through his usual blood-and-guts routine that day, my brain was working overtime to find a way out.

"Hurry up, Suzie, or I'm gonna give ya a beatdown!" Griner bellowed.

I sprinted to where he was standing by the corrugated-metal warehouse. Inside that warehouse was his carnival of horrors meant to "make your balls drop and turn you into a man." The heat was stifling in there and I knew I would be required to fight my way through a gang of shirtless psychopaths that Griner had bought like livestock from the warden at a nearby Mexican penitentiary. They would be armed with ax handles, chains, horse whips, and any other rusty implements Griner had lying around. If I didn't get there fast enough, he would just tie me up and let them beat me until I pissed my pants.

When I caught up to him, he flashed his sadistic grin and, with the wave of his oily Confederate flag bandanna, set his dogs on me. They were vicious, half-starved mongrels who had attacked me the first day I arrived there. After that, they had a taste for my blood. The alpha charged and leapt directly for my throat. I grabbed him by the mouth in midair and heaved him effortlessly at the other advancing dogs. He bowled them over and they scattered, whining and snapping. When he saw he had no backup, he ran to his pack, braying and covering his asshole with his tail. Griner laughed and locked them in their chicken-wire pen. This was his idea of entertainment, only because he was a mongrel himself.

He examined my hand and farted a "humph" of approval through his mottled, sneering lips. There was no blood. There had been no blood for weeks. My hands and feet were no longer instruments of my senses, sending the language of touch to my brain. They were knotted lumps of scar tissue. The nerve endings were destroyed by the merciless bludgeoning of wood and stone and by the flames of Griner's oil barrel fire. I could punch through a solid hickory door and use the same fist to smash a cinder block. I could kick through six-inch glass bricks barefoot without so much as a scratch.

I didn't walk on hot coals. I walked on fire.

Griner's philosophy was simple. Weapons are unreliable, noisy, and leave too much evidence behind. The more complicated the weapon, the more undesirable it is as a tool of the trade. Guns were a joke to Griner. We would go into the Mexicali slums for what he called "rooster fucking" and he would start trouble with the lowest snake-eyed degenerates he could find. They drew guns and he shoved the barrels up their asses before they could even think about pulling the trigger. To Griner, a hand holding a gun or knife was just another point of leverage, an invitation to have your arm torn out of the socket, which I'd seen him do more times than I cared to count.

To Griner, the only true weapon was the body. He didn't see

elbows, hands, feet, or heads. He saw points, edges, and rock-hard bludgeons. With the right amount of force and placement, a finger is ten times more deadly than a knife. Of course, Griner was not the originator of this method. It's a very old kung fu style called "Iron Palm." Legend has it that an ancient Chinese master whose daughter was raped and nearly killed by a roving gang of thugs created Iron Palm. So that she could never be hurt again, he slowly turned her body into a mass of hardened scar tissue and bone through the use of corrosive chemicals and repetitive hand and foot strikes on canvas bags filled with sand. Definitely not a Disney family. She eventually became one of the most feared warriors in China and never used a weapon. And as revenge for never getting to go to the prom, she caved her father's face in with her heel while he ate his breakfast.

As I said, I was running out of money and getting tired of playing grasshopper to Griner's Master Po. So, I had asked him that morning when he was going to send me out on a job, but he just grunted incoherently. Later that day, after vanquishing the dogs, I knew I'd made a mistake bringing it up.

"So you think you're ready to swing, eh, pussy mouth?"

"Yeah," I said with unwavering confidence.

"Bullshit. You're still a dickless crybaby." Griner laughed sadistically. "When you can take *me*, then you're ready."

To make his point, he hawked a massive gob of chewing tobacco in my face. When I wiped my eyes, I saw the long sunlit string of rancid brown saliva running from his mouth to my face bow and snap, leaving a quivering drool pool on his chin. I could feel the black rage filling my eyes. When he raised his hand to wipe off his chin, he exposed his rib cage. Without thinking, I focused all of my energy and slammed my open palm into his ribs. The impact shattered his rib cage, driving sharpened fragments of bone into his delicate lung tissue. He growled in pain, gasping for air, and settled himself, closing his body to me like an armadillo slipping into its armor. It was on. To maintain honor, he would have had to kill me or die trying. There was nothing in between.

"No better time than the present, you inbred fucktard," I said.

"Boy, you ain't got the sense the good Lord gave a shit fly. Now I'm gonna have to swat you like one."

Then he advanced, savagely pummeling me with rapid-fire side kicks. The broken ribs were just a distraction for Griner, and I knew it. He used his arms to protect his torso but that made no difference. His feet were even more nimble than his hands, powered by whip-like muscles. But thanks to Griner, my hands were like granite and they absorbed the strikes. My own ribs were rattling from the kicks to my elbows, which I used to protect my sides.

Then he unleashed a roundhouse kick that slammed my own fist into my head. I dropped to my knees, fighting to stay conscious. In that moment, I had to act or die. Griner punctuated this fact with a kick that rang my head like a bell. I could hear the distorted cacophony of his dogs in the distance, chewing their mouths bloody on the chicken wire as they desperately tried to escape their cages to assist Master Griner. At that moment, my only thought was about what *they* would do in this moment. And that's exactly what I did.

Griner went for the kill with a foot aimed at my temple. I ducked and launched myself off the ground with all of the force my powerful legs could deliver, my hands outstretched and shooting for his throat. He grinned and grabbed my wrists with his clawlike fingers, pulling me toward him for the knee that I could see rising to crush my face. But instead of attempting to free my hands, a move that would have only facilitated Griner's kill shot, I opened my mouth wide and sank my teeth into his throat. Having learned from the dogs, I knew the exact action to ensure a kill. My canine and front incisors gained purchase on his larynx and surrounding blood vessels and I closed my jaw down as hard as I could. Like the dogs, I matched Griner's struggles with violent side-by-side motions of my head, gnashing, tearing, goring. The ocean of blood that filled my mouth nearly drowned me and I fell away, retching and gagging. I looked up, expecting Griner's kill shot, but instead saw that I had mortally wounded him.

I staggered to my feet. Griner's thug posse, made of men who have seen and done it all, stood with their mouths wide in horror. Even the dogs had quieted in their kennels. Griner's face was a ghostly pale, mottled grimace, his lips white and his hands clutching desperately to stave off the bleeding. He attempted to rise into a crouching position, his instinct still driving him to fight, but I knew he only had a few seconds of life left. So, I took that opportunity to impart some wisdom of my own.

"The body may be a weapon, Griner," I said. "But the best weapon is the one you don't see coming."

I brought my heel down on the back of his neck and shoved his face in dog shit.

"To answer your question," I said. "Yes, I'm ready."

And I stepped down hard, snapping his neck like a dry twig.

26

A few days later I was a stowaway in the back of a cargo plane loaded with counterfeit cartoon character tchotchkes bound for New York, drinking a bottle of Griner's Scorpion moonshine. I wanted my entry back into Manhattan to have no electronic footprint, so I avoided commercial planes, trains, and automobiles. I was still a ghost and planned to keep it that way until it was time for my resurrection. And I was ready for a fight. Because of Griner, I was no longer afraid of hell, let alone Alice.

To me, she was simply a traitor, and the fact that she tried to kill me twice wasn't her highest crime. She killed what could have been an epic love affair, the antithesis of emasculating Match.com culture. We could have cashed out and raised a couple of young maniacs of our own. We could have gone to fucking Disneyland. As the landing gear doors opened and the first whispers of morning light surrounded me in a funereal haze, the wheels touched down and the empty moonshine bottle spun on the floor near my feet, threatening to come to rest and point itself at me, the kiss of death in its whirling promise. *Now it begins*, I thought, excited to make the first move in what was going to be an epic chess game.

When I was back in Manhattan the first thing I did, after kissing the ground and grabbing a slice, was procure myself a villainous lair to use as my base of operations. It had to be big and sinister and I

spent most of the night indulging in one of my favorite pastimes—
roof-hopping—which led me to an enormous SoHo loft, the home
of a German deconstructionist sculptor named Osgood Kurtz. You
may have seen his work if deeply obscure contemporary drivel sold
to bourgeois art hoarders is your passion.

Osgood was recently deceased and had no next of kin. Don't
worry. He died of self-inflicted natural causes. I could smell his exit
fumes from several blocks away as I leapt over the urban canyons.
Eventually I saw a cloud of bottle flies, my old pals, lollygagging
around Osgood's window. Unmistakable. The sweet stench of rot
was cutting through the hot garbage and Chinatown animal-market
reek. Home sweet home.

I climbed down the fire escapes until I reached his kitchen window. I could see him slumped over a work-in-progress bronze of
Hitler's head on the end of a six-foot, angry metal cock. Pedestrian
concept, but I must admit, flawless execution. Osgood's heroin gear
lay on the table next to his bloated still life of a body. Overdose.
From the look of the amber-colored resin on the spoon, our boy
wrecked himself on some musky skag that had probably been cut
with fiberglass particles. The Afghan mullahs running the opium
drug trade love to throw a bit of that into a random bail as a nice
screw you to American junkies. *Surprise, white devil! We just shut
down your heart with a massive arterial embolism and drove a chemical ice pick into your brain!* I bagged up old Ozzie and trucked him
off to an acid bath in Jersey—in his Maserati, of course—where his
final and most brilliant installation consisted of him turning from a
solid to a liquid to a gas in twenty minutes.

Then his casa was *mi casa*. As long as I kept paying the bills, no
one would ask questions, and I was pretty sure there was no way he
had any friends. I filled the place with blue curls of cigarette smoke
and deadened my aching wounds with the mellow twenty-five-year-
old Scotch Herr Kurtz left in his otherwise bare cupboard. With

each smoky, peaty sip, I came to the happy realization that Alice was finally out of my system. She had been a cancer that had spread to every cell. And as with most cancers, it took nearly killing me, in Mexico of all places, to be cured. It felt nice to be free to return to my old militantly egocentric self with no emotional ties to anyone or anything. Even my desire to find my real family had evaporated with the simplest of axioms: If they didn't want me, why would I want them? This newfound clarity enabled me to focus purely on finishing the job I had come to New York to do—execute the Alice contract quickly, cleanly, and with extreme prejudice.

But I needed assistance. I needed Sue. And I had to contact him in a way that wouldn't tip off Alice about my presence. Of course, the whole proposition was risky. Time had passed and there was always the chance that his fear of Alice had fostered some kind of Stockholm syndrome false loyalty. But I had no other choice. Without him there was no way I could get any reliable intel on her movements. One thing I knew about Sue is he *does* love the strip clubs. And, like all connoisseurs, he had his favorite, a dank skeez pit in the Bronx called Papa Cherry's. For all you haters, Sue wasn't proud of being a thong stuffer. He would have liked to have a steady girl, but like the rest of us, he learned early on (the hard way) that relationships were potentially lethal to significant others. So he burned his hard-earned cash on the ladies of the pole, often ending up in the sucker's paradise known as the champagne room, which is where we were reunited.

Sue pimp-rolled into the room with two girls. I was sitting in a dark corner, and as soon as they settled into lap dance mode, scored by the Johnny Cash song that was his namesake, I aimed the cork on the $10 bottle of champagne that was about to cost him $200 and popped it right into the side of his head. Sue jumped out of the chair and the girls went sprawling. Legs, hair, and curses were flying and Sue was frantically searching for his gun, which I could see was on the floor, covered by an electric-blue feather boa.

"It can happen that fast, Sue," I said, laughing my ass off. "One minute you're shellacking the canoe and the next your brains are all over the salad bar."

Sue whipped around, ready to fight, and saw me standing there. His instant smile and attitude change told me I had made the right decision finding him.

"Johnny fucking Lago!"

I looked down at the flag flying at half-mast in his trousers.

"I guess you're glad to see me?"

He laughed and went to hug me.

"I think a handshake will do," I said, but he hugged me anyway.

The girls were confused, so I spoke their primitive lipstick language by handing them a stack of hundreds.

"Thank you for a lovely evening, ladies," I said.

They exited, eager to hide the money from the house, and I took a good look at the boy named Sue. He looked strung out.

"Let's bounce," I said. "We need to talk and I need to keep a low profile. You know a place near here?"

"We can go to my old hood a few blocks down. That's as low pro as it gets."

27

Sue took me to a massive block of housing projects near Fort Apache in the South Bronx. This is a place abandoned by police and emergency responders. It's literally a lawless island on the end of an island and it's the least likely place to be under any kind of surveillance by the authorities. 911 doesn't exist there and even professionals like us stand the chance of being dusted by any number of gangs with ominous names and blank-staring youth soldiers. We drank beer in a burned-out apartment in the projects that used to be one of Sue's foster homes.

"You look like shit," I said to Sue.

"The dragon lady's added years to my life, JL. HR is a clusterfuck and I'm ready to tie a noose at the end of my rope. Good to see you too."

"What's been going on?"

"Alice is . . . man, she's a mess. Angry. Damn. Everybody on eggshells. And paranoid. Got a dozen mercs, armed to the teeth, always at her side. Surveillance everywhere. She's watching us all the time, even at home, like that dumbass show *Big Brother*."

"Any heat from the FBI?"

"Nah. None that I can see. I have seen a few ghosts, though."

"What kind of ghosts? Christmas past?"

"Spotters. Probably why Alice is freaking out."

"Think she's been greenlit?" I asked.

This would not have been outside the realm of possibilities. The FBI has a long history of using contract guns to do its dirty work. The long arm of the law is often attached to a big briefcase full of cash.

"If she has, they're taking their sweet time."

"We have to assume, at least, that whoever it is has her on twenty-four/seven surveillance rotations."

"Definitely. She opened the juice can this time."

"Yeah. More competition for me. Makes it interesting. How's business otherwise?"

"Popping. We always got gigs, but they feel like B-list marks. Come with a lot of low-life clients, which makes her paranoia even worse."

"What about Alice? What's she working on?"

"She's kept it pretty close to the vest, but I dug into it just to make sure she wasn't driving the bus off the edge of a cliff again, you know?"

"I don't blame you. I should have never agreed to the FBI job. I did it to placate her and ignored my instincts. Love . . . guaranteed to transform you into a complete dumbass by the second date."

"Won't argue with you there."

"What's she got cooking that's so top secret?"

"Looks like a cupcake. Chinese guy named Zhen. He's the CEO of some company I've never heard of called CIS, Inc. HQ is in Midtown."

"When's she going to initiate?"

"I think she already has. I haven't seen her as much in the office lately, thank God. Before, she was up our asses daily. I figure she's got to be working."

"How long you think?" I asked.

"Maybe a couple of weeks. I'll look into it some more, if you want."

"I want."

"Whatever you need, JL. I'm with you."

"Are you?"

"Hell yeah—"

"This is my fight, Sue. And it's going to get ugly. You can stand on the sidelines and feed me some intel and stay out of the fray. I don't expect you to take any bullets for me."

"You're my ticket out of this, JL. As long as Alice is taking up space, this gig is nothing but a black bag. Like you with Bob. Fuck that, man. Nobody owns me. Especially not some uptight white bitch with a loose screw. Whatever you got going, put me in the game."

"Thanks, Sue. I'm glad to hear you say that because, to tell you the truth, there's no way I could do it without you." I laughed.

We shook on it. Sue passed me another beer.

"So, where the hell you been anyway?" he asked.

"Church camp. I've seen the light."

"You look like you've been rode hard, put away wet, and burned up in the barn. Your damn hands look like beef jerky. Where the hell've you been? I thought you were dead for sure."

"I *am*."

"Why you got to lay all this cryptic nonsense on me?"

"The less you know about it, the better. I made some fairly serious enemies in my recent travels, people that will be looking to put my head on a spike at the town gates. I figure it's a matter of time before they track me down. Plus, I don't want you to know anything Alice could beat out of you."

"You'll buy me a shot and beer and regale me with your adventures when all this is under our belts?"

"Kid, when this is under our belts, you can have front-row tickets to John Lago, the Mexicali fucking musical."

"Let's do this. What do you need from me?" Sue asked.

"Just keep me fat on Alice intel until I can get her into a corner and give her a proper divorce."

"I'm on it."

———

While Sue worked on getting under Alice's skin, I gathered intel on her assignment, Fang Zhen. Definitely not a cupcake. Not even close. CIS, Inc., or Chinese Industrial Solutions, was a front for a global corporate and industrial espionage ring with ties to the Chinese government. Zhen was the CEO, but his real job was as a Ministry of State Security operative. The MSS is the arm of Chinese intelligence with an expanding global network of "nonprofessional" operatives. These operatives are businesspeople, intellectuals, teachers, doctors, engineers, and other field experts assigned to blend into foreign societies for the purpose of gathering information in those fields. Because of their legitimate qualifications, and because they aren't associated with anything political, they are rarely scrutinized as potential spies and can go for years gathering intel completely undetected.

Even though an MSS operative is not necessarily a professional, it's prudent to assume they are surrounded by them. Beijing tends to go to great lengths to protect their investments because, like with Zhen, the intel that MSS operatives provide is worth billions. Which is why it didn't surprise me that security at CIS headquarters was as tight as any modern military installation. Zhen rarely left the building, and when he did, an armored Chinese military helicopter disguised as a private helicopter service picked him up from the roof and transferred him to secret ground pickup locations that were part of an intricate network of commercial vehicles, including NYPD squad cars.

Sue and I met to compare notes, and he was already hitting it out of the park. He had put a tracking device on Alice's mobile phone, along with a wireless mic and transmitter like the NSA uses to turn our iPhones into 24/7 surveillance devices. As it turned out, Alice had already initiated her infiltration of CIS about a week before I arrived back in Manhattan. The more I found out about it, the more the whole thing seemed almost too good to be true. Because of the heavy security at Zhen's building, Alice would not have her usual doom squad there to protect her. They wouldn't even be able to monitor her with visual surveillance. And forget about weapons. Every employee was subject to a millimeter wave scan—just like at the airport—so she would be hard-pressed to get a nail clipper past the lobby. It was the exact scenario I needed to get to her. She was completely exposed. The only problem was, I would be too.

Sue and I got to work immediately on the difficult task of getting me access to the building. I no longer had HR behind me, so I couldn't gain placement through the usual back channels. There was really no other course of action than to go completely analog on their asses. So, I put on my best bright eyes and bushy tail and marched right into CIS, résumé firmly in hand. It took nearly two weeks of calling, dropping by, and general ass kissing before they decided to give me a shot. I'm sure the way they saw it was, here's this Harvard kid (hey, I went big) wanting to come get coffee and do grunt work for free. Guy won't take no for an answer, so he's a real go-getter. And his father has been part of the diplomatic corps in China for over a decade (nice touch). The bottom line is I got a foot in the door the old-fashioned way: I bullshitted my way in.

As I walked to the CIS building in Midtown Manhattan—a part of New York that could disappear tomorrow and only the tourists would miss it—I was invigorated by the fact that Alice and I would be on an even playing field. The prospect of having to mow down layers of security in order to get to her, like some geek playing a first-person shooter game, was not appealing. Also, that would have ruined all the fun. In my mind, meeting her face-to-face in our natural corporate habitat was the only honorable way to end our relationship. So, like the knights of old, I suited up in my trusty intern armor—brownish-green suit, sensible cap-toed oxfords, white button-down, and omnipresent LensCrafters glasses. If I wasn't able to shoot her, I could probably bore her to death.

28

One of my briefest, but most eventful, foster home placements was with a minister and his wife in Kilgore, Arkansas, a grease spot of a town with a main street so short you could spit the length of it. The only excitement we had were the junior high fights that went down at the flagpole after school. Pretty much every day you could count on fisticuffs—dudes duking it out, catfights, girlfriends beating up boyfriends, boyfriends beating up their girlfriend's other boyfriend, boyfriends scrapping with girlfriends' dads . . . It was a regular bare-knuckle cockfight with milk money and all manner of pocket collateral on the line. I'll tell you one thing, with the exception of my time with Griner, Kilgore was the place where I really learned to fight.

Every few months, we'd get treated to a bout between our own local Ali-Frazier combo, Russ and Travis. With their beards and bricklayer builds, these guys looked more like grown men than junior high school boys. They hated each other like poison and they were first cousins. I guess their dads were brothers with a blood feud and Russ and Travis carried on the tradition with dumb animal loyalty. Something would happen on the field or in the locker room or in class, one of them would start talking smack, and next thing you knew, everyone in school was whispering, "Russ and Travis at the flagpole, place your bets."

Half the school was ringside by three-thirty, making it rain with fistfuls of dollars. And those boys wouldn't disappoint. They'd fight like gladiators—brutal, grisly, and without mercy. With other fights, the principal usually only had to yell from his office window to break it up. Not with Russ and Travis. The sheriff had to be called. Large men working at the local pig slaughterhouse had to pry them apart. And the ground was covered in so much blood and hair you'd think it was the Roman Colosseum. Neither would yield. Their pride and family name were at stake. So, it was always the bloodiest draw you've ever seen and no one ever made a dime.

Until one afternoon in the spring of their final year before moving on to high school. Russ had missed a week of school with the flu. When he got back, he looked like death warmed over—pale, drawn, and weak. Travis smelled blood and wouldn't stop taunting Russ. He was like a stronger wolf pup trying to kill the runt. Russ was understandably reluctant to fight. He was still having trouble holding down his lunch and even passed out during gym class. When Travis heard about all of that, he turned up the asshole dial and pushed Russ as hard as he could to get him to fight. Word had it he even tried to pull Russ's girlfriend in the parking lot of the Tastee Freez. That was the last straw for Russ.

The fight was set for Friday afternoon and you could smell the confidence coming out of Travis like cheap cologne. Russ was looking like he regretted the decision and his girlfriend was trying to get him to just go home. Russ pushed her away and the two goons started circling each other. Travis took the first swing and connected with Russ's nose. Russ went down hard but got back up again, blood streaming into his mouth and onto his Motörhead shirt. Russ was wavering and seemed unsteady on his feet. Travis saw this and moved in for the kill. He started pummeling Russ and Russ just covered up and took the beating. That's when I noticed the look on Russ's face. He was waiting for Travis to tire himself out. Muhammad Ali called it the rope-a-dope, and that's what Russ was doing. The more Russ made it seem like he couldn't fight back, the harder Travis punched. But his punches were just hitting Russ in the arms and hands. Finally, Travis backed off, huffing and wheezing like an old man, yelling at Russ to stop being such a pussy. Russ called him a faggot and Travis came at him.

But before Travis could land a punch, Russ hauled off and hit him with a right cross to the jaw. You could hear the jawbone snap, and suddenly there was metal raining out of Russ's hand. He had just hit Travis with a roll of quarters—poor man's brass knuckles. Travis hit the pavement hard, smashing the back of his skull. The impact knocked him unconscious and he started going into convulsions. That's when Russ really went to work on him, kicking and snapping every rib and even curbing his ankle until it snapped and hung like a ragged L in the gutter. Travis never recovered. He spent his first year of high school in a wheelchair and dropped out later due to decreased mental capacity. Russ was never charged with anything because they were under eighteen, and because of the beating Travis gave him, they said Russ acted in self-defense.

The beauty of it was that Russ never even had the flu. All of that, and even the girlfriend thing, was part of the plan to make Travis vulnerable, and it worked like a charm. Ali had the rope-a-dope and Russ had the Bullshit Express.

The reason I bring this up is because even though it may seem like two people are evenly matched in a conflict, there is always room for an advantage. And that comes from one opponent being willing to do whatever is necessary to get it. There is nothing fair about a fight. A sense of honor and fairness is the invention of someone who never had a fight. A fight is very black and white. Winning is everything and you only win if you are willing to make the kind of sacrifices your opponent is not willing to make. Look at Vietnam. The Vietcong were willing to do *anything* to win, and they did it while the American war machine stood by, appalled by an enemy that they deemed to have no honor. Honor, my ass. There's nothing honorable about human beings slaughtering one another. It goes back to the animal in us. We are predators and our only objective is to bag our prey. Alice had made me the prey before, due to a sense of honor I had for her, but when I walked into the lobby of CIS, Inc., the tables had turned. And the one thing that was not going to happen was a draw.

The place looked like one of those office buildings in *The Matrix*—marble, metal, and glass with a high price tag and no soul. And, also like *The Matrix*, the place was crawling with guys in black suits and sunglasses with crew cuts and hardware bulges in their sports jackets. I checked in with the front desk and was escorted to the elevator by a man who never said a word to me, even when I asked him a question. I toyed with the idea of crushing his lower spine with a side kick and watching him crumple to the ground like a wounded gazelle, but it was my first day of work and I wanted to make a good impression. Mr. Nothing took me up the elevator and walked me to a windowless, wood-paneled conference room that reeked of bad takeout and worse coffee. It was empty. I sat down at the conference table and he quickly left the room.

To be honest, I was actually a little nervous. I hadn't had a real job in a while and I was eager to prove to myself that I could still perform at the same level as before.

I just needed some inspiration.

And then I got it—a dumpy, fast-food-poisoned office manager wearing what appeared to be a wool herringbone muumuu entered the room and sat across from me.

"I take it you're John," the muumuu said without looking up from her notepad.

"Yes. Hello."

"My name is Marjorie."

"Nice to meet—"

"Congratulations on being selected for our intern program. I'm sure you're aware of just how difficult it is to sit where you're sitting."

Marjorie looked at me for a nanosecond, deciding whether or not she should send my sorry ass packing right then and there. I respectfully lowered my gaze to show her she was in control. This seemed to satisfy her for the moment.

"I'll need you to fill out this paperwork."

She slapped down a thick pile of forms and a cheap ballpoint.

The door opened and another person sat down across from me.

"John, this is Alice."

I looked up, smiling. Alice looked at me, her face completely white. We shook hands. And the earth stood still. That was a great moment. Alice is a know-it-all and she gets physically ill if she is surprised by something she feels she should have anticipated. And this was the king of all surprises. I hung on to her hand for a bit too long just to annoy her.

"Pleasure."

"Hi," she muttered, jerking her hand back.

"Alice has been here a few weeks, so she'll show you the ropes," muumuu Marjorie chimed in. "If you have questions, please ask her and don't bother any of the salaried employees."

She slapped more forms down in front of me.

"New York State now requires that all interns are paid," she said sardonically. "Please fill these out so you may receive your gross weekly stipend of three hundred dollars."

Paying your dues for a price, I thought to myself. *The entitled generation is going to run this country into the ground.*

"As the only two interns here, I expect you both to conduct yourselves in a professional manner . . ."

While she droned through her intern orientation gibberish, Alice and I clocked each other, assessing, evaluating. Alice was wearing a designer suit. So much for subtlety. She made sore thumbs look anonymous.

". . . finally, we are in full compliance with the new Manhattan intern laws," muumuu Marjorie continued. "If you feel like your rights as an intern have been violated in some way, or you'd like to know your rights as an intern, please call the intern hotline. Eight hundred number is on this card."

Slap.

The intern hotline? I had to stifle so much laughter that I thought I was going to give myself a brain bleed.

"Any questions?"

"Not at the moment," I said. "If I do I'll be sure to direct them to . . . I'm sorry, what was your name again?"

"Alice," she said quietly.

"Right. I'll go ask Alice."

"Welcome to CIS," muumuu Marjorie said as she unceremoniously shuffled out of the room.

Alice and I just sat there, barely drawing breath, never taking our eyes off each other. There we were, interns again—professionals disguised as coffee jockeys at Zhen's military industrial complex outpost disguised as a nerd farm. Back in our natural habitat.

"John, how've you been?"

"Not so good, Alice. You?"

"Great."

"So I see. I like your suit. DKNY?"

"Don't make me laugh."

"I don't plan to. Not anymore."

"You look different, John."

"So do you."

"How so?"

"In this light your true colors make you look like a corpse rotting from the inside out."

"I was going to say the same about you, you fucking traitor," she said with a straight face.

I burst out laughing. I couldn't help myself. I was starting to believe I overestimated her intelligence, or sanity. She felt my mocking rattling her bones and tensed, as if she was going to make a move. This made me laugh harder.

"Shut the fuck up," she spat.

"Or what?" I said.

"Or maybe I'll kill you right now."

"If at first you don't succeed. Try, try again . . . and again . . ."

"You're not as clever as you think, John."

"Really? Did you know I was coming today?"

Silence.

"You still thought I was dead, didn't you?" I laughed.

"You were to me," she said.

"Oh, that hurts, darling."

"Not as much as it's *going to hurt*," she said.

"That's the spirit," I said coldly.

"Why are you here, John? I didn't know you were in town, so you had the element of surprise. What's the point of getting back into your tired old character?"

"I've missed him," I said.

"I'm going to tell Marjorie to fire you today. I have an assignment here, so if you want to settle something with me—"

"I do and we'll settle it here. I can make this assignment go away and you know it. Then you'll be at the mercy of your clients, and what would be the fun in that? You'd have to go to war with them and you'd be blacklisted for . . . ever."

"Fine. You've made your point."

"Not quite, Alice. My point is this: you made a mistake. Maybe the biggest of your life."

"Poor baby. You're just mad that I fucked you, kissed your earlobe and told you I loved you, then slapped you like a bitch."

Then she doused my crotch with the boiling-hot coffee in her cup. My junk is the one part of my body that is not a numb piece of scar tissue. The pain was shocking and took my breath away. My animal brain sent my hands to the rescue, covering my searing nuts, but my internal fighting brain knew this was no good and that point was proven when Alice rang my bell with a high-heeled side kick. I lost my balance and was on a head-on collision course with the monstrous snack machine. In that moment, we worked together to avoid this. If the Chinese cavalry heard my 190-pound frame shatter a five-foot-tall, one-inch-thick pane of glass covering rows of Bugles, Lorna Doones, and microwave burritos, they'd have been in there in seconds shooting first and asking questions later.

Of course, the moment I regained my balance, we were back in the trenches and Alice attempted to throat kick me. I caught her foot with one hand, ripped off her shoe, and whipped the sharp high heel into her ear canal. The only thing that kept me from bursting her eardrum and driving all six inches into her brain was her sinking her teeth into my hand. She looked at me, surprised at the fact that her bite didn't make me grimace in agony or draw even the slightest drop of blood from my rawhide skin.

"What the fuck?" she asked.

"I just don't have any feelings for you anymore," I said smugly and whacked her injured ear with an open-palm strike. The blunt impact and air forced into her ear canal instantly pulled the rug out from under her equilibrium. She swung her hands wildly through the air, attempting to throw up any kind of defense while her brain tried to reset itself. She fell to her knees and I was staring down the barrel of the one split second I had to finish her. This was the diamond emerging from the truckloads of coal that every fiber of my being had been compressing and smashing to make. This was the kill moment.

Because it was Alice, I quickly dispensed with all of the obvious choices—heart punch, pile driver to the back of the skull, back-breaking body slam—and went for something more intimate. I slipped myself around her like a boa constrictor, encircling her neck with one arm and locking it in place with the other. My legs bound hers, reminiscent of an old wrestling move known as the Guillotine. The fight she delivered was predictably fierce and would have easily thrown off a normal person with normal nerve endings. I was beginning to wonder if she would ever choke out when I heard the footsteps of what sounded like an army marching down the hall. They were chanting something in Chinese. I let go of Alice and we both waited to get gunned down in a hail of bullets.

The doors burst open and several people stormed in, armed with a birthday cake and some two-liter bottles of orange Fanta. They looked at us briefly as we smoothed out our clothes and smiled courteously. One guy winked at me, as if Alice and I had been getting busy in the conference room. Then they broke into song, belting out "Happy Birthday" in Chinese to a four-hundred-pound woman wearing what appeared to be Hello Kitty overalls.

29

After a few days of annoying intern orientation at CIS—a dog and pony show of training, actual Human Resources paperwork, and some serious ass kissing to curry favor with a middle manager who might give me a decent gig—I was ready to jump off the roof. A battle-starved, combat drone like myself draws nourishment from the gasoline of war, not the brown-water coffee, stale Danishes, and single-cell work tasks that were piled on my desk. After our stirring orientation, getting to Alice was virtually impossible, as she made certain we were never in the same part of the building at the same time.

On the positive side, the terminally lazy, entitled employees made it really easy for Alice and me to eventually secure excellent assignments. She was working in IT and I was sent to, get ready, *Human Resources*. Ah, the irony. You could have cut it with a chain saw. I knew being in Human Resources was going to expedite things in a big way, so the weekend after orientation week, I strolled into the office feeling like it was *anything can happen Monday*. I was optimistic about finding an angle, a way to eventually weasel my way into point-blank range of Alice. Being in my department, I could potentially gain access to the entire company because *that* Human Resources was always hassling everyone with reams of paperwork, flu shots, and annoying personality tests.

Fortunately for me, Alice was my only objective. Unfortunately for Alice, she had a much more difficult assignment in attempting to bag Zhen. Bob used to call this type of job a Moscow Circus—a moniker reserved for a gig with so many moving and intricately co-ordinated parts that a lack of precision in even the smallest of tasks could easily topple the human pyramid and result in the untimely demise of a recruit. Alice was staring at the twisted mess of rope that represented Zhen with very little hope of organizing it all into a tightly cinched execution scenario. First off, Zhen worked in an ivory tower and moved in a very controlled, protected, and highly unpredictable fashion. This type of security would have taken me weeks to penetrate and, even then, my chances for success would have been astronomically low.

Of course, Alice is the type of person who *always* finds a way, and I had to be there when she did. If I allowed her to kill Zhen, she would disappear back into the safety of HR, Inc. and I would be pursued like a dog until I either left town again or they took me out. In a diabolical twist on my former intern gigs, I actually had to keep the target breathing in order to flush Alice out but also to catalyze her failure. I was not only determined to exterminate Alice, but I also wanted her death to mark the end of Human Resources, Inc., a blunt-force eraser in the history books with nothing but blood and bad memories left behind. It was the least I could do for the recruits, and the preservation of my sanity demanded it. The flesh-and-bone chess game with massive stakes had begun. And for every move Alice made, I had to counter like Garry fucking Kasparov and knock the wicked queen into the cheap seats.

That was not going to be a walk in the park because Alice was work-ing in the one department that had more company-wide access than Human Resources—IT, or Information Technology. I'll admit I was impressed that she was able to get into that department. Most IT managers think women are intellectually inferior, which makes me laugh, because women are tailor-made for IT work. Unlike men, they actually care about details. Show me a thousand lines of raw code and I'll be hard-pressed to find more than ten errors that could cause a full-system crash. Smarter dudes might find twenty if they've had a good night's sleep and a gallon of espresso. Alice could probably find hundreds. Women need to stop striving to be seen as equal to men because they're actually far superior. And as soon as synthetic sperm hits the shelves next to the mascara and maxi pads, men will become an endangered species.

The first thing I did when I got access to the personnel databases was to look up Alice's manager. Her ability to move freely was going to be directly related to him. I knew she would be deploying her considerable talents to attempt to manipulate him into giving her greater responsibilities, so I tracked down his profile. His name was Gavin and he was not what I expected. Normally, IT managers look like aliens who just landed on earth yesterday and hurriedly threw together a "human look" in an attempt to blend in. Gavin resembled a sporting goods catalog model—rugged good looks, youthful build, and sneering confidence.

The way I saw it, that was either a good thing—Gavin already got more ass than an airline toilet and wouldn't be easily manipulated— or it was a bad thing—Gavin wanted to add Alice to his ass-trophy case and the "manipulation" would be consensual. It turned out to be the latter. Two days after he started at CIS, Gavin took Alice to dinner. According to Sue, they went back to his place. She didn't stay over, but the fix was in, and I had to assume Alice already had him eating out of her hand, among other things.

Data security is a joke. When you are dealing with communication of any kind, the more entities you have communicating, the more opportunities for potential security breaches. And then you add human beings to the mix and you've got red carpet access to just about anything. Once Alice got her Jimmy Choo in the door, she could gain access to any and all information associated with CIS and its global enterprise network and easily expand her access, maybe even as high as Zhen's executive level.

She got lucky on that note, but just having access to data doesn't mean you have the time to actually process and scrutinize it. That's what makes me laugh about the NSA "listening" to millions of Americans' phone calls or reading zillions of texts and e-mails. Who's doing that? Do they have cube farms somewhere in the Nevada desert filled with 35,000 trained analysts, with security clearances, poring over the data to find anything suspect? Dream on. The U.S. government is about as efficient as a deaf and blind elephant. You want something stepped on, call Uncle Sam. For everything else, you're on your own.

Data is like a virus that grows in size and complexity, and attempting to analyze it all at once is something that could take years. So, I still had time on my side, but I wasn't going to wait around for Alice to get lucky again. Sue and I needed to anticipate her moves so we would know what they were before she even had a chance to make them. I figured that even though the lower floors of CIS were the front company, there had to be at least one channel of communication between Zhen and someone on that level. He would need to oversee that operation, just like anyone cultivating and maintaining a cover, especially since it was a legitimate business. If the financial markets caught wind of CIS being a beard, that would draw the kind of attention to Zhen that could destroy his entire operation and land him in a hard-labor prison.

So we started looking for at least one person working on the lower floors who might report directly to Zhen. We figured it had to be a midlevel manager who would be able to oversee the entire operation and report back to Zhen in a comprehensive way. A higher-level executive would be too risky, as they are always under scrutiny due to their ability to affect the stock price. We needed to find Zhen's bitch and clip his string before Alice did and got him to spill his guts.

30

Alice was in the perfect position to track down Zhen's connection. All she had to do was look for encryption code on internal communications—probably similar protocols used for their external communications, as they wouldn't want to try to integrate two separate systems on the same enterprise. I have worked in many IT departments and I know how the geek cookie crumbles. If Zhen was talking to someone in the lower level of the building, he would have wanted it to be as secure as everything else he did. I had to assume Alice had thought of that and had to find my own way of acquiring e-mail data.

That's where Rebecca, Sue's new girlfriend, came in. Rebecca was a new recruit whom Alice had taken under her wing as a potential protégée. I found out later that the reason for this was Rebecca's prowess with technology. A self-styled "data curator," Rebecca had a unique talent in that she was able to pull data pretty much out of the air. Alice had bragged that Rebecca's equipment cost her nearly half a million dollars but it was worth every penny. I knew Alice would put Rebecca on the case, so I made sure I put Sue on Rebecca.

After a night of Korean barbecue and live-band karaoke—two of Rebecca's favorite things—Sue found out that she had written a program that Alice installed on the CIS network. It monitored all outgoing communications from lower-floor employees and sniffed out those containing heavy encryption. Then it gathered all of these types of messages and analyzed them for similarities in the return encryption. When it identified messages from the same "family," it then analyzed where they traveled. If their destination was singular, then they were largely ignored. However, if they bounced all over the world and never really had an identifiable landing spot, then they were collected under the category of impossible to trace, the gold standard of truly secret information transfer in the age of Big Brother. It was actually genius. Too bad for Rebecca that her lips weren't as tight as her coding skills.

"Harold Leung," Sue announced.

"He's our fish?"

"Oh yeah. My girl sniffed him out pretty easily."

For the next part, I had Sue crawl up Harold's ass and set up camp.

"Sue, I want this guy on twenty-four-hour surveillance. I want to know everything about him."

"Copy that. Comic books to cock rings."

Within twenty-four hours, I owned Harold Leung. I had access to his office and apartment, keys to his car, and I knew the names and addresses of everyone who meant anything to Harold. Rebecca's program hit the bull's-eye. Harold was basically the caretaker of the legit business Zhen had going on the lower floors. He was very efficient and had actually managed to make CIS not only legit but also profitable. At that point we started monitoring and decrypting every message Leung sent. For the most part, Leung would only contact Zhen on the internal system from 7:00 A.M. to 9:00 A.M. each day. The timing of Zhen's response, from him pressing send to delivery in Leung's in-box, led us to believe that this was most likely the time each day when Zhen was actually in the building. And if she could work Harold over for the location intel, this would also likely be the time Alice would try to pop a cap in Zhen's ass.

Which is why *I* needed to throw Sue out of Harold Leung's ass and crawl up there myself and wait for Alice to make her grand entrance. Getting access to Leung was the easy part. He had no security detail, an apartment that a twelve-year-old junior smash-and-grabber could pop in thirty seconds, and highly predictable patterns of movement. Weirdo ate a Happy Meal for lunch at the McDonald's around the corner from the office every day and lined up the toys on his credenza. Who the hell does that? And every night he took the same bus home, ate Lean Cuisine with his wife, and watched reruns of *Who's the Boss?* I think maybe part of me wanted to kill him for being such a loser. The hard part was going to be coordinating it so that Alice and I got access to him at the same time.

31

Eventually I got a break and saw Alice getting ready to make her move. The previous evening, the IT department auto-message server (Alice) had sent out a laptop system software-upgrade notification to several employees. Harold Leung received it and so did Zhen, his BFF. I knew it because Rebecca spilled the beans to Sue about the brilliant rig she designed for Zhen's laptop. Clever girl. Just in case Alice didn't go through with it, I had to make sure it wasn't obvious that Sue was burning my end of the candle with Alice's intel. So, I volunteered to pass out dental plan pamphlets all over the building (greater access), so I could stalk her that day. I made sure she saw me clocking her moves several times so that her brain would simply assume that I was able to intercept her because of my own wily surveillance techniques, which was true, because I also had the wiretap unit on her iPhone.

What Rebecca had designed for Alice was a virus that would shut down the entire internal network. This would necessitate quarantine for the offending machine and any other machine that IT had been repairing at the time, because they would take down the individual unit firewalls for repairs. Basically, Alice created a way to keep both laptops for several hours, during which Rebecca was undoubtedly going to analyze both machines in order to be able to track Zhen's movements. She would then quietly give the laptops back and Alice would stick an ice pick in Zhen's wishbone the next time he surfaced outside of his protective office hive.

Frankly this seemed like a very roundabout way of doing things. But it did give me an idea . . . one that would require me to return to my past life as a street illusionist. You heard me right. The reason I didn't say "magician" is because I wasn't a kids' bday party clown. I was more of a hustler. Hey, when you're always broke, you find ways to make money in New York. Some guys sell handbags they stole off a boat. Some blow conventioneers or beat the crap out of construction workers looking to go on the disability dole. You do what you got to do. For me, it was card tricks—up close and personal. And I was good. But the cops weren't too pleased about the fact that I was using the card tricks as a distraction so I could filch pockets, Italian gypsy–style. I used to bag three or four fat stacks a day. Anyway, I had to channel my three-card monte persona to execute my fiendish plan.

On the day that all of this finally went down, Alice went to Leung's office to return his machine and the machine of "his colleague from China." You so crafty, Mr. Happy Meal! We would have never guessed you were talking about Zhen, the dark overlord! Amateur. I had made eye contact with Alice thirty minutes prior across a sea of cubicles, so she wasn't all that surprised when I walked into Leung's office a few minutes after her. I had with me the currency of Human Resources departments everywhere—paperwork—and I had a strong heel-toe-heel-toe urgency gait as I walked up and rapped my knuckles on the doorframe. I didn't wait to be invited in. I strode with official purpose into the office and slapped a pile of paperwork down on Leung's desk. I told him if he didn't resubmit some of his health insurance claims, his wife's back surgery (cruise ship chocolate fountain accident) would not be covered and he'd be liable for the $87,000 tab. That got his attention.

While he looked at the pile of incomprehensible insurance hieroglyphics, Alice looked at me, her mind racing. She knew I was up to something but had no idea what. Trying to kill her in Leung's office would have been insane, even for me, so her mind scoured itself for alternative explanations. Leung sighed wearily and looked up to me, wishing he could formally behead the messenger.

"Can I deal with this later?" he asked me. "I really need to get some work done."

He opened his laptop and logged in.

"Of course, Mr. Leung."

I began gathering up my papers, but ended up dropping them all over the desk and floor. As I bent down awkwardly to pick them up, I snuck a quick look at Leung's laptop. Mind you, it was very subtle, but Alice has an eye for detail you wouldn't believe. *Pick a card, any card* was what I thought as Alice, in turn, looked at the laptop. I didn't look again because that would have been a "tell," and Alice would have called my bluff. I was deliberately looking at other things, which was also a "tell," but in my favor, as Alice's viper brain was certain I felt I had made a strategic error by looking at the laptop in the first place and was trying to compensate by not looking again. You think this little mind fuck is complicated, you should have seen what went down when we were married.

"You know, Mr. Leung, there's one software upgrade I forgot to add," she said, improvising. "Let me just run it back to IT for a few minutes."

One hook. One pretty mouth. *Ace of spades, David Blaine.*

"No. You've wasted enough of my time. You can do that later. I have work to do," Leung protested.

She had to go big or go home.

"Okay, can I borrow your pen?" Alice asked as she reached across the desk.

Leung grunted and lifted his hands from the keyboard to make room for her to reach it. Then she knocked his full cup of coffee into the side of the laptop and all over the keyboard.

"Shit!" Leung yelled.

"So sorry," she said, groveling.

He stood up, furious.

"Idiot!" he said to Alice.

Then he stormed out of the room to clean his pants. It was a race to grab the laptop, but I let Alice win. She snapped the lid shut and I smiled at her.

"I don't think he likes you," I said, smirking.

"Fuck you," she said.

Then I kicked the switch on the specially modified surge protector I had swapped and plugged into Leung's laptop while I was struggling with my papers on the floor. Seventeen hundred volts of electric current—the amount they used to run through "Old Sparky," the electric chair they used at Sing Sing prison—*surged* into Alice's unsuspecting fingers. She fell to her knees, her face twitching and pale from ventricular fibrillation, and went limp on the floor. I checked her pulse and was very pleased to find none whatsoever.

"No, Alice," I said quietly. "Fuck *you*."

At that point Leung stormed back into the room with a huge wet spot on his crotch. He saw Alice on the floor and looked like he might faint.

"She just collapsed!" I blubbered.

"Go get help!" he screamed.

I ran out the door as he was picking up the phone to dial 911. I figured Alice had less than two minutes before brain death, and in that part of the city an ambulance can sometimes take an hour to arrive. It didn't matter. As luck would have it, for Alice anyway, one of the CIS employees on Leung's floor had been an army corpsman. And, to add insult to injury, management had recently added a defibrillator to the first aid kit in the break room. The guy zapped her sorry ass back to the land of the living in less than forty-five seconds.

As they carted her out, I walked with them, futilely looking for ways to finish the job.

"John?" she half whispered.

"What?"

"When I was having my out-of-body experience, I noticed you're getting a little thin on top."

"Bullshit," I said and instinctively touched the top of my head.

"Made you look, asshole."

32

After my zany joy-buzzer attempted-murder gag, Alice was game for a little intern-on-intern action of her own. She took advantage of the fact that I am a shamelessly materialistic, name-dropping snob, priding myself on my unique and difficult-to-acquire possessions. Near the top of the list was my favorite fountain pen—a Montblanc Bohème Pirouette Lilas. I bought it on our Italian honeymoon, fancying myself some kind of writer after I saw how well received the handbook was among the old recruit class, many of whom barely had an eighth-grade education. So, while I was at lunch, Alice somehow managed to replace the ink cartridge on my precious pen with one of her own, containing a special shade of black.

Then the dominoes of vengeance began to fall. First, Alice flagged my employment file in the Human Resources database as "eligible for promotion." She knew I wouldn't question this because of the high opinion I have of myself and because of the advantages being a paid employee would afford me in terms of greater access at CIS. I received the application packet from a third-party placement firm (invented by Alice—nice touch) due to the conflict of interest that would have existed had I, a member of CIS Human Resources, gone through the screening process in my own department. Yes, this *is* getting good, isn't it?

The promotion packet, assembled by Alice, included several personality inventories, many of which had been designed to help identify someone who might be a potential office threat. Ha! From the Minnesota Multiphasic to the Keirsey Temperament Sorter, I spent half my workday busily filling in answer dots and completing story problems. Because I *worked* in Human Resources, I didn't question any of it because I had seen it over and over. I felt like a high school kid sweating the SAT.

Here's the really good part. Commercial paper is largely made up of bleached wood pulp. The bleach is what makes the paper a nice bright white. Alice replaced my ink cartridge with one that contained highly concentrated ammonia—the same grade they use for pesticide production and sewage treatment. The ammonia was mixed with actual ink and a chemical agent designed to mask its horrifically pungent odor. And the paperwork itself had been treated to an even higher concentration of bleach. Thus, when I started filling it out, the ammonia-laced ink came in contact with the chlorine in the heavily bleached paper and produced highly toxic chloramine gas. You've heard of housewives accidentally offing themselves by mixing chlorine (Comet) and ammonia cleaning products (Windex), right? It produces chloramine gas, which, in the right concentration, will cause a severe chemical burn in your lungs that can drown you in your own fluids.

Wait, it gets better! The elegance of Alice's poison pen gag was that it was more of a slow burn so I wouldn't notice what was happening before it was too late. While I spent hours figuring out the color of my parachute, I was exposed to several hundred microbursts of chloramine, which has the unique property of bonding with oxygen atoms in the lungs. So, once it gets in there, it's very hard to get out. While I worked, I had a bit of a cough, but nothing that was going to stop me from acing my exams. By the time six o'clock rolled around, so much chloramine gas had built up in my lungs that I went into respiratory arrest and they found me facedown in the break room with a broken coffee mug in my cold, nearly dead hand.

I was rushed to the hospital, where I spent nearly a week. My lungs had suffered a severe chemical burn, so most of the time I was there I was coughing up blood or sucking down oxygen. But it was a beautiful rub, what Alice pulled. I almost fell back in love with her the more I thought about how she came so damn close to capping me in a way that would have made the Marquis de Sade rethink his whole game.

Admittedly, I had to take a little credit for it as well. I don't claim to have ever taught Alice much, but creativity is one thing I helped her cultivate in her work. She just isn't a creative person in the traditional sense. Her mind doesn't work that way. It's more logical and methodical and, well, boring. I was always asking her to imagine how *I* would do something. WWJD? She thought that was funny as hell at first, but she saw the light when we worked together—albeit briefly—at HR. Like with Dr. Love. It was my idea to use a composite pistol, but it was *her* idea to load it with a diamond. It was a stroke of genius for Alice, much like the poison pen. And as much as I wanted to gloat about it, I had to face the fact that she literally almost took me out right under my nose.

33

Speaking of which, I think my most creative—and insane—hit came when I was nineteen. Bob was mad at me about something, said I was getting soft or some nonsense, so he put me on what he thought was a cupcake job. I was supposed to snuff some ex-hippie politico who had faked his way into a job at an oil company with the intention of blowing it up and sabotaging all of its offshore oil rigs. And if that wasn't enough, he intended to burn the CEO at the stake outside the UN and pass out marshmallows. Actually, I was a little bummed out I had to whack him. He was kind of a modern-day corporate anarchist.

Anyway, even though it was a cupcake, it was also a political can of worms. Turned out the guy was the CEO's nephew, and the CEO was the one who had him greenlit. Nice, right? Because we were dealing with the backstabbing Family Robinson, we had to think of an execution scenario that would not arouse suspicion with the nephew's parents, upon whom the wicked CEO had to rely for money and political favors. It wasn't like I was jumping into the jaws of danger, but the situation was definitely a clusterfuck of T-shirt slogan proportions. MY PARENTS WENT TO GSTAAD AND ALL I GOT WAS A LOUSY BULLET IN THE HEAD.

That's where creativity came in. You can't always simply analyze your way to victory. Like Tom Cruise in *Risky Business*, sometimes you just got to say "What the fuck. Make your move." Since hippie boy wasn't likely to try to whack me back, that's exactly what I did.

It was basically a two-stage execution scenario. Stage one was the loss-of-all-credibility phase. After the guy was gone, office drones needed to be round the watercooler discussing how they saw it coming or were surprised it hadn't happened sooner. This was mainly for the benefit of his parents. They were über wealthy and powerful and needed to be embarrassed into keeping the cops or feds out of it. Stage two was the kill itself. Self-inflicted was our first choice, but I know firsthand that there are Grand Canyon–size pitfalls in that approach. So, we needed to create more of an "assisted suicide" hybrid scenario to ensure our kill and put the right spin on things for mumsy and dada.

Even though I dug his politics, I hated him the second I came in contact with him and immediately nicknamed him Yoko. He was a self-righteous know-it-all who had the breath of a dung beetle, a gray ponytail he barely pulled together from the bozo ring of hair clinging to his balding, freckled dome, and loved to drink, of all things, tea. Usually it was some sickly sweet-smelling herbal crap that was made in the hippie wasteland of Boulder, Colorado. The box was festooned with the image of a happy, dancing bear in a field of multicolored flowers and the tea had some idiotic name like Tai Chai. After work one evening, I snatched the box of tea bags from the break room and changed the recipe. I wasn't really worried that any other employees would use one of the tea bags because NO ONE DRINKS FUCKING TEA AT WORK, especially not the totally useless, noncaffeinated fairy tears reserved for old maids to sip while they watch *Murder, She Wrote* in bed with their legion of cats.

The day I initiated Stage 1, I posted up in an empty cube near the break room. Like clockwork, Yoko walked in and boiled hot water in the electric kettle while he whistled "Puff, the Magic Dragon." Then, per his habit—well documented by me of course— he dropped in the tea bag and let it steep while holding it under his nose. He loved to breathe in the steam coming off the dancing bear's nuts like some Z-list actorbator in a Lipton commercial. And that's where the fun began. As soon as the tea bag hit the water, it activated my special ingredient mixed with the tea leaves, and the steam emitted from the cup contained massive doses of BZ, a super hallucinogen the U.S. Army developed as a chemical warfare agent in the 1960s. The theory was that they could use BZ to control the minds of the Vietcong, but the reality was that all BZ did was make someone a balls-tripping-to-the-wall adult baby on the verge of a complete psychotic break.

Effects of this little gem known as "Buzz" are hyperrealistic, multisensory hallucinations, hysterical confusion, drunken stupor–like affect, and total removal of inhibition, often resulting in base, primitive behaviors. I know what you're thinking. Government-grade fun powder is enough to blow his mind but isn't going to blow him up. You're right. What I gave him was not lethal but it was enough to completely fry his brain, create that total humiliation scenario I described earlier, and put him in harm's way . . . mine. From there I planned to implement Stage 2, but *the best-laid plans of mice and men* . . .

When I saw Yoko casually returning to his desk, I was more than a little bit perplexed. He should have been on his hands and knees begging Satan to stop playing the drums so loud. So, I did what every stupid nineteen-year-old would do. Without thinking first, I sniffed the tea bag when he left the break room. I thought maybe he had had Earl Grey today instead and sideswiped my whole plan. And, of course, I dosed myself. When I went looking for him, he wasn't at his desk. So, I went to the bathroom and found him standing in front of the mirror, touching it and speaking in tongues.

"Yoko," I said as I stood behind him.

He whipped around quickly to look at me, thus sloshing the blood in his brain around in the same direction. I could tell the Buzz was beginning its long, merciless peak, making his heart thump like a jackhammer, immediately intensifying the hallucinogenic component. I knew this mostly because I was experiencing the same thing.

"Are you feeling okay, Yoko?"

He flinched as if I had just thrown battery acid in his face.

"Why are you yelling at me?" he asked.

When the words came out of his mouth, it sounded like a super-amplified scream wrapped in a pink noise blast. Then the entire scene turned into a garish, color-dripping Kabuki theater in which everything moved at a maddeningly glacial pace. I have done many drugs in my day and I immediately knew I had just saddled up on the Seattle Slew of hallucinogens. I was hyper-aware of everything around me as stimuli attacked from all sides. Because my brain was being unrelentingly assaulted, my body was releasing so much epinephrine that I could feel my heart pounding in my eyeballs and I could barely keep from grinding my teeth down to nubs. My diaphragm was so constricted I felt like I'd been swallowed whole by an anaconda and was forced to take what seemed like hundreds of shallow, painful breaths. But I had to keep it together and finish the job or Bob would have me killed in one of the gruesomely fantastical ways that kept flashing onto the IMAX screen in my head.

I had one lucid thought in the moment and that was to escape the bathroom and find a way to even out. Yoko and I were both in the same boat, but at least I knew what kind of wind was hitting my sails. I just needed to gather my mind up like pickup sticks and get to work before I had an uncontrollable urge to crank Phish and do a ribbon dance in the parking garage. I knew one of the admins was a convicted sex offender taking a court-ordered Benperidol—a powerful antipsychotic drug used to curb hyper sexual behavior—so I raided his desk and dry-swallowed a few tablets. After what seemed like several decades, but was actually only a few minutes, I floated back down to earth. The Buzz had been relegated to a low machine hum in the back of my mind and I was ready to get on with Stage 2. I just needed to find Yoko, who I figured by now might be trying to dive for pearls in the handicap stall.

When I turned to get out of my chair, he was standing at the entrance of my cube like a zombie who had come to suck out my brains.

"You're going to die," he said, and held his hand up like one of those saint statuettes you buy off a blanket peddler on St. Mark's Place.

34

Next thing I knew one of our lonely heart cube mates was stand-ing there, smiling. He was wearing a T-shirt with a Mickey Mouse glove hand pointing to his face that said I AM STUPID.

"Hey, you guys want to hit Taco Tuesday?" he asked jovially.

I looked at Yoko. He was admiring one of those desk tchotchkes of a little bird that perpetually tips down to drink from a nonexistent water source. He turned and regarded Stupid for an uncomfortably long time.

"So sweet of you to ask," he said, and proceeded to kiss the poor dumb bastard square on the lips.

Stupid recoiled in horror, which I appreciated, because then I knew I wasn't hallucinating the whole thing.

"Gaaaaahhhhh," he groaned, shaking his head like a wet dog, spitting and wiping off his tongue and lips.

His face turned crimson and he looked like he might pop like a boil, but instead he did an about-face and went off to have tacos with some other members of the office who would soon find out about Yoko's psychotic behavior. That was when I realized Stage 1 was right on track and nearly broke my arm patting myself on the back. But it didn't end there. Yoko went on a tear, skipping through the office and making strange bird sounds. He stripped off his shirt and crouched on top of someone's desk, scooping candy from a jar and shoving it in his mouth, wrappers and all. By the time he was finished, he had an orange Starburst goatee and his mouth was actually foaming from having eaten too many bags of Pop Rocks.

When I saw the office security guy coming down the hall, I had to intervene. I had to improvise . . .

"Yoko, they're coming for you."

"Who?" he said, instantly terrified.

"Aliens. They're dressed as security officers, as the prophecy says."

I was really winging it. My own brain was about to spontaneously combust and I was trying not to talk too much because, to me, my voice sounded like a robot trapped in an aluminum can full of angry wasps. Yoko saw the security officer's head bobbing down the hallway and crouched to the floor.

"Don't look," I poured it on. "He's carrying the anal probe."

"Sweet holy Jesus lizard," he said. "What do we do?"

"Follow me," I said in my best Dora the Explorer voice.

I took him to the twelfth floor, where they had been doing a lot of construction. It was a bank holiday, so the workers had the day off. The construction was so unfinished that there were many sections cordoned off for safety. I took him by the arm to a construction area that was still more in the framing stage and had no windows.

"Where are we going?" he asked.

"Rendezvous point. I called in a rescue ship."

"Oh good," he said, as if that made perfect sense.

Then he started to gag and dry heave, his system overloaded by the drug and wanting to eject it. The sound of it was unbearable and I started to get sick myself, so I slapped myself hard and then slapped Yoko, nearly knocking him over.

"It's time," I said to him sternly, leading him to the open windows.

"For what?" he said, rubbing his cheek.

"If you stay here, *they* will drag you out of here and give you the anal probe. Do you want that?"

"No! What can I do?"

"You have to recon with the rescue ship."

"How?"

"Stargate portal," I said, pointing at the huge open metal window frames 150 feet above the street.

"Right," he said. "Of course."

I looked at my wrist, which contained no watch.

"The ship is here," I said and patted him on the shoulder.

"What about you?" he asked, genuinely concerned.

"Don't worry about me," I said. "I'll come through the portal right after you. Only one can go at a time."

He went to kiss me on the lips, but I stopped him.

"Go, young soldier. Your bride awaits."

"Oh," he said, his eyes lighting up.

And he walked right out of the building. I looked down and saw him land on top of a combination hot dog cart and novelty balloon stand. When he hit it, the explosion of pork, meat water, and multi-colored sodas, followed by the rapid, vertical exodus of balloons, looked like a supernova, and I was so mesmerized I nearly fell out the window myself. It wasn't pretty, but it was one of my most creative hits, and if I was going to out-Lago Alice, I needed to think outside the box—mainly so I could fill it with high explosives and burning dog shit and leave it on her doorstep.

35

The day I left the hospital, as I was walking out, one of the receptionists in the lobby ran up to me, holding an enormous helium balloon bouquet that she could barely herd across the lobby. The balloons were all Disney characters with the words GET WELL! emblazoned in their bursting speech bubbles.

"Sir, these came for you. Since you requested no visitors or deliveries, we kept them in our gift shop."

The way she was smiling at me, you'd think she had found my pot of gold at the end of the rainbow.

"Must be a mistake," I said.

"The delivery company listed your specific room," she said.

"Was there a name on the card?'

"No."

"Of course not. Thank you, ma'am, but I'm sure they were intended for someone who would appreciate them . . . like a child or circus clown."

"Okay," she said, completely crestfallen.

Sue . . . guy thought he was hilarious. Balloons. Obnoxious. That morning he texted me and said he needed to meet with me as soon as possible to get me up to speed on Alice. I had him meet me at the Rusty Knot bar on the West Side Highway, a no-questions-asked enclave for professional drunks and the skinny-jean set. When Sue arrived, he looked flustered.

"Hey, man, you feel better?" he asked.

"If by better you mean do I feel like I've been sucking the tailpipe of a diesel garbage truck in Mexico City, then yeah, I feel aces."

He was too distracted to care about my answer.

"Good, man. Good. Becca just hit me with something we need to handle—"

"Becca?"

"Yeah."

"You're starting to shit where you eat, aren't you?" I asked. "Rule number five."

"No, man—"

"Never mind. Say what you got to say before you pop and make a terrible mess."

"Alice is gonna move on Harold Leung tonight. She didn't find any good intel in the laptops."

"Shocker."

"Right? Anyway, she's going to black bag him tonight and go to work on him at HR with a dental drill and a couple of hungry sewer rats."

"With interns like these . . ."

"Yeah. On the guy's birthday too. She's so cold you must've got frostbite on your dick, JL."

"That's the funniest thing you've said since we met. Nice work."

"Thanks. What do you want to do about Leung?"

One of the things I have always loved and hated about this work is the necessity to improvise. Thinking on one's feet is a critical skill because nothing ever goes according to plan, especially when you're dealing with Alice. Obviously, I couldn't allow her to torture Leung to get intel on Zhen. I was certain Leung didn't know enough to be of consequence because Zhen wasn't that stupid, but on the off chance he did know something, I needed to be proactive.

"We need to take him out. Right now."

"That's what I figured."

"Any ideas?"

"A few. None—"

"—of them good. I know. You say that about all your great ideas, dummy. Speaking of bad ideas, thanks for sending me the FTD 'I heart blowing my cover' balloon bouquet."

"What?"

"You didn't send me balloons at the hospital?"

"Hell no. Balloons? What do I look like, a—"

Before he could finish, I got up and sprinted out of the bar.

"Hey!" Sue yelled and followed me.

We got into the lobby of the hospital and I nearly jerked the poor receptionist out of her chair.

"Where'd you put my balloons?!"

"I thought you didn't want—"

"I want them now, goddamnit."

I was trying my best to keep my voice down. Sue was clocking the security guys, getting ready to sweep some legs.

"Okay. Okay. We took them to the maternity ward," the lady said.

"You what?" I said, sweat pouring down my face.

"I'll go get them, sir. Please calm down."

But I was already sprinting away. I scanned the directory while Sue stabbed the elevator buttons. It was taking forever, so Sue and I hoofed it as fast as we could up the stairs to the tenth floor. My lungs felt like they were going to explode in my mouth.

"What's up, JL? What's with the balloons?"

"If you didn't send them—"

"Oh shit," Sue said.

We made it to the maternity ward and saw the balloons gently bumping against the viewing glass outside the nursery.

"Mother of God," I said under my breath.

"Can I help you?" said an old crotchety nurse, standing between the balloons and us.

"Yes, ma'am," Sue said, making himself sound mentally slow.

The nurse thought he was adorable.

"I work for the florist and I delivered them balloons to the wrong hospital. This is my boss. We got to get them to the right place or my boss will take away my Lego money."

"Okay, son, you may take them. But please be quiet. We have a lot of sleeping babies."

"Yes, ma'am," he said, nodding his head vigorously.

We pretended we were just trying to be quiet when we carefully removed the balloon bouquet like guys from the bomb squad.

When we got outside, I breathed a sigh of relief. There's one gas that is lighter than helium, could easily be used to blow up balloons, and is readily available: hydrogen. The difference is that helium makes you talk funny and hydrogen—in high enough concentration—is highly flammable, even explosive. Just ask the thirty-six passengers who were incinerated onboard the Hindenburg, the first lead zeppelin. Since Sue hadn't sent me the balloons, I had to assume Alice had, and she wouldn't have gone to all that trouble for helium. I gave Sue the balloon bouquet while I took one from it and poked a small hole in the bottom. I let most of the gas out and when the balloon was the size of my fist, I lit my lighter next to the hole. A five-inch flame shot out and melted the balloon in half a second.

"Damn," Sue said.

"Dirty pool," I said, disgusted. "And these are Mylar. She could have blown up half the hospital."

"We sure she did it?" Sue asked.

I looked at him like he was insane.

"What do you think?" I asked.

"I think we better do something about Harold Leung," Sue said.

36

The office cake ritual is well documented in corporate lore, most pointedly by Mike Judge in the modern cinema classic *Office Space*. It is an unwritten rule that, in order for morale to be maintained, cake must be served at least once a week. The occasion for the cake is far less important to those standing in the chow line than a guarantee that everyone will get a piece. And the best part is that there is never, *ever* enough cake. Blame it on portioning or surreptitious seconds, but it is an axiom—some Milton will always be left standing with an empty paper plate and a full cup of bitterness.

Being in Human Resources came in handy again when I returned to the office that day, with some fanfare, and was asked to help plan an impromptu conference room birthday party for Harold Leung. I love a good party, so I really put my back into the work. Like docile livestock, everyone gathered in the break room and sang "Happy birthday to you" to Harold in English and Cantonese, which sounded more like a call to arms than a birthday tune. And, as is the custom, Harold was given the first slice of cake. I know what you're thinking: *He's going to kill Harold with his own birthday cake.* As cruel as that sounds, the thought *did* cross my mind.

And, of course, I've been there, done that, and bought a T-shirt. I had to whack a dirty CFO once and couldn't use poison because I would risk killing the whole office—*or at least those who got cake*—

and that's just not very professional, is it? So, I had to do a little bit of medical history research on my mark prior to his big office celebration.

At sixty-five, he was a fairly healthy man. However, a quick perusal of his medical records yielded an exotic diagnosis: myasthenia gravis. This is a neuromuscular disease that, in layman's terms, causes intermittent muscle fatigue and weakness. Severity ranges from mild symptoms like droopy eyelids and slurred speech to life-threatening conditions like poorly functioning breathing muscles. Obviously, this guy fell into the mild category because it was not noticeable and he smartly used up all of his sick days to avoid being seen at the office during attacks.

The interesting thing is that, for ER docs, it's one of a few "boogeyman" conditions that keeps them up at night. If someone with myasthenia gravis needs to be intubated, just like everyone else they receive a neuromuscular blocking agent, which is used so docs can feed a tube down someone's throat without having the gag reflex cock block their whole procedure. Unlike for everyone else, these drugs can be potentially lethal to someone with myasthenia gravis because they can cause profound muscle paralysis for extended periods of time, resulting in respiratory and cardiac arrest.

So, guess what the secret ingredient in the buttercream icing on my target's cake was? With the addition of a minimal amount of a neuromuscular blocking agent, the rest of the folks who ate the cake were probably more affected by the sugar crash than the drug itself. But it proved fatal for my target. They found him that afternoon, stone dead in the bathroom stall, still wearing his SpongeBob party hat.

As for Harold Leung, I had not delved into his medical history, so a cake gag was out. But lucky for him, there was a surprise that was sure to put a smile on his face waiting in his car when he left the building: a beautiful bouquet of balloons! When he saw them, he stood in the parking garage, staring like an awestruck child at all of his favorite Disney characters, whose maniacally cheerful faces were pressed up against the windshield of his car. But instead of inviting him to join them on an enchanting trip to the Magic Kingdom, they detonated somewhere in Queens, and by the time they got the fire out, all that was left of Harold and his car could fit in a Folgers family-size coffee can.

My ad hoc execution scenario was the car itself. Harold drove a 2002 Pontiac Grand Prix. Righteous wheels, I know. The beauty, or beast, of this car was that it contained the GM 3800 Series II V6 engine. About 1.2 million GM vehicles with this engine were recalled by 2009 because it was prone to oil leaks, which would cause the car to burst into flames if the oil hit the engine manifold. Once it got lit up, all the petroleum-based plastic was highly combustible and the car would burn down to the frame. If you've ever seen one of these smoking ruins on the side of the road, you would have questioned the driver's chances of survival. So, when they found Harold's smoking ruin, it was assumed the car was the cause of the blaze, as only a demented freak would blame it on a friendly bouquet of birthday balloons.

Rising higher than the noxious odor of burning plastic and melted aluminum was the smell of Alice's desperation, which Sue said was palpable back at HR. According to him, I had not only pushed Alice's panic button by killing Leung, but I had also broken it in the "on" position. Morale was taking a nosedive, and because of Alice's focus on Zhen, other clients were breathing down her neck. I knew time had become a luxury she could no longer afford and I wasn't surprised to hear that she was considering trying to hit Zhen head-on, old-school, with no foreplay.

So Sue and I started running scenarios. Doing him at CIS was a nonstarter. He was always traveling, so if I were Alice, I would have tried to exploit a weakness when he was on the road with a smaller security detail. Of course, Zhen didn't travel light. No matter what was transporting him by land, air, and sea, it would be heavily armored and well guarded. She was going to need some serious military hardware if she wanted to try to get him with a full-court press.

Where does one go when one needs modern weapons of mass destruction on short notice? The Russians of course! In an attempt to keep me from picking up her trail, she dug deep and chose the dirtiest, most obscure Russian mobsters she could find. But she and Rebecca actually took Sue with them when they traveled to a ten-thousand-acre compound in some godforsaken part of Wyoming and he gave me the play-by-play when he got back. Those chain-smoking creeps had *everything*, including helicopters and an ancient, but fully functional, Soviet MiG-25 fighter jet. The place was like the Walmart of wildly outdated weapons of mass destruction and it was run by one of the shadiest Russian mobsters in the business.

Yuri, as he referred to himself, was wearing knee-high English riding boots, a scarf, and no shirt. His boys, also cut from the same tick, were hustling buyers, passing around Cuban cigars and absinthe in Boy Scout canteens. Shirtless Yuri was a former colonel in the army, even served with Putin. The other guys were some kind of Special Forces types. They spoke very little English, but that didn't matter because Alice let her suitcases full of cash do the talking.

With her paranoia at an all-time high, she had refused to tell Rebecca and Sue exactly what she purchased until the day she planned to use it. When they got back to New York, Alice put Rebecca and Sue to work trying to find any information they could on Zhen's travel plans. They also spent days going through surveillance footage captured outside the CIS office building. Anytime a car left the garage, a helicopter landed and took off from the pad, and delivery trucks came to the loading docks, they recorded it. They were attempting to analyze for patterns and identify any anomalies that might indicate Zhen's movements. It was a long shot, but it's all Alice had. And, thanks to Sue, I had it too.

37

Alice's plan wasn't exactly good news. The fact that she was pre-pared to go completely off the reservation with a hit that might make the St. Valentine's Day Massacre look like a purse snatching meant she wasn't thinking clearly, and that could be a very danger-ous thing indeed. When someone like Alice is backed into a corner, the outcome can be very difficult to predict and the potential for collateral damage is massive. Whatever she was planning would have to be countered with superior strategy and firepower if I had any hope of taking her out. Knowing what Alice is capable of made this a profoundly daunting task for someone like me with limited resources.

On the other hand, I could see some logic, albeit reckless, in her desire to cut to the chase. The traditional work-your-way-up-the-ladder-to-access-intern gambit was simply not going to work and time was of the essence. Alice and I had reached a stalemate in our intern chess match, and even if someone had weeks to try to get close to Zhen in the conventional HR way, it would still be dicey. The Chinese MSS have mastered the art of avoiding any type of routine that could be captured and time-logged by even the most sophisticated surveillance rotations. That's why they are able to stay embedded for decades without rousing suspicion.

Because I didn't have the resources Alice had, I figured I would have to try to gain the upper hand by getting to Zhen before she did. That way, I would have some element of surprise when she showed up to reprise the Tet Offensive on Zhen and his crew. So, I started looking for other access points to Zhen and turned my sights on his bread and butter: corporate espionage. I needed to find one of his prime intel sources and tap my own needle into that vein. Disrupting the flow of invaluable information to Beijing would not only get Zhen's attention, but it would also flush him out of his natural habitat and put him on the warpath.

"When your enemy makes his battle cry is when you reach in and pull his nuts out through his neck," Griner used to say.

He was right. We're never more vulnerable than when we're on the attack. And to get Zhen to that point, I needed to get my hook into his biggest fish, one that could drown him and take his three wishes with it. So I did what any decent FBI agent would do and I followed the money. Whoever was getting the biggest payday from Zhen was going to become my bestie.

This is where Harold Leung came in handy. When Alice first started stalking him, I had Sue break into his car and install a modified RFID reader, similar to the ones thieves use to steal your credit card numbers just by standing near your wallet. While he drove home, the reader captured and uploaded his laptop data. Within twenty-four hours of Leung's demise, I checked the data dumps and found a client list. To say it was shocking is the understatement of the century. Suffice it to say that the Chinese government owns this country. We are the lion at the end of the tamer's whip and every advance we make is assimilated and perfected by them. Put simply, American "progress" is the fuel that they will use to burn us out when they are no longer amused with our stupid movies and require a million acres of our Pacific coastline to establish a new province.

Every industry, from agriculture to medicine, to electronics and utilities, and everything in between, had blue-chip players on Zhen's roster. Want to know what Apple's iPhone is going to look like in ten years? Ask Zhen. How about which big pharmaceutical company may have a cure for cancer in five years? Zhen plays golf with their CEO. But, as you can imagine, all of these things were of minor importance to Zhen's MVP squad—military weapons contractors. Want to know how to shut down our missile defense systems and conquer the greatest country in the world in fewer than forty-eight hours? Zhen has the blueprints and the companies that our government pays to develop technology handed to him on a silver platter.

Enter Craig Davison, CEO of Bear River Industries, named after Craig's hometown in Idaho and, incidentally, the site of the worst massacre of Native Americans in U.S. history. Ain't white folks grand? Craigy was one of the richest men in the world and his specialty was feeding the U.S. military's hunger for "push button weaponry." Basically, Americans don't like to wage war with actual people because they end up dying and making everyone feel bad. George W. Bush and his cronies introduced the erroneous notion that you could sit your sorry ass in a Barcalounger and blast bitches into submission before last call. Despite reams of evidence to the contrary, this philosophy is not only going strong but is also well funded by the Pentagon.

Craigy was truly an enemy of the state. Not only was he selling his own product intel to Zhen, but he was also using his security clearance to help Zhen access other DOD information he was privy to. Craig Davison was robbing Peter to pay Zhen and putting the American people at risk. And Zhen had him so deep in his pocket he was going to become a piece of lint any day. There's no telling how many American soldiers have died in Iraqistan because of Craig's treason. All I needed to do was position myself between Craig and Zhen and I would have my access point.

Now, let's go back to the world's greatest treasure trove of knowledge: movies. No matter what, I can design any scenario based on what I've seen in a movie. For this little caper, *Scarface* came to mind. There was a sequence in that movie when Tony Montana was trying to work his way up to doing business with Alejandro Sosa, the über drug lord living in Bolivia with the CIA in *his* pocket. Tony quickly realized that Frank, the guy who brought him into the big show, would make a pretty convenient stepping-stone to Sosa. So, he exploited Frank's increasingly apparent weaknesses until Frank fucked up royally and tried but failed to take Tony out.

Tony knew that all he really needed to do was replace Frank with himself and everyone could go on with business as usual, with very few ruffled feathers. Not only did Tony pull it off, but he also managed to take Frank's wife, Elvira, played by the sublime Michelle Pfeiffer. After that, he had free access to Sosa and from there he built his massive, albeit relentlessly tacky, empire. Who buys a tiger? Imagine the cage cleanup for an animal that devours ten chickens a day. Anyway, Craig had to go out and I had to slip into his skin in a smooth and inconspicuous way that maintained the flow of information critical to Zhen's survival. If I pulled it off, I would be in the inner circle of the lucrative supply chain in record time, and Zhen would demand an audience with me shortly thereafter.

For that kind of access, I would need to be a new and improved version of Craig, capturing Zhen's attention with more lucrative intel and prompting him to relax a little with his trust issues. Once I had his ear, Alice would go into full panic mode, wondering if I intended to kill him or expose her, or both! Of course, I had no intention of killing Zhen. I would simply use him to flush her out and force her to make a move on him out of pure desperation. And when one fails to look before she leaps, one tends to land in a pit of sharpened bamboo punji sticks coated with human feces. Just saying. I rousted Sue and we got to work. Right away Sue pulled together a highly actionable plan to get Craig in our net. Things were starting to look up, but that's usually when you don't see the size-twelve, steel-toed boot that's about to land square in your balls.

38

When I showed up to work at CIS on a Monday morning, Alice had gone AWOL. I did my rounds, looking for her in the usual places, but she was nowhere to be found. I had Sue track down her phone and it was somewhere on the twentieth floor. That was the floor just below the penthouse level, where Zhen worked. I didn't think it was possible that she was going to attempt to break through the ceiling or scale the glass outside, but I wasn't taking any chances. I had put her in a desperate position and Alice never thought twice about resorting to desperate measures.

Getting to the twentieth floor was no joke. I was in the Donkey Kong world of Draconian corporate hierarchies and CIS was the pinnacle of that ethos. Everyone had a key card that contained the secrets to their status and the keys to their relative kingdoms. As I was a lowly intern, my key card had limited access to the building, but it was slightly better than most because I was in the Human Resources department.

My supervisor had the ability to swipe it and give me temporary access for special circumstances. Rhonda-Pat was a chunky soccer mom with a cubicle full of kid and pet photos and the persistent smell of canned tuna. She loved coffee and she especially loved the coffee I made for her, which was a rare Peruvian bean that, unbeknownst to her, had been cured in a vat of goat cud for six weeks before being bagged and shipped to market. The fermented ruminant (basically goat puke) gave the coffee a peppery aroma and flavor, much like a complex rye whiskey.

I deliberately didn't bring her a cup at the usual time so I could get her jones going. Then I got to work running around the office looking busy. She finally intercepted me in the hallway with that smile people give you when they are either going to change your life with horrible news or they want something petty and are afraid to ask. I preempted her question, relieving her of the embarrassment while ensuring her cube stayed vacated for a while.

"Hey, Rhonda-Pat. Sorry. I have a pot brewing in the kitchen right now."

I looked at my watch.

"Ten minutes tops."

"Oh, John. That's wonderful. Maybe I'll just—"

"You should go wait for it. A couple of guys from Risk Management were milling around in there—"

"Thanks!"

And she took off like a shot. I had set the coffeemaker to start just prior to seeing her, so I knew it was going to be more like fifteen minutes. I went straight to her cube, typed her cat's name in the password field, and authorized my card for the twentieth floor.

When I finally made it up there, Sue vectored me into Alice's location. Based on the coordinates, she was smack-dab in the middle of the men's executive washroom. I crept up to the door and put my ear against it. I heard something but I wasn't sure what at first. Then it got louder and I realized it was Alice. She wasn't speaking, just making odd sounds. They got louder and then I knew what I was hearing.

It was the sound of Alice having sex.

In the throes of passion, she would coo, almost like a dove or a baby dolphin. It would get louder and louder until . . . well, you know the rest. It was getting louder and louder and in about ten seconds flat I went from cool, calculating assassin to raging, jealous husband. Next thing I knew, I had barged into the bathroom and locked the door behind me. As soon as I entered the absurdly luxurious bathroom—complete with espresso machine, bar cart, and leather furniture—the noise stopped. The stall door was closed. I looked under the door and saw nothing. But there was no place else for them to hide, so I figured they must have had their feet up and out of sight.

"Alice?"

No answer. I gently nudged the thick stall door. It was locked.

"Banging our way to the bottom, are we? You make me sick."

Still no answer. Not a sound.

"I know you're in here. You and your mark. I'll bet his name is Mark. That would be perfect. Fuck you too, Mark."

Total silence.

"I'm actually glad it's going to end this way. I wasn't sure if I could go through with it, killing you, but now I know it won't be a problem at all. A pleasure, in fact. I'll even enjoy killing you, Mark. She may have led you in here by your angry inch, but she's still my wife, mother—"

"—fucker," Alice said, *behind me.*

I turned and the barrel of a Kimber Tactical Pro II .45 with a barrel suppressor was in my face. Alice grinned at me triumphantly.

"Let me guess. No funny stuff?" I said.

39

You were actually jealous, John." She laughed.

I was so enraged I could feel my fingernails cutting into my palms as I clenched my fists.

"On your knees."

"Nope," I replied casually.

She cocked back the hammer.

"Okay, that's your final 'I mean business' move," I said. "Looks like all you have left is to shoot."

I spit in her face and used the half second afforded me by her knee-jerk repulsion to grab the suppressor on the gun. She managed to fire a round that whipped past my face and punched a hole in the brass paper towel dispenser. I then tore the gun out of her hand and threw it through the window in one motion. Alice's trigger finger was bleeding as the Kimber sailed to the street below.

We stared each other down in a Mexican standoff scored by a hideous Muzak version of "You Light Up My Life." In moments like that, it's important to have a strategy well before first strike. It's not a time for improvisation. So, we did the same thing—faced off, clicked into a premeditated plan we hoped would give us each a slight advantage, and waited for the other to make the first move.

"You first," I said.

"Age before beauty," she said.

Then she kicked me in the chest with such force, I flew back into the wall and shattered the ceramic tile. I countered with a savage front kick to her stomach. She gasped and retched as her mouth filled with blood. But this didn't slow her down. Instead, she spat the blood in my eyes and started beating my head and neck with the marble towel rod she tore off the wall. I snatched the rod in midstrike and twisted it with all of my strength, ripping it out of her hand and burying it in her kneecaps. She went down hard on the floor. I went to body slam her and she rolled, causing me to hit the ground with my full weight on my elbow. Then she jumped on top of me and circled her arm around my neck.

She applied a choke hold called Silkworm. Its origin is unknown, although many speculate that it comes from Naban wrestling, which originated in ancient Burma. The choke arm encircles the neck and is locked into place by the other arm, which twists through it like a pretzel and holds fast on the back of the attacker's neck. It's so tight initially that the inexperienced fighter will black out instantly. I was able to get my chin in the way just before she locked it off, so she was only cutting off blood flow in my right side carotid and subclavian arteries and I could still barely draw breath.

At first, I thought about trying to flip her over my head. But then I remembered that would have been a very bad idea. If I had flipped her and she had maintained her grasp, she would have rotated in midair like a gymnast and used what's called axial loading to break my neck. So, instead, I started lifting her off the ground, duping her into thinking I was going for the flip. She tightened her hold but then had to reposition her arms to maintain her balance when I quickly brought her back down on the floor. That shift was all I needed to rotate my body into a position wherein we were chest to chest. Before Alice could unlock her arms, I had already encircled them with mine in another famous hold—the Bear Hug. At that point, I just needed to hold her still enough to deliver a deathblow from my forehead, driving her nasal bones into her brain. She closed her eyes, seemingly waiting for death, but then pulled the one move I wasn't expecting.

She kissed me.

I'm not ashamed to admit it was the hottest kiss I've ever had. I kissed her back and we switched gears so hard from homicidal rage to carnal fury that I thought we might spontaneously conceive a love child right there in the executive washroom.

Then someone started knocking on the door.

We heard urgent voices calling for whoever was in the bathroom to unlock the door. They were concerned someone might be dying in a stall and said they had called 911. Then we heard the heavy boots of the facilities maintenance crew pounding down the hallway and the telltale sound of master keys jangling from a belt holster. With the sound of the key in the lock, I threw my jacket over the window and Alice kicked out the glass. When they opened the door and started jabbering in Chinese about the damage to the bathroom, we were already outside, standing on the window ledge. By the time the hoary janitor poked his head out the window, we had both jumped to a construction scaffold attached to the building next door and gone our separate ways.

Just another day at the office.

I must admit, part of me was excited by our one-round knockout lavatory tryst. Clearly, the fire between us was still lit. But the next time I saw Alice, I found out the hard way that it was burning out of control.

40

FBI-NCAVC, Quantico, Virginia
Present day

I'm beginning to understand why you want to see Alice again,"
Fletch says smugly.

"Why is that?"

"You're still in love with her."

"Whatever you're smoking, have some sent to my cell."

Fletch seems almost touched by the idea that my motivation to
see Alice one last time is strictly romantic. This is a good thing in his
mind because the holy grail of interrogation is finding that one personal hook that strikes the right chord on the subject's heartstrings.
Every terrorist has a soft spot for someone or something. Every serial
killer has a favorite teddy bear. Fletch wants me to have my teddy
bear to keep me cozy at night in my cold, dank cell. In this way he
is a father figure and a savior all in one, bearing loaves and fishes to
save my soul.

"Are you denying it?" he asks, sounding oddly adolescent.

"I'm denying you the satisfaction of familiarity, Fletch. Seeing
as you've taken everything else from me, I think I'll keep that to
myself."

"That's fine, but our only concern about you seeing Alice has been one of safety. You can imagine the kind of shit storm that would roll in if you managed to harm or even kill her in our custody."

"Not to mention the paperwork."

He ignores my bad joke and glances at the two-way mirror.

"But if I knew your intentions for seeing her were . . . more innocuous—"

"I get it, Fletch. Does admitting that I love Alice help my cause?"

He shrugs a "maybe" and waits to be right again.

"Fine. I love her. I've never stopped loving her. Happy?"

He smiles. I think he really is happy. But clearly he's not aware of the "thin line between love and hate" the Persuaders so elegantly exposed.

"Can we move on or do you want me to show you the Alice tattoo on my d—"

"Let's move on. Tell me more about Craig Davison."

41

I hate golf. It's an impossibly difficult game or sport or whatever you want to call it, but it's played by the fattest, drunkest brain-dead honkies on the planet. And I hate Florida. For all the same reasons. But there I was, John Lago, a highly trained killing machine, fresh off the red-eye wearing yellow pants and taking practice swings at Ben Hogan's favorite course, the Seminole Golf Club in Juno Beach. While I obsessively washed my ball and tried to wrap my head around "the kiss," my new foursome partner Craig Davison joined me in the tee box. The other two players had not yet shown up yet. Hmm . . . I wonder why.

Craig would have been the perfect intern if he weren't in his mid-forties already. He had the ideal build and looked to be a world-class wallflower. I was chatting at him a fair bit, trying to get him to open up to me using good old boy small talk. But he was a pro and knew exactly how to say a lot without saying anything. While we waited our turn to tee off, I poked at his Teflon facade a bit more.

"What kind of work you in, Craig?"

"Sales."

"What's your product?"

"Tech sales. Not very exciting," he whispered, slightly annoyed.

"I worked in tech for a few years," I whispered back.

"What field?"

"Information systems mostly."

"Man, we're both as boring as we look." He grinned.

"You got that right. Sometimes I think watching paint dry would be more exciting than my life," I said.

He courtesy laughed and headed up to the tee. After an eternity of warm-up and ceremony, he shanked the damn thing into the woods with a wicked slice. Needless to say, he was not pleased with my arrow-straight 350-yard drive that cut the fairway in half.

"Nice shot," he mumbled. "You play a lot?"

"Hardly ever," I said, chapping his ass.

We got into the cart and I could smell the rabid desire to win coming out of Craig's every pore. Of course, I was playing an amazing game and he couldn't make a putt to save his life. As we progressed from hole to hole, I began to see that all-too-familiar frustration and angst that come with a poor round of golf. In fact, he was getting downright pissed but keeping his feelings very close to the vest. And he started drinking. That was exactly where I needed him to be. The back nine on that course is notoriously difficult. Fairways are exceedingly narrow and the rough is the forest primeval. By the time we made the turn and finished lunch, Craig was half in the bag, had no confidence, and had his nose buried in his iPhone, pretending that he was too busy to care about his game.

Around the sixteenth hole, he sliced the ball a country mile into the woods. It's amazing what a slight adjustment to a five iron will do to your game. Oh yeah, I forgot to say that Sue and I completely reengineered his clubs prior to tee time. Oops! I could hear Craig quietly cursing as he stormed off to retrieve his ball, refusing to accept a ride from me on the cart. He was in the trees awhile, hunting around and stomping like a child having a tantrum. Finally, he gave up and turned to head back to the fairway but ended up turning right into me.

"What the—" he started to say as I Tased him in the neck. Craigy then dutifully slumped to the ground, out cold. Sue was waiting for us in a grounds-crew cart, so we loaded him into the equipment trailer and covered him with a tarp.

"Cinderella story," I said in my best Bill Murray accent, which basically sounded like an Australian leprechaun.

"What's that mean?" Sue asked.

"Bill Murray? *Caddyshack*?"

"Doesn't ring a bell."

"Kids. Jesus. If a movie doesn't end up on a McDonald's drink cup, it doesn't exist."

42

Sue drove the landscaper cart out of the golf course grounds and we dumped it in the weeds. Unconscious Craig assumed the position in the trunk of our rental car and we took him out on a nice little boat ride—on his own 350-foot super yacht. When he came to, Sue and I were drinking his champagne and smoking his $10,000 Cuban cigars.

"I hope you don't mind that we made ourselves at home," I said.

"I'm on a boat!" Sue sang out.

Craig's eyes went wide when he saw Sue. All black people are presumptively angry and murderous to palefaces like Craig, which is why Sue was the perfect cracker interrogator, sitting backward on a chair and staring wide-eyed at the poor bastard. Sue had immersed himself in the persona of a gacked-up crack baby trying to decide if he should waste a bullet on you or just pistol-whip you to death.

"Who . . . who are you?"

"I'll ask the questions," I answered. I'd always wanted to say that. Sue backhanded him to drive the point home.

"I have money. Whatever you want," Craig pleaded.

"We know you have money," I chimed in with a calm but menacing FM radio voice. "You've been selling out our beloved country to the Chinese, you filthy traitor."

Sue slapped him like the bitch he was becoming before our very eyes.

"I don't know what—"

"Don't!" I bellowed in his face.

"Let's smoke this fool!" Sue said in his best *Shaft* voice and shoved the barrel of a .45 into the side of his head.

Sue never spoke like that and it sounded funny, so I had to stifle laughter. When he saw I was trying not to lose it, he made it worse by turning the gun gangsta sideways.

I sat across from Craig and looked at him with the piercing X-ray vision of a police detective.

"We're going to kill you, Craig. You know that, don't you?"

Craig nodded, his shoulders slumping.

"You know you deserve it, right?"

He hesitated to react.

I reached out and took hold of his chin, pulling it up and down in a nodding fashion.

"You sold radar tech to the Chinese. They sold it to a bunch of scumbags in Afghanistan. The scumbags used it to target three, count 'em, three American troop choppers. All three were shot down. Thirty-two American soldiers smashed into the mountains and burned to death in a coffin of twisted metal and glass—on foreign soil, thousands of miles from home. Their families buried an empty box, Craig."

He looked at me like he'd seen a ghost. That's because he had. What I had told him was true.

I laughed at his shocked look.

"Craig. Seriously, don't insult me with that look. Did you actually think your crimes were victimless?"

No reply. Sue walloped him in the balls with the butt of his gun. He screamed in pain and tried to double over but I backhanded him and his chair fell over. I picked him up by his hair and set his chair up again.

"Linda. That's your wife, right?"

"Oh God . . ."

"I'll take that as a yes. You don't want anything to happen to Linda, do you? Although, she *is* fucking most of your friends."

"No. What? Please. Whatever you want to know. Anything."

Craigy was having a hard time processing the thing I said about his wife, which was also true.

"Good. I want you, and her future second husband, Ronnie the pool boy, to know that you can trust us with her safety. As long as you give us what we want."

He nodded.

"Do you trust me, Craig?"

He looked at Sue like you would look at a pit pull on a choke chain.

"Look at me, Craig. I need to know you trust what I'm telling you."

He looked at me. The fear on his face gave way to surrender and he nodded. Craig knew exactly what he'd been doing. I smiled, acknowledging what was now a constructive rapport unclouded by emotion or false expectations.

"When I leave here," I continued, "I'm going to have to be you. I have to replace you as a source for your buyer, Mr. Zhen. So, I need you to tell me absolutely everything I need to know. And . . . this is important . . . I need you to help me set up a meeting with Zhen."

"If I'm dead or missing, he'll run for cover," Craig said blankly.

"You'll be neither to them because you decided to take your boat out fishing. You needed some alone time to relax after your pancreatic cancer diagnosis. Zhen will understand."

"I don't have—"

"According to your medical records, you do. So, I've taken care of Zhen. Now you need to take care of me."

For the next twelve hours, Craig spilled his guts to us. I kept him "inspired" by peppering in more of his personal information—where his kids go to prep school, the name of his invalid father and his nursing home, the kind of knowledge that froze the blood in his veins. Like all educated white boys with no street smarts, Craig didn't even try to be vague or deceitful. When I knew he was completely tapped out on information, we put him out of his misery (in a nice way) and gave him a moving burial at sea. Then we set his GPS headings for Cuba—they can always use a decent boat—and went back to shore on his diving Zodiac. And I had the keys to the kingdom, as it were.

Zhen's people were understandably skeptical, but when they saw Craig's medical records, Zhen sent him best wishes and accepted a meeting with me, Craigy's new wunderkind protégé. I was told the meeting would not be scheduled in advance and I would be summoned when they needed me.

Then Sue and I agreed to part ways for a while. Alice was wondering where the hell he'd been for twenty-four hours and his story about being laid up with the swine flu was starting to wear thin. He no longer needed to risk his ass hanging around with me anyway and he served a better purpose getting back to Manhattan to keep an eye on her for me.

"Thanks for your help, kid."

"You know how you can thank me, JL? Kill that witch and pry my nuts out of her claws. Think you can do that for me?"

"With pleasure," I promised.

A couple of days later Sue told me Alice was waiting for me to make a move so she could whack Zhen and me together. I told him they had contacted me to set up a meeting and she would have her chance in less than twenty-four hours.

43

Zhen's people communicated with me via a series of highly encrypted electronic messages. I had been told to provide a P.O. Box number, where they mailed me an ancient pager for this purpose. The messages traveled from Zhen's mobile device to a Chinese spy satellite and down to me in the form of a numeric page. The page had to be processed through three different cipher programs before I could read it. They sent me to several locations for bogus meetings just to see if I would show up and also to get a decent look at me. I made that almost impossible because I always wore a baseball cap and sunglasses and never looked up to provide any eyes in the sky with a positive ID.

Meantime, I managed to put together a weapons package that was highly portable and that I could deploy at a moment's notice. All of it fit into a large metal briefcase that I schlepped at all times. I was pretty impressed with it. Alice had all the money in the world but I had to get creative, and I totally nailed it. Although, I shuddered a bit to think that I might have to actually use it. I'd been *in the shit*, as they say, but never actual combat. Alice had obviously assembled some kind of WMD arsenal that she was waiting to uncork, and God only knew what it was. I had some ideas, which helped me decide how to put my own arsenal together, but I wasn't looking forward to being right.

The morning of my meeting with Zhen, I spoke to Sue one last time and told him to stand by and be ready.

"What's she been up to?" I asked.

"No idea. Keeping her movements very close to the vest. Bec . . . Rebecca doesn't even know."

"Then *Becca* has outlived her usefulness," I said. "You need to kill her and dump the body, Sue."

"What?" he asked defensively.

"Just kidding."

"Ha-ha. You got the goodies for Zhen?"

"Yeah, I have an encrypted data drive with data on all the new weapons Craigy had promised him for Christmas."

"Outstanding. Wait, what if something happens to you and Zhen gets his hands on all that intel? He might start World War Three," Sue said, legitimately concerned.

"Don't get your panties in a bunch. The drive contains a virus designed to wipe the data in seventy-two hours. And it can't be copied."

"Sounds like you got it dialed in, JL."

"We'll see."

The day of my meeting with Zhen, he sent me no fewer than a dozen false times and locations, so I spent hours going to different parts of the city to meet with him, only to get a new location. I finally ended up at South Street Seaport. I waited there for two hours and heard nothing. So, I walked back to my apartment and when I got there, a Rolls-Royce Phantom limousine was waiting by the curb. Not good. Somehow he knew where I lived. Really not good.

At first glance, the Rolls looked like the usual rich-asshole-mobile. But closer examination revealed it to be heavily armored against a sophisticated attack with military ordnance. Windows were narrowed and thickened and it was rolling heavy on the tires—which were no doubt Kevlar lined and built to function even when riddled with bullets. The vehicle weight was due to the two-inch thick bulletproof-glass windows, the ballistic steel covering the engine, gas tank, and battery, and, more important, the thick layers of composite armor beneath the vehicle's original body design. Based on what I could see, the entire vehicle was impervious to handgun and submachine gun rounds and maybe even small explosives. Again, not good.

The rear, impenetrably black tinted window slid down a crack. I sat there for a beat, waiting for a bullet to spray my brains all over my stoop.

"Get in," a voice inside whispered.

The back door opened with a pressure-releasing hiss and I slid inside. The limo cabin looked like a well-appointed private jet. Zhen was sitting farthest from me, near the driver partition. His men occupied the seats on the side. One of them was casually pointing a QBZ-95 Chinese military assault rifle at my face.

"Just so you know, Marshal Dillon," I said to him, "that rifle has an effective range of four hundred meters and firing it point-blank into my face would not only turn my head into a grenade with razor-sharp bone shrapnel, but also the slug would most likely ricochet throughout this heavily armored vehicle and could, depending on what the oddsmakers in Vegas say, end up in your boss's face."

Feathers ruffled all around and a collective scowl was aimed in my direction by Zhen's men. Zhen laughed. Then he said something reproachful in Chinese to the man holding the assault rifle. The man lowered his head, and when the car began to speed up the West Side Highway, he opened the door and ejected himself. Behind us, I saw him rag doll under the wheels of a semi. The only pink slip you get from the MSS is a thirty-foot blood smear on the asphalt.

"Pleasure to finally meet you, Mr. Lago," Zhen said quietly.

Motherfucker.

44

I guess I wasn't completely surprised that someone in Zhen's position had figured out my identity. It was just a pisser because I figured next they were going to take me somewhere to pull my skin off with a cheese grater and make me eat my severed balls before burying me alive in a pine box full of starved badgers.

"You are either very brave, Mr. Lago, or very stupid."

"What kind of stupid ever got himself into *this* seat?" I inquired.

"Excellent point. Which is why I'm not going to kill you. At least not right away."

"That's mighty white of you."

He laughed.

"You are a capable man, indeed. Most men shake in their boots at the sight of me. But you, you just tell jokes like we are old friends. I like this. The English had a saying when I was in school: *You can be cordial at the gates of hell.* I couldn't agree more."

"So, what happens next?" I said.

"I am aware that I have been targeted by your former organization. My security forces are robust but, as we both know, there is no substitute for someone with your training. So now you work for me."

Great minds think alike.

The door to the Rolls-Royce hissed open and the roaring eighty-mile-per-hour wind outside was nearly deafening.

"Or we can always hold you by your feet until the pavement grinds away your face," he said with the same ease someone might suggest going to brunch.

"That won't be necessary. When do I start?"

He nodded slightly and the door to the Rolls closed and left us again in the hermetic silence of luxury. He shook my hand and then examined it closely.

"Iron Palm," he said with great interest, like a wine connoisseur examining a particularly good vintage.

He showed my hand to his men. They Tonto-grunted their approval.

"Gentlemen, take a good look. John is a man with no worldly price and no instinct for self-preservation. All he wants is revenge so that he can make right an imbalance that has destroyed everything dear to him. In many ways, he is the most dangerous man you will ever encounter."

They all bowed gracefully. I'm pretty sure I blushed.

"Do you know how I knew your name, Mr. Lago? How I knew where you lived and about your history?"

"You read my book and you're a fan?"

Zhen laughed so hard the Beretta in his shoulder holster almost went off.

"I don't read books like that, Mr. Lago. The reason I know you is because of the man who hired Alice to kill me."

The little hairs on the back of my neck stood up.

"And who might that be?" I asked.

"I am not at liberty to say and you are not at liberty to ask."

I changed my tack.

"May I ask why he wants you dead?"

"He doesn't. He wants *you* dead. You and your lovely wife."

I felt the blood drain out of my face. The whole thing was a setup—the FBI mole, the mystery client . . . I knew the *what* but the *why* was what I was trying to Scooby-Doo as we hurtled to an uncertain fate in the back of Zhen's limo. It must have been a play for HR, revenge for our hostile takeover. The FBI gig was meant to get us both smoked. When he realized we were going to make it out, he went for the divide-and-conquer package. After all, who better to kill us than, well, us? He played us with our own dissonant chords of paranoia, lack of trust, and homicidal rage. He made us mortal enemies, and I had no way of telling Alice the truth. She was coming for us with everything she had and the only thing I could do to stop her was kill her.

"I believe Human Resources, Incorporated may have reached its expiration date," he said. "What do you think?"

"I think you're right as rain, Mr. Zhen."

For the life of me, I could not think who our mystery enemy could be. With both Bobs out of the way, I would somehow need to get that information out of Zhen. But I would have to deal with that later. As we drove on in silence, I was paying close attention to the landscape outside, racking my brain on how to communicate with Alice. If I went for my phone, they would blow my brains out. Short of smoke signals through the sunroof, I was SOL.

We appeared to be heading north, upstate, and into a remote area. The road was narrowing and we were climbing much of the time. I could also see a stone safety wall on the side of the road with a significant drop on the other side. Then I recalled several car commercials I had seen that were shot on this road. We were on the scenic byway near Port Jervis and Hawk's Nest, New York. The drop on the other side of the stone wall was probably forty to sixty feet, with the Delaware River at the bottom.

"Where are we going?" I asked.

"You'll see," he said quietly and lit a cigarette.

No sooner did the words and smoke exit his tobacco-stained lips than I heard the distant sound of helicopter rotors.

"I'm wondering if there's an alternate route."

"Why?" he asked.

"Because my first duty as your employee is to inform you that you are about to be ambushed by what sounds like an Mi-24 Russian attack helicopter."

45

Zhen looked out the windows, searching the skies.

"I don't see anything."

"She won't parallel us until she's ready to engage," I offered. "My guess is that she's about twenty or thirty clicks east flying below radar, striping us with GPS."

"She?"

"My wife."

"How would she know our movements?"

"That's what she does. What you need to worry about right now is the fact that this road is a death trap for the next twenty miles and all we have to look forward to is a long suspension bridge, which absolutely defines the phrase *sitting duck*."

"We will stop and go on foot into the forest."

"Infrared will track us and the .50 caliber miniguns will shred us in less than sixty seconds. This car is our best line of defense."

"Against antiaircraft missiles?"

"Yeah, well, we still need to make sure those don't come into play or we'll be proper fucked."

"How do we stop them? With small arms? Don't be ridiculous."

I could hear the chopper more clearly now.

"May I use my phone? I'm going to try to call her."

Zhen considered this and then nodded in agreement. I pulled

my phone out and tried over and over to call and text Alice, but to no avail, and I wasn't surprised. If you think texting and driving is deadly, try texting and flying a combat helicopter.

"Do you have a police or military radio?" I asked.

"No," he said.

"Looks like Plan B."

I put my phone away and went to open my briefcase. Zhen's men immediately put their guns in my face again. The whole scene was starting to play like a Mel Brooks musical. *Christmas with Chairman Mao!*

"What are you doing, Mr. Lago?" Zhen said.

"If you want to live, we need what's in this case," I said.

"What is it?"

"Let me show you."

"Open it," he said to his men. "What is the combination?"

"Triple zeroes."

One of them opened my case. Inside was a flight control stick, additional controls, and avionics displays and gauges.

"What is this?" Zhen asked.

"It's a portable flight console for a Wing Loong drone."

Zhen raised an eyebrow.

"Funny, right? It's the knockoff of the U.S. Reaper drone your government built based on hacked U.S. military tech stolen by you. Kind of like the almost-Nike shoes you've been selling for years. Got it for a good price, actually."

"Why would you bring that to meet with me, Mr. Lago?"

"Because, Mr. Zhen, until about five minutes ago, I was using you as bait to draw Alice out and kill her."

"What?!" he screamed.

"Yeah, sorry about that. But after what you told me, things have gotten exponentially complicated because I don't want to kill her anymore."

He put his own gun in my face.

"If you don't, I'll kill you."

"Mr. Zhen, that's not the best motivator for me. And if you shoot me, there will be nothing to stop her from putting an antitank missile in your glove compartment and turning this thing into a five-hundred-thousand-dollar Crock-Pot."

He was seething but realized threats were futile and put his gun away. He had no choice but to trust me. He started speaking to his men in Chinese, isolating me. But I knew they were talking contingency plans. I was just hoping that didn't involve group suicide. I had heard that Chinese agents were big on punching their own ticket to avoid capture or if they were facing disgrace. I laughed to myself, thinking I might actually have to protect Zhen from himself, along with everything else.

"How soon can you get the drone here?" he asked me.

"Ten minutes or less once I deploy. We may not even have that much time."

"Do it," he said.

His men handed the drone console to me. I fired it up and bounced the telemetry signal to its command satellite. It came online immediately. I pulled up the LCD display with video and data feed and commanded the drone to our location, and we watched the video from the nose-cone camera as the drone flew inland from the Atlantic. While it vectored itself to us, my mind was working overtime to solve the world's most deranged word problem: "John is traveling north at 90 mph in a car. Alice is capable of closing on John from 20 miles away in a Russian attack chopper traveling east at 150 mph. A Wing Loong drone is flying toward John and Alice from the south at 350 mph. Who will reach John first? (a) The chopper, (b) The drone, or (c) All of the above." I've never been great at math, but statistically speaking, we were probably all going to come together and die at once.

Chasing the ultimate long-shot bet—save Alice *and* Zhen and ride off into the sunset—I fired up the drone video feed on my console and switched through all camera angles, seeing it had a full 360-view around itself. While the drone hauled ass to our position, we heard the chopper rotors much louder. It sounded very much like Alice had decided to move on us, which made sense due to the fact that our position on the road gave us zero escape options. As that thought crossed my mind, the first pass of Alice's .50 caliber minigun rocked our world. If you're unfamiliar with a minigun, think one of those old-school Gatling guns but about a thousand times more powerful, firing rounds as big as the head on a lucky Chinese cat statue. The blazing hot meteorites of lead and metal hit the car with such force that Zhen's driver could barely keep it on the road. I was quietly impressed that the bulletproofing could withstand munitions that large, coming in that hot.

Zhen took cover on the floor of the limo. I looked out the window and laid eyes on the chopper as it turned to come back for a second pass. I was banking on Alice wanting to avoid a U.S. military response and to use her missiles only as a last resort. I checked the drone-targeting screen. GPS put it in striking distance and I had a visual of the chopper. Then I had a visual of the drone through the car window. Decision time.

46

I immediately thought of the time Bob initiated me into HR, how he subjected me to a merciless onslaught in the middle of the woods until I had no fight left in me. He wanted me to be willing to accept death. That was the lesson. And I never would have learned the lesson without Bob's total commitment to making me feel like I had no control over the situation and death was imminent. That's what I decided I needed to do with Alice in that moment. Evading and defending would only incite her predatory instinct more. She would assume weakness and do whatever she had to do to exploit it. I didn't want to kill her. In fact, I had never been more motivated to protect her in our lives. However, I needed her to believe that I not only wanted to kill her, but that I also had complete control and her destruction was imminent. She still had a much stronger survival instinct than me, so I believed she would retreat if need be. That was the goal. But until then, I had to walk the tightrope, with killing her for real on one side and getting myself killed on the other. The thought of never being able to tell her the truth fueled me to the core and I deployed every ounce of skill, experience, and intelligence to ensure that did not happen.

I pointed the drone right at her and gunned it. She immediately took evasive action. I whipped through the air like a cobra head and opened up on her with my own minigun, being careful not to hit her but attempting to get close enough to make it feel real. Despite its age, the Mi-24 is more nimble than it looks, and she dove out of the way of my fire. I made another aggressive pass. Alice banked hard right and tried to fly low to get the drone to overshoot and pass overhead. Nice idea but I anticipated that move and the drone glided back in just behind her. You do not want a drone on your ass under any circumstances. That's the tactical equivalent of dropping the soap in the shower of a Turkish prison. I fired up the drone's advanced weapons systems. My targeting grid started tracking Alice's chopper, working to execute a missile lock. I'm sure this lit up her radar board and she banked hard left and flew right at the limo, strafing us again with her miniguns.

The impact shook the car so violently that the driver smashed his head on the bulletproof window and was knocked unconscious. When it rains, it pours! All hell broke loose as the big tank of a car started swerving all over the road, pitching Zhen and his men and their guns all over the place. I had to get Alice off our ass so I could regain control of the car, so I deactivated my target locking systems and fired a missile in her general direction. The missile wasn't locked on her, but it came close enough for me to achieve my objective. While she took evasive action, I blew open the driver partition with one of the assault rifles and climbed into the driver's seat. I drove the car with one hand and operated the drone with the other. Now that's multitasking!

As the missile I had fired plowed into a hillside and exploded, blowing a hundred-foot burning black dust cloud into the sky, Alice turned to come in for another pass. I flanked her with the drone, forcing her to engage with it and not the limo. Every time she tried to maneuver to get a clear shot, I mirrored every move she made. This really pissed her off and she aggressively tried to peel away with a diving side turn. The tail yawed wildly and she nearly went into a death spin, but after a few harrowing moments Alice righted the ship. And when she did, the drone was right next to her again, mirroring the chopper's every move, flying within a quarter mile of it at all times. Her overtaxed engine began to spew black smoke but Alice kept pushing it, so I backed off.

Bad idea. Next thing I knew, Alice's chopper had disappeared into a ravine. I pursued her with the drone but lost her briefly around the high tree canopy. I slowed my air speed and switched it to a search mode. Still no sign of her. I didn't like that at all. Then I remembered why the helicopter is superior in combat to a fixed-wing aircraft: a chopper can hover. She was behind that tree cover somewhere, watching me, waiting for me to slow my drone's air speed and come looking for her—which I had done. The drone doesn't have an actual pilot with the ability to hear the rotors and triangulate location. My video feeds had nothing but the drone's own engine sounds coming over audio.

I tried to accelerate and get the drone out of there, but it was too late. Alice knew this was her only chance to kill my drone and she took it. She rose straight up behind me and opened fire with everything she had. The drone was peppered with .50 caliber rounds and my warning lights started to flash. She had missile lock on me. I switched to my rear camera in time to see her fire a 9M17 Skorpion missile. The good news is that the Mi-24 is more of a tank buster, so this type of missile is usually reserved for fixed targets on the ground. It has a minimum range of 500 meters and a max of 2,500—not one of your sophisticated antiaircraft missiles. The bad news is that I was not even 1,000 meters from the chopper when she fired it.

I turned the nose on the drone to the sky and maxed the throttle. It went straight up through the clouds and the missile followed it. Drones are very difficult to hit, even with a hard missile target lock. They're agile and able to make moves a human pilot in a much heavier aircraft couldn't pull off or physically endure. So, I pulled out every evasive maneuver I could think of and sent that missile on a wild-goose chase, hoping to shed it like a cheap suit. After threading the needle between two massive oak trees with a sideways vertical pass, the missile hit a grove of trees and exploded.

Meanwhile, I steered the Rolls-Royce tank through the winding roads and saw what was ahead—the Roebling Delaware Aqueduct suspension bridge. The limo would never make it across that bridge because Alice would simply blow it and send us plummeting into the drink, where she could pound us until there was nothing left. I estimated I had about three minutes before reaching the bridge. Then she put all of her cards on the table. She target locked the limo *and* the drone and fired two Skorpions at once.

The way I saw it, I had two choices: either ditch out the driver's-side door of the limo and lose any chance of getting a name out of Zhen, or attempt to shoot down the incoming missile with my drone missile. Since my missiles were ten times more sophisticated than hers, I decided to go for the latter. It took me forever to lock on to the limo-bound missile because my drone was simultaneously evading one missile while trying to target lock and destroy another.

I finally locked it and fired but I wasn't even sure my missile would hit the Skorpion before the Skorpion stung us. I was about a hundred yards from the bridge when I saw both missiles come raining down toward the limo, their warheads pointed like the end of a middle finger right at my face. Then we hit the bridge, way past the point of no return. When both missiles were less than a quarter mile from impact, I slammed on the brakes. Within seconds of that move, my drone missile hit the Skorpion head-on and scrubbed it.

The problem was that this impact took place less than 300 yards from the limo. The explosion lifted the front end of the car so far off the ground it must have looked like a dog begging on its hind legs. When it came down again, it smashed into the concrete bridge wall and stalled. I was thrown up against the dash and rolled down onto the floor. With one hand, I was trying to pull myself back into the driver's seat. With the other I was clutching the joystick on the drone flight module. I could see the second missile closing the gap on the drone as I hung there, totally useless.

When I finally got back into the driver's seat, I looked out and saw that the second missile was dangerously close to the drone. So, I pinned the throttle on the drone and ran continuous 360-degree loops around the chopper, maintaining a distance of no less than 200 yards. As the drone dropped into orbit around the chopper with the missile on its tail, Alice opened fire, blasting her heavy guns in a futile attempt to slow down the drone. I knew immediately that Alice had made a fatal mistake because the much stronger heat signature coming from her machine guns and her overheated chopper engine caused the missile to lock on to her as its new target.

It went straight at her and it was way too close for her to evade it. I hit the afterburners on the drone and chased the missile, unloading my miniguns at it, doing everything in my power to get it off Alice's ass. Alice attempted to move to a lower altitude near the forest to try to lose the missile in the trees but that did nothing. It was headed straight for her cockpit. I had no choice but to try to shoot it down, even though Alice was directly behind it in my line of fire. I hit the miniguns again and managed to blow the tail off the missile. Without its tail wings, it veered wildly off course. I hoped it would just fly past her but it clipped Alice's rotor head fairing and blew off two of her five rotor blades, stopping the main rotor dead and turning the chopper into a lead balloon that plunged straight down into the forest. After it disappeared into the trees, its fuel tanks exploded on impact, setting the forest ablaze and filling the sky with black smoke.

I got out of the car and tried to see it but it was gone.

Alice was gone.

47

I sent the drone crashing into the river below and looked into the back of the limo. All of Zhen's men were dead. Judging from the bright red color of their skin, they had swallowed cyanide capsules. Zhen was nowhere in sight.

I looked back at the flames and the loss of Alice hit me like a bullet in the chest. She was dead. In trying to save us both, I had killed the woman I loved. I had risked my neck so many times to show her I loved her. The only thing that had been important to me *was* loving her. It was even more important than living. It was what made me truly strong, even if for a brief time in my life. The rest of me, the violence and destruction, the soullessness and depravity, were what made me weak. With her, I was solid as a rock. Without her, I was nothing.

How had I lost that? At what point did I decide to abandon my conviction, my truth? In her own moment of weakness, she falsely accused me of betraying her, and even tried to kill me as a traitor, but I should have seen right away that we'd been set up. And I should have demanded she allow me to prove her wrong. I should have done everything in my power to make her trust me again. Instead, my ugly, vicious ego stepped in and I did what I do best. Kill things. Even when I'm trying to do right, I kill things.

And all I could think was *What now? Where do I go from here?* Sure as hell not back to HR. *I should have ended this in Mexico,* I thought. I had my chance to rid the world of me and I punked out. And after seeing Alice die, killing myself felt like another selfish, bullshit, escapist John Lago card trick.

Now you see me . . .

"Lago?" I heard Zhen's weak whisper from inside the limo.

I looked inside. Zhen was sitting against one of his dead men with a huge gash on his forehead. His pupils were as big as dinner plates and his face was pale. His shirt was soaked through with his blood. When I looked closer, I could see that his head had more than a gash. It was a bullet entry wound. Based on the amount of blood, he was already breathing on borrowed time. He looked at me for a long beat, as if he were trying to remember something he wanted to say.

"Zhen," I said.

"I am dying," he said.

"Do you want me to call for help?" I asked, knowing there was no way I was going to do that.

He chuckled slightly and coughed up a bit of blood.

"You amuse me, Lago."

"Happy to oblige. Now maybe you can oblige me with the name of your friend."

"Come closer. There are eyes and ears everywhere, John."

I moved closer and he whispered the name in my ear. It hit my brain like a sledgehammer.

"What do you plan to do?"

I was so stunned, I didn't even hear him at first.

"John."

I turned to him.

"What are you going to do?"

"I think we know the answer to that question," I said quietly.

"You can't just kill him. You have to destroy all of it. There are others, but he's the leader. If he's dead, and there is nothing left to salvage, then your revenge is complete."

I thought about the sheer insanity of what I had to do.

"I'm not sure I have the means," I said absently.

"I will help you."

"How?"

"Money. With money, all is possible. All is . . ."

He wavered dizzily and fought to remain conscious.

"Listen and remember," he said and gave me the number of an offshore account.

"There is more than enough . . . I am very—"

He tried to hug himself for warmth from shock but could barely move his arms.

"Cold," he said, and died.

Then I heard a chirping sound. It was the sound of my phone, somewhere in the car. I searched for it among the stiff and stinking corpses of Zhen's men. When I found it, there must have been fifty missed calls and text messages from Sue. I looked at the latest text:

Alice is alive. She's been calling me for help. What happened? Where the fuck are you? Call me!

48

I ran flat out toward the chopper wreckage. It must have been a solid five miles from the bridge but I didn't care. Surrounding the wreckage was a massive forest fire. The smoke was thick and I had to crawl for what seemed like hours trying to find Alice. Sue was guiding me with the GPS, but the smoke and the heat and the weak phone signal made that spotty at best. I could feel my body being singed and seared by the flaming debris falling from the sky, but I pushed through it, keeping my face up and away from the heat as best I could.

When I was on the verge of exhaustion and smoke asphyxiation, I heard Alice calling weakly in the forest. Then I found her hanging from a burning tree by her parachute, upside down and beat up, but alive. I called Sue and told him to get his ass over there to pick us up. He had stolen a jacked-up Ford Bronco from some Brooklyn hipsters and was off-roading to our location. I climbed up the tree, the callused flesh on my hands sizzling and smoking like pork chops on a grill, to get Alice down. She looked at me as if she were dreaming.

"John? What . . . are you doing here? I must be dead. We're both dead, right?"

Her eyes were glassy and she was on the edge of losing consciousness, so I figured that was no time to start splitting hairs over semantics.

"Yeah, we're dead. And we're in hell," I said as I blew out the flames on my fingertips and worked on getting her out of the parachute harness.

"That explains the fire."

"Right. Can you pull your arm out of there?"

Then she punched me right in the face.

"Motherfucker," she whispered and passed out.

I anchored myself to the tree and with one of her parachute lines pulled her the rest of the way out of the harness. Then I threw her over my shoulder and climbed down the tree. She was still out cold, so I carried her two miles out of the blazing forest to the rendezvous point where Sue picked us up.

He drove us into the city in his urban hillbilly wagon with Alice passed out in the back. On the way, I filled him in on the situation, about the mystery puppet master that Zhen had named for me and how we'd been set up by that motherfucker from the moment Alice and I started running HR. Sue seemed relieved, like a kid whose parents told him they'd decided not to get a divorce after all. It was weird, in an *Outlaw Josey Wales* kind of way, but it felt like we were all one big happy family on a road trip.

When we got back to Manhattan, we went to my favorite cash-only chop shop hospital for wounded bad guys. They sedated Alice and treated her for smoke inhalation and a couple of broken ribs. I treated Sue and myself to a bottle of their low-grade mob doctor Scotch from the medicine cabinet while she got some rest. Sue polished off half the bottle in one gulp. Kid can drink like a Siberian oil worker who just lost his woman and beaver socks in a card game. I sent him to check in on HR so I could be alone with Alice when she woke up.

"Mom and Dad need some quality time," I said.

"Hit me when you're ready to circle the wagons, JL."

It was around midnight when Alice came to. She started crying when she saw me sitting next to the bed.

"What's wrong?" I asked. "Aside from all the obvious things?"

"I'm sorry," she said.

She saw the utterly bewildered look on my face.

"I heard what you and Sue were talking about in the car. I feel like such an idiot. Even worse, I'm the traitor for not trusting you. You should put me out of my misery, right now. I'm not worth it, John."

I hugged her tightly, being careful not to squeeze her ribs.

"We both stopped believing in each other, Alice. Never again."

"Never again."

She pulled me closer and winced from the pain.

"Broken ribs. You need to sleep," I said.

"Don't leave," she said wearily.

"I'll be right here," I said.

She started to doze off but then grabbed my arm.

"John?"

"Yeah?"

"When I wake up, promise me we're going to kill that motherfucker."

"I promise," I said, kissing her on the head. "Sweet dreams."

49

I got a call from Sue early the next morning. He had been locked out of HR. When he tried Alice's access code, same thing. Later that morning, when he went looking for Rebecca to figure out what was up, he found her dead in her apartment. She'd been shot in the head and her body was in the tub, decomposing in an acid bath. Professional job, albeit sloppy. Someone was cleaning up.

Sue was completely freaking out, rabid with anger and raw with grief. I told him not to go home and to get off the street. There were no safe places left and we had to assume anything that was a part of our lives before was now part of a very intricate death trap. He pulled himself together and met us at the chop shop hospital. Alice tried to comfort him, but he was in a very bad way about Becca. And it hit too close to home for me. Eva all over again.

We had to make a move on the puppet master. With what had gone down at HR, it was a solid bet we could find him there, no doubt holding the recruits hostage until he decided either to kill them all or find them another slave master. When I wrote *The Intern's Handbook,* my intention was to help the recruits, to lend guidance where I'd had none. I failed. If anything, I was the reason they were all staring down the barrel of yet another person in a position of power looking to use them up and throw them away. *No más.* It was time to end the nightmare and try to salvage what was left of those poor kids. It was time to destroy HR from the top down.

The three of us stayed holed up at the hospital for the next few days. As long as the money kept flowing, I could rely on the ghoulish docs there to keep their traps shut. In that time, we worked out our entire plan to take down HR and our own personal Wizard of Oz. Zhen's account had roughly $80 million in it. He was right. It was more than enough. Infiltration wasn't all that complicated, as Alice and I had designed the HR security system and there was no way they'd had time to replace it in her absence. All we needed was some backup.

"How many swinging dicks you think we need, JL?"

"At least twenty."

"Thirty," Alice said. "Let's stack the deck."

"Thirty it is. Now, where are we going to find thirty cold-blooded killers who know how to handle a gun and won't soil their britches when they see someone pointing one at them?" I pondered.

Sue started laughing.

"What?" I asked.

"I got this," he said and started making calls.

It was going to cost us a good chunk from Zhen's war chest, but Sue guaranteed we'd have the ballers we needed to get the job done. Alice and I worked on the weaponry. Within twenty-four hours, we had everything and everyone we needed to turn Human Resources, Inc. into a smoking ruin. The problem was, we had no idea what had happened to the recruits because Sue had not heard from any of them since he'd been locked out of HR.

50

The night before the siege on HR, I carved out some much-needed alone time with Alice. Since being reunited, all we had done was draw up battle plans and spend copious amounts of money on weapons and ammo. I needed to take a moment with her because, quite frankly, I was fairly certain we were not going to survive another day in Oz and I wanted to make up for lost time. When darkness fell, I handed Alice a Barneys bag and told her to get dressed. She looked stunning in the Helmut Lang black jumpsuit and black Belstaff boots.

"What's the occasion?" she asked. "Alice Cooper's funeral?"

"We're going out," I said. "And by out, I mean . . . out."

I donned my all-black Ralph Lauren Black Label gear and escorted Alice to the nearest rooftop, where I uncorked a 1988 Krug champagne. We drank straight from the bottle.

"Darling wife?"

"Yes, handsome husband?"

"I'm going to take you on a little adventure tonight."

"Really? Do tell."

"As you know, I'm fond of rooftops. I chose this particular rooftop because, from here, we can go on an entire date without ever touching the sidewalk."

"Sounds lovely," she said, kissing me.

"Are you and your ribs up to it?"

"Absolutely. Oxycontin is my new best friend."

"Outstanding. Shall we go to dinner?"

"By all means."

We finished the champagne and went roof-hopping. Alice loved it. For dinner, we landed on Ichimura, my favorite sushi restaurant. The chef himself had prepared a private rooftop dinner for us and we ate under the stars, just a normal couple, enjoying an evening out. We actually talked about subjects that had nothing to do with high-velocity ammunition or the most stable explosive compounds.

After dinner, I had a real treat for Alice. I took her back to the Four Seasons, where we got married. We couldn't be seen checking into a hotel, so we hopped on the lower-level roof and took the service elevator to the top. The Ty Warner Penthouse, our old stomping grounds, was still being renovated from when we blew a nine-foot hole in the floor and massacred Bob II and his goons. So, the suite was vacant for the night!

Sue had already dropped off my supplies for the evening—via a construction crew drink cooler—earlier in the day. I had a full bar with mixers, snacks from Dean & DeLuca, and other . . . things that Alice was fond of . . . We walked in and I lit some candles and made us both a drink.

"John, what did I do to deserve you? I am racking my brain and nothing but bad things come to mind."

"Maybe that's it. I'm opposite karma. I'm what you get when you live an evil, murderous existence."

"When you put it that way, it actually makes sense."

We kissed and I walked her to the spot where we had our ceremony. The hole in the floor was still there, although partially repaired.

"What are you doing?" she asked. "We're going to fall in."

"We're going to finish what we started here."

"Is there someone else down there for us to kill?"

She peered into the hole.

"No, we never said our vows on our wedding night and, if you don't mind, I'd love to say them now."

"Oh, honey." She kissed me. "But we don't have the preacher man and that . . . book."

"The Bible?"

"Right. That one."

"We don't need either. Let's just say what's in our hearts. I know it's cheesy, but I feel the need to do it. To voice our truth about each other. Man, that's even cheesier. Sorry."

"It's not cheesy," she said, tears welling in her eyes. "I want to do it. You go first."

I held her hands and looked into her eyes and we both started laughing immediately.

"Okay, sorry," I said.

"Yeah, me too. Serious now," she said.

And that made it worse. We were both laughing so hard we could barely breathe.

"I got this!" I said. "Sorry . . ."

We both took a deep breath and Alice kissed me.

"Ready?" she asked.

"Ready."

She held my hand.

"Then please proceed."

"I, John Lago, being of somewhat sound mind and ripped body, take you, Alice, being totally insane and with smoking body, to be my wife. I promise to love you, above all else, and to never go to bed mad—or to engage in hand-to-hand combat with you, shoot, stab, burn, or bludgeon you, or fire an air-to-air ballistic missile at you again. I promise to trust you with my life, to allow you to trust me with yours, and to always have your six, even in a noncombat situation. Till death, or a lengthy prison term, do us part."

Tears were streaming down her face. And she was still laughing.

"That was beautiful," she said.

"Now you," I said.

"I, Alice, take you, John Lago, to be my hot husband. I promise to love the shit out of you, maybe even until it hurts. Actually, definitely until it hurts. I promise to be an aggressive, predatory, highly disagreeable bitch to everyone *but* you, and I promise never to attempt to maim, cripple, or kill you, even if you leave dishes in the sink."

"I knew you hated that."

"So why do it? Anyway, shut up, I'm not done. I promise to trust *you* with not only my life, but also my soul, and I promise that you can trust me with yours. And I promise to always make love to you with rabid enthusiasm and a willingness to try anything at least once. Oh, and I promise to do old-school wife things for you, even though I don't have to—like cooking, buying you cool clothes, and running a bath for you when you've had a hard day—because I want to, because I love you, John. I fucking love you, baby."

We were both crying at that point.

"You may kiss the groom," I said.

We kissed and melted into each other, and with half of Manhattan glancing away from the TV to witness, we made love like two people who meant everything they just said.

51

The next night, we drove a tour bus full of weapons and explosives to the Bronx to pick up our new crew. When we arrived, thirty street-hardened black men stepped out of their luxury rides. These guys were muscle, pure and simple. And judging from their cars and clothes, they were high-priced muscle who made reams of paper working for drug dealers, made guys, and anyone else who wanted their problems to go down in a blaze of glory.

"You guys selling candy bars so you can go to Disneyland?" I asked.

They laughed. Good. I wasn't going into HR with a bunch of loose-cannon hotheads. These guys were pros with a quiet, menacing ease. One of them approached me carrying a gold-and-onyx-plated Uzi. He walked up, his barrel less than two feet away, and smiled a mouth full of gold fronts with "187" laid out in diamonds on them.

"You got the money?" he asked.

I pulled my jacket back, revealing my souvenir from Mexico—the gold-plated .45 with a platinum Virgin Mary inlaid in the grip.

"As a matter of fact, I do," I said.

Sue showed them thirty black duffel bags, stuffed to maximum capacity with hundreds.

"I don't know how you come up with that much cash so quick," he whispered, "but you just bought up the whole playground, G."

His crew laughed.

"Let's go smoke some bitches, shall we?" I said.

"That's what we do," he said, and we loaded up on the bus.

On the way to HR, our gangsta crew was playing puff puff pass with a spliff the size of a baby's arm. They offered it to me but I needed something opposite for my pregame.

"Got any ups?" I asked.

They laughed. One of them produced a Ziploc bag full of drugs that could have housed a Thanksgiving turkey.

"Put your ass in the stratosphere if you want."

"I want."

I pulled out a stack of hundreds.

"Nah. Put that away. First taste is always free."

He assembled four different pills and a minuscule plastic vial of bluish powder on his dinner plate hand.

"I call this the V12. You got your Mexican Molly, Dutch Molly, OG Dexy, and a Calcium Channel Blocker to keep your heart rate and blood pressure even while you busting out on all twelve cylinders."

"What's the powder?"

"Pure ginseng root. Couple hours after the hit you piss all the poison out. Hopefully on the face of the guy you just capped."

"Remind me to get your pager number after this. You're my new best friend."

I hit his V12 cocktail, as instructed, and it was everything he promised—high-octane brain clarity and a physical rush that had me convinced I could do anything Iron Man can do but without the suit. Took the cardiac meds next. Worked like a charm. Even. Smooth. Clear.

"We're getting close," Alice said. "Gear up."

"Yes, ma'am," I said and strapped myself with two SIG MPX-K submachine guns, a dozen 9-mm twenty-round mags, and two SIG P226 pistols with eighteen-round mags. And stylish Kevlar body armor, of course.

"What'd you guys knock over, the Department of Defense?" my new drug dealer best friend asked.

"Yeah, man," another one said to me. "We're keeping this G.I. Joe shit after the gig. Feel me?"

"You walk away from this gig and you can keep whatever you want," I said.

They laughed. Confident. Cocky. These guys had no idea who they were dealing with. We rounded the block and the location was in sight:

Human Resources, Inc.

We parked in the loading docks in the back of the building. When Alice, Sue, and I stepped out of the bus, we stood at the entrance of HR for the last time. The street was strangely quiet.

"Welcome to Human Resources, Inc.," I said.

"You'll go to interesting places," Alice continued, "meet unique and stimulating people from all walks of life—"

"And kill them," Sue said.

"Let's do this," I said.

Alice kissed me.

"I know part of why you did what you did last night was because you're afraid we won't make it out of here," she said, "but I promise you there's no way we're going to lose."

"Hell no," Sue said. "Failure is not an option."

"We need some kind of Three Musketeers call to arms thing," I said.

"Smart-ass." Alice smiled.

Our gangsta army filed out, bristling with weapons like urban Marines on an assault mission. We locked and loaded outside because as soon as we breached the doors, it was going to be on, and we needed to be ready. I was ready.

I was matte steel and composite . . .

Smooth black Kevlar . . .

Powder, lead, and fire.

I was the bullet. And I had a name etched on my dull gray face, just above my gaping hollow-point mouth. That night I was going to break the place and the man that made me.

52

We opened the loading dock doors with military breaching charges that didn't sound like much more than a car backfiring. But we knew it was going to be enough to alert whoever was inside to our presence. When we got inside, we were fully expecting a firefight, but the place was empty. Lights were out on all the floors and there was no sign of life.

We were about to call it a night when I remembered the subbasement. That part of the building was the original HR back when the rest of it was full of legit businesses. Over the years, Bob had acquired the rest of the building and closed it off. I knew about it because I'm nosy and I used to steal what Bob stored down there — booze, pharmaceuticals, money, guns, ammo, IDs, credit cards, and the occasional stinger missile.

We used the service stairwells to head down there. When we opened the access door, one of my gangstas peered out onto the subbasement's main floor. It was dark and all was quiet — a very bad sign.

"All clear," he started to say. "Let's—"

A metallic *zip* sound preceded his brains being blown all over us and the back of the stairwell.

"Follow my lead," I whispered.

I slammed two titanium combat knives into the metal fire door and motioned for one of the thugs to grab them like handles. Then I shot the hinges off the door and we advanced into the room, clustered behind the door. Silenced 9-mm rounds were spraying the door and ricocheting all around us. We watched our flanks, blasting anything that moved. We lost one of our crew but managed to take cover in another room with only one access door. We donned night vision specs and I surveyed the scene.

It was a death trap.

An unknown number of shooters started blasting and I made everyone lay low while I counted weapons and rounds. Sounded like maybe twenty of them. I knew exactly what subs they had and exactly what sidearms, and since they were going all redcoat on us with the firing line, I was able to guesstimate when they were tapped. As the silenced hellfire started to peter out a bit and I could hear slapping mags, we busted out of there like Pamplona bulls looking to gore-fuck a few tourists. Turned out this was a gangsta specialty. These guys were like Spartan soldiers in a frontal assault. Anyone they didn't fill with lead they eviscerated with brass-knuckle knives.

Blood flew like ocean spray on the bow of a ship and bodies fell all around these man mountains in basketball kicks and leather coats the size of a full steer hide. It was beautiful! But I was also on a 50,000-volt high, moving, shooting, cutting, punching, and kicking like Van Damme in fast-forward. And Alice and Sue were right there with me.

My gangstas were gaining ground and control of the enemy thugs, pushing them back with their fearlessness and new-school Wild West gun-wielding skills. This allowed me to penetrate deeper into the maze, where I heard the sound of voices yelling for help. I tracked down the source of the sound. It was coming from a room behind a locked metal fire door. Alice blew off the hinges with her MPX-K and I kicked the door in. It flopped straight down and skidded across the floor and Alice and I ran in with some of our gangstas.

That's when I saw all of the recruits.

They were zip-tied at the wrists and ankles and lying facedown on the floor. Sue ran in after us.

"All clear out there," he said.

I pointed to the recruits. Then we heard the electronic pop of an M7 blasting cap and the back wall burst into flames . . . followed by the wall next to it, then the next, until the room was engulfed in fire.

"It's a trap! We need to get them out of here!" I bellowed.

"John, look!" Alice yelled.

Sue and I followed her gaze to the ceiling, which was wired with what appeared to be enough explosives to demo the whole building. They were the C4 charges I had planted at HR long ago. We had a matter of seconds before the heat or flames set them off.

"Move!"

We snapped out our blades and cut the zip ties as fast as we could, getting the recruits to their feet, then we ripped the duct tape off their mouths and jerked them back to reality.

"Go! Now!"

Everyone sprinted back through the cavernous subbasement maze. There were bodies everywhere and we had to pick our way through them while being blinded and choked out by the smoke. Then one of the members of our street crew ran up to me.

"Place is crawling with feds outside!"

"What?"

"We're surrounded. My crew and I are going to shoot our way out. Fuck trying to beat a federal rap. Sorry, man. Much respect."

He and his crew took off up the stairs. We followed them back up to the loading bay, where I could see an army of feds and local cops outside with their guns drawn.

Then the first round of explosives in the subbasement detonated.

"Get down!" Alice and I both yelled.

We all hit the deck as the building shook violently from the blast.

Outside, the feds and cops scattered, afraid the whole building was coming down on their heads.

Everyone headed for the loading bay doors. Just as we made it through the doors, one of the cops saw us.

"Freeze!" he yelled.

"Move now!" I screamed through the smoke and dust.

I opened fire on the cops and feds while Alice and the recruits made a run for it. When my mag ran out and I went to reload, the cops scrambled up from their cover positions and opened up on me. I felt a bullet rip through the side of my hip and the sudden agony made me drop my weapon. I had no real cover to speak of and the cops were getting ready to blast me into oblivion when the rest of the explosives in the subbasement detonated. A hail of brick, glass, and wood shrapnel exploded into the street. The concussion knocked the cops on their asses and the loading bay floor collapsed underneath me. I fell to the floor below and hit so hard I was knocked out cold. I'm not sure how long I was out, but eventually I started to see bright lights flashing in my eyes.

When I finally came to, a firefighter was standing over me, shining a flashlight at my pupils. He draped me carefully over his shoulder and carried me out of the rubble. The EMTs loaded me onto a gurney and two federal agents handcuffed me to it. My eyes searched for Alice and Sue in what looked like the aftermath of an urban war zone, but they were nowhere to be seen. As they quickly wheeled me to an ambulance, I watched Human Resources, Inc. finally implode and disappear from the Manhattan skyline.

53

I've been in custody now for a couple of weeks while Assistant Director Fletcher and his cronies decided what to do with their favorite insect specimen. Which makes me laugh, because the choices are pretty straightforward: death or a fate worse than death—life in this hole. I'm trying to imagine choking down the creamed spinach, creamed corn, creamed broccoli dinner rotation for the rest of my life, and all I can think of is hanging myself with a rope that I slowly weave out of the horrific cadaver meat they serve in the cafeteria.

I have one piece of good news. Recently, Assistant Director Fletcher's office sent me word that they were granting my request to see Alice. As you know, in exchange I had to give them information that led to her capture. Truth be told, I'm really looking forward to seeing her again, because as long as our target is still alive, neither of us has a snowball's chance in hell at surviving till next quarter—and that's being generous. Guys like him can do anything they want to anyone they want.

Anyway, my old buddy Fletch called me personally this morning to tell me that they have Alice in custody and they are bringing her to see me. So, I'm back under the bright fluorescent lights of my windowless cinder-block bug jar at Quantico, handcuffed to the chair and waiting to bask in the dawn's early light of my fate. I asked for a creepy Hannibal Lecter psycho-ward mask to try to lighten the mood, but Fletch didn't find that at all amusing. I'm actually a little nervous, which surprises me considering I truly have nothing left to lose. Fletcher walks in, smiling broadly like a dad about to surprise his son with a Red Ryder BB gun on Christmas morning.

"She's on her way, John."

"Somebody get me a mint," I joke.

Fletcher lights a cigarette. He doesn't offer me one. We hear footsteps coming down the hall. The tension is palpable. There is a knock on the door and Fletcher practically jumps out of his chair to open it. He's so eager it almost makes me ill. They wheel Alice into the room in a wheelchair. Her upper right arm and lower leg are both in casts.

"You've got five minutes, so make it count," Fletcher says. "You understand that anything you say is admissible as evidence?"

"I wouldn't have it any other way," I say.

Fletcher turns to Alice.

"Alice?"

"Yes," she says quietly, smirking at my partial body cast, which is itching like a son of a bitch.

"Guess they took the fight out of you in the first round, eh, John?" Fletcher asks, taunting.

I ignore him.

"What happened to you?" I ask Alice.

"Actually, I got pretty banged up during our Wild West show at HR. I was a week away from getting my casts off when, thanks to you, the feds found me this morning . . ."

"I'm sorry, I—"

"Please save it, John. I'm here now. You got what you wanted. And as the man said, you've got five minutes."

She glares at Fletch.

"Pretty inequitable exchange if you ask me," she says.

"Can we have a minute?" I ask him.

"Sure," he replies, gloating like a school bully.

They wheel her up to the table and position her on the opposite

end, handcuffing her to the chair and chaining it to the table. A
DON'T FEED THE ANIMALS sign is the only thing missing. Fletch and
company leave the room but I can see them peering through the
steel-reinforced window on the door.

Alice and I look at each other for a long time, both of us breathing the other in. She softens a bit and even manages a smile.

"How have you been?" I ask.

She looks at her leg and arm.

"Great. You?"

"Never better."

We laugh a little.

"I'm sorry, Alice."

"No you're not."

"I know you don't believe me."

"Why would I?"

"Because I really do love you."

"If you loved me, I wouldn't be here, John."

"You know the opposite is true. And you know you still love me,"
I say.

"Perhaps. But, like a chronic viral infection or a bad president,
I've learned to live with it," she says.

"Don't be bitter. We both know this is for the best."

"For who?"

"For us."

"John, is this why you brought me here? To tell me you're sorry
for bringing me here?"

"I needed to see you. After today—"

"Don't. This is pathetic enough as it is," she says.

"Is that all you have to say?" I ask.

She looks away for a beat, trying to hold back tears.

"You know, John. You weren't the only one who made a deal."

"What's that supposed to mean? I never made any deals."

I look at Fletch outside the door. He's pretending to be interested in his files while I know he's listening closely to everything we say.

"I figured since you ratted me out to save your ass, I should use whatever chips I had to stay out of the death row game."

Fletcher walks back in the room.

"I never ratted you out to save my ass."

"That's enough," he says. "Five minutes are up."

"What kind of deal did you make with Alice, Fletcher?"

"I said that's enough."

"I said I would give him the name of the person who really runs HR," Alice says defiantly. "And finally get this target off my back."

I look at Fletch for verification. He motions for his boys to come in the room and wheel Alice out.

"In exchange for what?"

"One of us has to die, John. You realize that, right? They can't just let both of us keep on breathing after everything we've done."

"Alice, if you tell him, we *both* die."

"You never give up, do you, John? Maybe I'll just tell him right now, in front of you, make our little visit that much more special," Alice says.

"Get her out of here," Fletcher says, moving closer to my end of the table.

"Don't you want to know the answer, Fletch?" she asks.

"Shut the fuck up, Alice," I say. "He's a liar. This is what he's been gaming for the whole time."

She turns to Fletcher. He puts his hand on the back of my chair.

"Don't listen to him, Alice," he says. "And don't say a word."

"Why not, Fletch?"

"Alice, you're on thin ice," Fletcher warns.

"I know why you don't want me to say it, Fletch," she says, leering at him, "because *you're* the person running HR . . . and you always have been."

54

Assistant Director Fletcher stares at her for a long beat. Then he looks at me. It's difficult to tell if he's angry or shocked or about to have a stroke. Finally, he grins, the corners of his mouth quivering slightly.

"I'll be filing both of your cases as enemy combatant status. You're both going to burn. But not until we drown you for information first. And this conversation is over."

"Then you'll burn with us, Fletch," I say.

And I lock his wrist in the handcuff I just took off of mine.

"What the fuck?" he says, reaching for his gun, which I am now holding.

I hit him upside the head and knock him into his chair. Agents draw their guns but before they can even think about pulling the trigger, I shoot them both in the feet and drop them, guns clattering, screaming in agony. Then I rest the barrel on Fletcher's head.

"Crawl your asses out of here now," I say to the wounded agents, "or I'll do him. And lock the door behind you. No one comes in!"

They comply, moaning like a couple of pansies the whole way.

"How did you get out of the cuffs?" Alice asks.

"You'd be surprised at all the fun and useful items you can buy from a prison guard. Those guys are like walking convenience stores."

Fletcher goes for the gun. I elbow him in the face and break his nose. Blood gushes down his shirtfront. Storm troopers are assembling outside the door. No doubt the place is going into lockdown. I wheel my chair over to Alice and point the gun at her face.

"So, this is it?" she says.

"This is most definitely it," I say.

"You figured we'd go out in a blaze of glory, huh?"

"Something like that," I say.

"Your Clint Eastwood complex is getting out of hand, John."

She closes her eyes.

"Okay. Blaze away."

"On three," I say.

Together we say, "One . . . two . . . three . . ."

And I lean over and kiss her.

Our kiss is deep and passionate. It's the kind of kiss that sucks all the air out of the room and if you aren't one of the two people kissing, you are dying to get out of there and catch your breath.

While Fletch looks on in shock, I unlock Alice's handcuff. She throws her good arm around me and practically pulls me off the table.

"I hope you're enjoying yourselves, because you're both dead. Try to find a place to hide. It doesn't exist."

"We don't really need to hide anymore, Fletch. We brought along a couple of get-out-of-jail-free cards."

Alice and I quietly pull thin metal cables hidden inside our casts that split them in half and lay both sides open. The insides of Alice's casts contain detonator wires. She pulls the metal bar from her arm cast—a stroke of genius to get her past the prison metal detector—and unscrews the end. Blasting caps slide out of the bar. She attaches them to the wires and I attach all of that to my two casts, which are made of high explosives.

"What the hell is that?" Fletcher says.

"Pretty cool, right?" Alice says to him and to the camera in the room.

I give him the two-cent tour.

"Fletch, you may want to take some notes. My cast is made of a very exotic military-grade explosive, a not-so-garden-variety cocrystal mixture of HMX, aka octogen, and CL-20, aka some shit I can't pronounce."

"It's used in armor-piercing missile warheads and there's easily enough here to take out everything in this building . . . and everything else in a quarter-mile radius," Alice adds.

"If you think that's going to get you out of here, you're sadly mistaken," Fletch warns.

"Oh, but this isn't our only party trick, Fletch."

"No way," Alice chimes in. "This is the FBI, right? Quantico. You got to go a lot bigger than this."

"Huge," I say.

"I'm calling your bluff," he says. "Take them out!" he yells at his men outside.

They start to come in and I clap twice, like the old guy on the TV commercial turning a lamp on with the Clapper. A nearby explosion—a sizable one based on the sound—rocks the room like an earthquake.

"What did you do?" Fletcher asks, legitimately shaken by the reality check that just kicked him in the nuts.

He puts his hand up to stop his goons from "taking us out."

"That was an old storage room where the FBI keeps illegal wiretap records on American citizens. Buh-bye. No one went to G-man heaven yet, but if we blow what's in both of our casts right now— along with all the other devices we've planted—there's enough of this shit to vaporize your entire beloved Quantico and all the fresh-faced recruits in it."

Fletcher's eyes are darting around. He's trying to think of something, anything.

"I don't know if he's convinced, Alice," I say.

"Yeah, Fletch, how about another demonstration."

I raise my hands to clap.

"No!" he says. "I believe you."

"Good," I say. "I'm glad we're finally on the same page."

"I need to tell the duty commanders about this. Otherwise, they'll send the cavalry up here. If they haven't already."

"We thought of that too," I say.

"We're very thorough," Alice says.

"Hey, Sue!" I yell.

Sue appears on the security monitor in the corner of the room. He waves at the camera like a fanboy on *Good Morning America*. He's holding a SIG MPX submachine gun.

"Hi, guys!" he says. "Check it out. I brought some friends with me!"

The entire recruit class of HR, Inc. files in behind him, also holding MPX rigs and also waving like dumbasses.

Fletcher looks at the video screen, incredulous. All of the lobby personnel are zip-tied and gagged on the floor.

"That's your lobby," Alice says, "and that's your duty commander zip-tied to the potted palm."

"And those are the illustrious HR recruits," I say proudly. "While your men and the cops were trying not to get shot by me and running for their mamas when the building blew, they all skipped out, along with our new friends from the Bronx."

"Honey, you're my hero," Alice says. "Staying behind to take the heat for all of us."

"You're worth it, darling," I say.

"You wanted to get caught," Fletcher says.

"Of course," I say. "But I figured if I turned myself in, you might get a little suspicious."

"And while you and your cronies decided my fate, Alice and Sue worked out the details of sealing yours. Sue, show Fletch what's behind door number two."

The security monitor switches to a live feed from the main security HQ at Quantico. The entire staff is bound and gagged. An explosive device is positioned next to them. Fletch can't believe what he's seeing.

"Yes, Fletch," I say, reading his mind, "we got them covered too."

"How did you gain this kind of access?" Fletcher says, totally bewildered.

"Access is what we do, baby."

"But what about the cast with the explosives?"

"Again, getting things in and out of prison, not a problem. All of this was waiting for me before I even got here. I just needed to get into a fight, go to the infirmary, have my chop shop doc, who got in there with a Photoshop ID and a smile, put on my special cast . . . It was so easy, it's almost embarrassing."

"There's a Marine squad assigned to this building," Fletcher starts. "I need to inform them—"

"We took care of that too," Alice says. "Show him, Sue."

Security monitor switches to the Marine squad barracks. The gangbangers from the HR siege have them all facedown on the deck, with zip-tied hands and guns to their heads. They're passing a joint and laughing as they blow smoke in the Marines' faces.

"God, they're cute," Alice says.

"Knock it off, darling."

I turn to Fletch and help myself to one of his cigarettes.

"Looks like you've covered everything," he says.

"Fletch, don't act so surprised. After all, you're the one who created us. This is *your* monster."

"I don't know what you're talking about." He laughs.

"Let's get past the whole denial thing, shall we? Your decades-long role as the secret head of HR is well documented in the evidence jacket we provided the FBI director and your colleagues here at Quantico with. After Mr. Zhen was kind enough to reveal your identity, we did the due diligence to back up his claim. I have to admit, we were pretty impressed when we reviewed all the financial files and, you're going to love this, CIA files. Turns out they've had their eye on you for some time."

"We were even able to trace the money you sent me for the Zhen job," Alice says proudly. "Face it, Fletch. We have evidence to convict you twice."

"What you're saying is ludicrous," he protests, shaking his head.

"I know, right?" I say. "A well-respected, decorated FBI agent, an assistant director no less, running a placement firm for elite assassins who pose as interns? Ludicrous."

I backhand him to stop his head from shaking.

"Listen, Fletch, this little performance you're putting on for your golf buddies is not only stupid, it's also distracting you from a very important choice you need to make right now."

"What choice is that?" he says, defeated.

"Either you let us walk out of here or we blow this taco stand with everyone in it. Right, darling?"

"Without question, sweetheart," Alice says. "And great use of *taco stand*."

"But just to be clear, this isn't just about an exit strategy. If all we wanted to do was get away, we would have never let you catch us in the first place."

"I don't follow," he says.

"You will. See, this is *your* party. And we want everyone to know all about our guest of honor."

"Think of it like a roast, but with guns," Alice says.

"For years, you have exploited young people like us and traded our lives for profit. For years, you have been a traitor to the government that pays your salary. For years, you have been Assistant Director Fletcher. But today, you're the man who started Human Resources, Incorporated. And that's how you'll be known from now on."

"That's why we're here," Alice says. "Judgment day."

Fletcher is pale. The storm troopers standing outside our door are still and silent, undoubtedly gut-punched by what they just heard. Part of me is surprised that they're surprised. Guys like Fletcher have been butt-fucking the American Dream since before the ink on the US Constitution had time to dry. In some ways, the exploitation of the poor by the wealthy power elite *is* the American Dream.

"I love you, John Lago," Alice says.

"I love you, Alice whatever your name is."

She kisses me. Our kiss is interrupted by Sue's voice, crackling over the security monitor speaker.

"Tap the keg. We got us a party, kids."

Sue cycles through all the monitors, showing SWAT and DOD Security Forces surrounding the outside of the building. On the inside of the building, our HR forces have sealed and secured every exit and every member of the internal security detail has been inca-pacitated. Basically, we've engineered the biggest Mexican standoff in history.

"Clock is ticking," Alice says to Fletch.

"Tick. Tick. Boom," I say.

Fletcher watches the monitors intently and then looks back at me.

"I have just one question," Fletcher says.

"Shoot," I say.

"You say you know who I am, but *who are you*? Really?"

I lean in closer to him and smile.

"My name is John Lago, motherfucker. And you got five minutes, so make it count."

55

Fletch looks at me, resignation in his face.

"I'll give you what you want," he says, nearly choking on the words, "but only to protect this agency."

"Good. What I want is a 777 commercial jet with a crew, topped off with fuel for its full eight-thousand-mile range, waiting for us at Reagan airport in two hours. And I want a charter bus to take us there in one hour. And that's just for starters."

"I have to speak to the director to order something like that."

He rattles his handcuff to make his point.

"We'll have a phone brought to you. In the meantime, Alice and I will be needing our civilian clothes."

Fletch makes his calls and they bring us our clothing. By the time we're done getting changed, he gets a call.

"This is Fletcher," he answers. "Yes, sir. I'll tell them."

He hangs up the phone and looks at us apologetically.

"Fletch, that's not the look of a man who is about to say yes," I say.

"The director says we need more time for your request."

I turn to Alice.

"I feel like I was fairly clear about our request, don't you?"

"Yes," she says, "crystal clear. Maybe they're trying out some new-fangled hostage negotiator technique."

"The director understands your request. We just need more time."

"I gave you two hours. A lot can happen in that amount of time."

"John—"

"Fletch, we don't negotiate here," I say, echoing his previous admonition.

He makes another call and speaks to the director. Actually, from the looks of it, the director does all the talking. When he hangs up, he looks like he's been beaten with a phone book.

"He said he would try."

"He better try hard if he doesn't want to lose Quantico and everyone in it."

"I understand," Fletch says.

And we wait. Five minutes before my deadline, Fletch's phone rings. Fletch answers.

"Fletcher."

He says nothing, just listens. Then he hangs up.

"John, I'm sorry—"

"Not as sorry as I am," I say and clap again, detonating another charge and rocking the building.

"John, stop this! I get it that you want me dead, but there are hundreds of innocent people working here. I find it hard to believe you're going to kill them too."

"Is that what the director told you to say?" Alice asks.

"Neither of us think—"

I clap and another explosion shakes the room. Dust falls from the ceiling.

"Think what, Fletch?" I ask. "Think I have it in me to kill all those *innocent people?*"

I shove the gun barrel in Fletcher's face.

"In case it slipped your mind, I'm an assassin. I kill people for a living."

And I shoot him in the head.

"Sue, blow it all!" I yell.

"Roger that!"

A series of explosions starts to shake the room in a violent cadence.

"We should probably go," Alice says.

We run out of the interrogation room. A few more explosions detonate and it feels like an earthquake that never ends. As we run, no one tries to stop us. It's every man for himself as the human stampede smashes through glass doors and runs people down in a panicked exodus. I know what you're thinking. Would I really kill all those people? Of course not. The explosions are from charges we planted in the twenty-five-odd records warehouses spread out all over Quantico. The only thing we're killing is years of data that has been illegally collected on American citizens since J. Edgar Hoover. No matter what happens after this, at least I can die knowing I did my civic duty.

Alice and I recon with Sue and the recruits near the lobby.

"How are we looking, Sue?" I ask.

"Cops and SWAT have backed off to protect their people. Devices are kicking up so much smoke and debris they've pulled back air support. They're totally blind right now, just waiting for the smoke to clear and the chaos to subside."

"Perfect. Then I guess it's checkout time."

We all sprint out the lobby doors and through the wooded portion of the grounds used by the academy for training. We run for two miles until we reach a switching station for the Quantico railway lines. There's a big freight train sitting on the tracks. The engine is firing up. Our gangsta crew runs up and recons with us there. I see the crudely spray-painted graffiti on the side of the train:

BULLSHIT EXPRESS.

Alice and I laugh.

"You like?" Sue asks.

"You've out-Sue'd yourself, Sue."

Sue opens the freight car doors and we all load in—Alice, Sue, the recruits, the gangstas, and me. The cars are spartan but Sue has filled them with couches, chairs, food, drinks, and battery-powered LED lights. It's not the *Orient Express*, but it's a nonstop express train all the way to Manhattan and the least likely mode of transportation the feds would expect us to take. Personally, there's no way I'd rather travel.

Epilogue

As we ride the *Bullshit Express* back to New York, everyone retires on the couches and chairs to have a drink, smoke some green, and get some rest. Alice and I take that opportunity to walk up to the engine and watch the lights of Philly slowly start glittering across the dark water of the night.

"I think this is the part where we say we did it," I say.

"And the part where we congratulate each other on a job well done," Alice replies.

"Good, I'm glad we got that out of the way."

We laugh and I kiss Alice for the first time as a free man.

"I have something to show you," she says, smiling.

"I love it when you talk dirty," I say.

"It's not *that*. Look."

She pulls her left hand out of her pocket and shows me the Harry Winston ring on her finger. I can't believe it.

"You went back for it?"

"Yeah," she says coyly.

"Why? You had disowned me."

"John, I thought you were dead. I know it sounds sick, but I needed something to remember you by."

"That's not sick, it's sweet," I say as I slip the ring from her finger and throw it off the side of the train.

"John! Why the hell did you do that?!"

"Alice, I bought that ring with Bob's blood money, under false pretenses, back when everything about us was a lie. We need a fresh start and I need to buy you a ring that means something."

She smiles and kisses me.

"That's beautiful. And to tell you the truth, I didn't like it that much anyway."

"Here we go . . ."

"No, seriously. It's . . . was . . . an amazing ring, but the diamond was just way too big and flashy for my taste. I'm more of an understated girl."

"Really, I didn't know that about you."

"Honey, there are a lot of things you don't know about me."

"Then it's a good thing we have whiskey and a ways to go."

We kiss and I smile at her. Then it hits me . . .

"Wait," I say, "do I even *want* to know more about you?"

"What, are you afraid I'll tell you something disturbing?"

"Should I be?"

Alice smiles and whispers in my ear.

"Yes."

Acknowledgments

Book two . . . the Minotaur. I charged into the labyrinth and slew this infernal beast driven by the love, support, and healing alchemy of Amanda Kuhn and my warrior clan—Skoogy; Kenners Bear; Jo Mama; Mary B; Ky; Ozzy; Brad Pearson (chief medical officer); Samacolada and the Kailua boys; the metal and muscle of the ruthless Simon & Schuster army—Sarah Knight (her name befits her gallantry and superior battle skills), Marysue Rucci, Jonathan Karp, Elina Vaysbeyn, Kate Gales, Kaitlin Olson, and Roberto de Vicq de Cumptich; the trusted guidance of my war council—Hannah Brown Gordon, Brad Mendelsohn, Kirsten Neuhaus, Elena Stokes, and Tanya Farrell; the courage and loyalty of my allied forces abroad—Alexander Elgurén, Ed Wood, Ida Cornelia Rahbek Manholt, Rachel Clements, Stephanie Melrose, Sarah Shea, Gemma Conley-Smith, Pantagruel (Norway), Sphere/Little, Brown (UK), DuMont (Germany), Sonatine & Univers Poche (France), Fanucci (Italy), Euromedia (Czech Republic), Ikar (Slovakia), AST (Russia), Europa (Hungary), and Alnari (Serbia); and the spiritual protection of my underworld sentinels—Kenneth, Tina, Kara, Margaret, and Gilbert Kuhn, Warren and Bernie Witham, Nana DuWors, Big Bri Mahoney, and Nixon. With this victory, the gods are pleased and the Fates spin a thread of ass-kicking destiny.

About the Author

Shane Kuhn is a writer, director, and producer working in the entertainment business and advertising. He is one of the original cofounders of the Slamdance Film Festival and he's currently developing a novella and television series about a highly sophisticated international heist ring for the European market. He lives and works in Colorado, Los Angeles, and the Bay Area. He is the author of *The Intern's Handbook,* bought for film by Sony Pictures, and *Hostile Takeover*, the second book in the John Lago thriller series.